To Heal a Heart

by

Jana Richards

The Masonville Series, Book 2

To Heal a Heart

Cover Art by *Rae Monet, Inc. Design*

The Wild Rose Press, Inc.
PO Box 708
Adams Basin, NY 14410-0708
Visit us at www.thewildrosepress.com

Publishing History
First Champagne Rose Edition, 2020
Print ISBN 978-1-5092-3154-6
Digital ISBN 978-1-5092-3155-3

The Masonville Series, Book 2
Published in the United States of America

"You should be ashamed of yourself." She swept out her free hand, indicating the hip bone protruding from the horse's flanks. "Look at this animal. He's been starved."

"I know, but—"

"There's no excuse for it." Nothing angered her more than the mistreatment of an animal. "And look at all his sores and welts. He needs veterinary attention."

Unsmiling, the man crossed his arms over his broad chest. "I plan to get him looked at right away."

"Good. Make sure you do." Should she believe him? He was big and mean-looking. A scruffy beard covered his jawline, and his hair was disheveled, as if he'd just rolled out of bed. Worse, she smelled alcohol on his breath, even in the distance between them. Yet somehow, there was something familiar about him.

He reached out one large hand, palm up. "I'll take him home."

Blair clutched the rope against her chest. "How do you plan to do that? You don't have a horse trailer."

"I'll walk him."

"What about your truck?"

He shrugged. "It's not going anywhere."

All kinds of questions trembled on her tongue. Was he equipped to look after this horse? Did he have other horses in this kind of shape? Who was he and why did she feel she'd met him before?

Praise for Jana Richards

"Talented author Jana Richards, with her gift for creating snappy dialogue, honest, lovable characters —human and canine—has given us another winner. Do not miss *CHILL OUT*. You'll be as entranced as I was."

~Wild Woman Authors blog

~*~

"The reader is skillfully transported to 1942 occupied France....Whether or not a reader is familiar with (or even interested in) this particular historical era, she will find *FLAWLESS* a terrific read both for suspense and romance."

~Judy Nickles, The Word Place

~*~

"What a great read! ...If you are looking for a sweet tale of true love, *BURNING LOVE* is perfect for you!"

~M. Dobson, Sizzling Hot Book Reviews

Dedication

To the friends whose help has made this book possible.
To my writing friends with
the Saskatchewan Romance Writers,
thank you for the encouragement and great ideas.
To my friend Ishbel
for not pulling any punches in her beta-read.
Much appreciated!

Chapter One

The acrid smell of smoke and burning fuel hung thick in the air. His lungs burned with the smell, and his head pounded. Blood trickled into his eyes. He couldn't move, couldn't escape the burning vehicle. Noise surrounded him. Men shouted and groaned and screamed in agony.

Hands grabbed him and pulled him free. He cried out at the excruciating pain shooting through his right leg. It was like nothing he'd ever experienced before. He'd once broken his leg, and it was painful, but this agony was a thousand times worse.

This was bad. This was real bad.

"Saunders!" Someone shook him hard, making his teeth rattle. "Garrett Saunders! Can you hear me?"

"Yes." His voice was rusty, his throat dry. He forced his eyes to open, to focus. "Where's Tommy and Chris? They okay?"

"Chris is fine. He pulled you out."

"And Tommy?"

No answer. He grabbed a handful of the medic's uniform, his forehead breaking out in sweat and his body shaking as he pushed himself up onto his elbow.

"Where is Tommy Carmichael? Tell me!"

The medic's eyes filled with pity, and Garrett knew even before he heard the words. "He didn't make it."

He released his hold on the medic's uniform and

fell back against the ground, oblivious now to the medics working on him and the pain in his leg. His best friend was dead.

Garrett Saunders woke with a start, gasping for air. He scrambled to get his bearings, to remember that he was in his childhood bedroom in his parents' house in rural North Dakota, on a farm a couple of miles outside the small town of Masonville. Afghanistan was far away, and only existed in his nightmares.

Nightmares were something he was well acquainted with. They'd dogged him since the Humvee he'd been a passenger in encountered a suicide bomber almost two years ago. Twenty-two months and two days, to be exact. He'd been told that although the Humvee had been retrofitted with armor plating and other modifications to make it safer, the explosion had been so strong no amount of armor could have protected them. The explosion had taken his best friend's life, part of his own right leg, and much of his peace of mind.

Garrett pushed himself to a sitting position and scrubbed a hand over his face. Though bone weary, there was no point trying to get back to sleep. Bitter experience had taught him that.

He grabbed his prosthesis from where it rested against the bedside table and set it on the bed beside him. He'd had to learn patience putting it on, something that hadn't come easily to him. If he didn't use an appropriate thickness of cotton sock liner beneath the silicone liner and the prosthesis itself, the prosthesis wouldn't be snug enough. His stump would slip and move inside the device, which was uncomfortable, and more importantly, unstable. He'd also discovered that if he didn't properly line up the silicone liner that went inside the prosthesis, it wouldn't fit the way it should and he'd have to start the whole procedure all over again. Sometimes it took him several tries to get it right.

He swung his legs to the side of the twin bed he'd slept in since he was nine and sat on the edge. Sighing, he blew out a breath.

Please God. Give me patience.

He opened a drawer in the bedside table and grabbed a handful of cotton. He rolled one cotton sock liner over his stump and then another. He turned the silicone liner inside out, placed it at the end of his stump, and carefully rolled it over the cotton socks. Finally, he pushed his stump into the prosthesis and stood, taking a few tentative test steps. His stump sat comfortably inside the prosthesis and everything lined up perfectly. Garrett marveled at getting it right the first time.

It wasn't so bad, really. Sure, he missed all the sports he used to play, but there were still plenty of things he could do, like walk. And breathe. Tommy couldn't do that anymore.

The night was hot, with no cool breeze coming in through the screened window. The clock radio on the table flashed three twenty-four a.m.

I need a drink.

Not bothering to put on a shirt, he left his room wearing only his boxer shorts. He navigated the stairs of the old two-story farmhouse with the help of the handrail. His physical therapist at the VA hospital had recommended using a cane for stability and balance, but he'd be damned if he'd use an implement meant for an old man.

Or a cripple.

Moving as quietly as possible so as not to wake his parents, he made his way to the kitchen. Opening the fridge door, he stood in front of the appliance for a moment and enjoyed the coolness before reaching in to grab a can of beer. He pulled back the tab and tipped the can to his lips. The cool liquid quenched his parched throat, and he drained the can in a few gulps.

He set the empty can on the counter, then stared at the closed refrigerator. Damn, he wanted another. Hell, he wanted another six. Anything to take the edge off and help him sleep.

Help him forget.

But his mother kept a close eye on the number of beers he drank. She worried about him, fussed over him, drove him crazy. He loved his mother, loved both of his parents fiercely, but their concern was suffocating him.

Now that his military career was over, he needed to find his own place, and a new life. He was thirty-one years old. He shouldn't need to rely on his parents as much as he did.

You can't hide out here on the farm forever.

Garrett pushed the thought from his mind. He wasn't hiding out. He was working on it. Twice now he'd put in offers to buy a farm, and twice his plans had ended in disappointment. The most recent offer had been on a neighbor's farm. If he'd been able to purchase Everett Branson's place, he would have had a couple of thousand acres of land and his own house. Not that he had any idea what to do with that land. Or with the rest of his life. But at least he would have had the solitude he needed to figure it out.

His plans had been thwarted by Everett's sudden decision to take the farm off the market. Simply one more disappointment in a bitter couple of years.

If I'd really wanted to farm, I would have stayed in North Dakota and taken over the farm from Dad instead of joining the marines at eighteen. Now the land is gone.

Garrett pounded his fist against the counter in frustration, then immediately regretted his outburst. He held his breath and listened, hoping he hadn't woken his parents. When everything remained silent, he breathed a relieved sigh.

After Garrett joined the marines, his father Robert sold the land, believing his son wasn't ever coming back to North Dakota. And until his Humvee met that suicide bomber, Garrett had had no intention of coming home. But right now, it would have been nice to have the land to fall back on.

It didn't matter if farming wasn't his first occupational choice. His first choice was gone, and he had to do *something* with his life or go crazy. Without his leg or a college degree, his other options were limited. He'd find some land somewhere else. Someday. Even if he didn't know what the hell to do with it.

Quietly, he made his way back up the stairs to his room. He carefully closed his bedroom door before making his way to the locked trunk on the floor of his closet. Opening the combination lock from memory, he rummaged under old uniforms and ten years' worth of memories until he found the bottle of bourbon he'd hidden there.

He made himself comfortable on the bed and stared

at the crescent moon through the open window while he drank. The chirping of crickets helped to sooth his restless brain until the Jack Daniels worked its magic and carried him away.

****

The next morning a headache pounded, and the inside of Garrett's dry mouth tasted like mothballs. He ignored the evidence of his hangover and slammed shut the gate that trapped a frightened, struggling horse inside a chute. He'd promised his brother-in-law, Cole Walsh, that he'd help him this morning at the horse auction, and he never went back on a promise.

Well, almost never.

Cole, a veterinarian, had been hired to examine the horses up for auction to ensure they were healthy enough to either be sold to new owners or enter the food chain. Garrett pushed away the distasteful thought of these beautiful, frightened animals being turned into dog food.

While the horse was pinned securely inside the chute, Cole ran his hand over its flanks. He'd explained earlier he was looking for any obvious tumors, hernias, or signs of disease. As Garrett watched, Cole checked the horse's legs and hooves and listened to its heartbeat and stomach sounds with his stethoscope. Removing the earpieces, he turned to Garrett. "This one's ready for auction."

Garrett nodded grimly, then opened the front end of the chute. The horse ran into the next enclosed pen, probably relieved to have escaped the tight confines of the chute. He was glad the horse didn't know what was coming next.

Handlers in the first paddock separated a gray

gelding from the rest of the herd and forced it into Cole's chute. Once it was inside, Garrett closed the gate behind it, trapping it. The gelding snorted and tossed its head, making its displeasure known. Garrett stroked its neck and spoke in his calmest voice. "Hey, buddy. It'll all be over soon."

The gelding's ears perked at the sound of his voice, and it immediately quieted. One eye locked on him, and in that moment, Garrett's world narrowed to this barn and this horse. As the horse gazed deeply into his eyes, acceptance and empathy flowed between them. The horse understood his frustration and anger, and the gelding's fear shot through Garrett's body like a launched rocket.

He staggered back a step. *I must still be drunk.*

The gelding tossed his head, struggling once more to be free. Garrett stroked its neck, hoping to calm it long enough for Cole to finish his examination. He didn't blame the horse for resisting its confinement. He understood what it meant to be trapped, to have no place to go. He understood fear.

Panic rose in his throat, threatening to choke him. He couldn't permit this animal to die.

"I want to buy this horse."

Cole pulled the stethoscope from his ears. "What?"

Garrett cleared his throat. "I'm buying this horse."

"This is not a good example of great horseflesh."

"I don't care. This is the horse I want."

Cole ran his hands along the gelding's bony flanks. "I think he might have been a nice working quarter horse at one time, but that's a few years in the past. He's emaciated and there could be an underlying cause aside from being denied food. He's got some welts, too.

Makes me think he was abused. And he's at least fifteen years old, possibly older. If you really want a horse, we can find something better."

Garrett stared into the horse's eye once more, unable to look away. The gelding needed him, and he had the frightening suspicion he needed the gelding. They were both a little beat up, but still proud.

"I don't want anything better. I want this horse."

"Where are you going to keep him? Your folks don't have a fenced paddock or a barn. It's not like he's a dog you can keep in your room."

Garrett thought fast. "He can stay in Dad's garage."

Cole shook his head. "You've got to be realistic. You'll have to find someone willing to board him. And feed him."

"I'll figure something out." He didn't have a clue who'd be willing to board the horse for him or how much that would cost. Garrett only saw he had to do it.

Cole gave him a hard look. "If you're sure—"

"I'm sure."

"Okay. We'll separate him from the rest and tell the auctioneer. Maybe we can borrow someone's horse trailer to get him home."

Garrett nodded in relief. Then inwardly groaned. He'd never cared for a horse before. He hadn't ridden since he was a kid, and even then, not much. What the hell was he doing?

He stroked the broad white stripe that ran from the gelding's forehead to his nose. He was doing what he was meant to do.

****

Blair Greyson sped down the gravel road, glad the

farm was only about two miles from her workplace in Masonville. She wouldn't make a great impression if she was late on her second day of work at the Masonville Veterinary Clinic.

Her grandfather had wanted to talk, so she'd spent a few extra moments listening to one of his stories and making sure he downed his heart medication. So now she was breaking the speed limit on the gravel road. And hoping a police officer with a radar gun wasn't lurking around the next bend.

Up ahead, something approached her on the road. She slowed her truck. Not a vehicle, but some kind of animal. As Blair grew closer, she saw it was a horse with a dappled gray coat and a white stripe on its forehead. A rope dangled from its bridle.

Blair thought about continuing on her way. It was only her second day of work, and she didn't want to be late. But she couldn't abandon the animal to its fate. Obviously, it had escaped from wherever it belonged. She couldn't in good conscience leave the animal on the road. What if it got hit by a vehicle? They weren't far from the Interstate. Blair didn't want to think about what might happen if the horse wandered onto the main highway.

With a sigh, she stopped her truck and turned off the ignition before getting out.

The horse grazed on the new grass at the side of the road. Blair approached cautiously, letting the horse smell her. He lifted his head, ears twitching, but didn't run.

"Hey, big guy," she said softly. "What are you doing here?" Fortunately, he didn't seem alarmed by her presence. Perhaps, at one time, he'd been someone's pet and was used to people. But as she got closer, she saw exposed ribs and healed abrasions. If the horse had been cared for at one time, that was no longer the case. Anger grew in her chest. How could someone treat a beautiful, sentient creature so cruelly?

The horse allowed Blair to come close enough to grab the rope. Now what did she do? She had no horse trailer with her. Did she walk the horse the mile to her farm and put it in the corral with her own two rescue horses?

She groaned as she stroked the horse's neck. She was going to be very late for her second day of work.

Another truck approached, plumes of dust billowing behind it. With any luck, this was the owner looking for his horse.

Blair straightened her shoulders. If it was, he'd better be prepared to have a strip taken off him.

The truck stopped in front of hers. A man got out and walked across the road to where she and the gray horse stood. Blair lifted her chin. "Does this horse belong to you?"

"Yeah, I—"

"You should be ashamed of yourself." She swept out her free hand, indicating the hip bone protruding from the horse's flanks. "Look at this animal. He's been starved."

"I know, but—"

"There's no excuse for it." Nothing angered her more than the mistreatment of an animal. "And look at all his sores and welts. He needs veterinary attention."

Unsmiling, the man crossed his arms over his broad chest. "I plan to get him looked at right away."

"Good. Make sure you do." Should she believe

him? He was big and mean-looking. A scruffy beard covered his jawline, and his hair was disheveled, as if he'd just rolled out of bed. Worse, she smelled alcohol on his breath, even in the distance between them. Yet somehow, there was something familiar about him.

He reached out one large hand, palm up. "I'll take him home."

Blair clutched the rope against her chest. "How do you plan to do that? You don't have a horse trailer."

"I'll walk him."

"What about your truck?"

He shrugged. "It's not going anywhere."

All kinds of questions trembled on her tongue. Was he equipped to look after this horse? Did he have other horses in this kind of shape? Who was he and why did she feel she'd met him before?

She looked at his hand. The fingers were blunt, and there was a scar running across the palm, bisecting the lifeline. Reluctantly, she handed him the rope.

"I swear, if I hear of this horse being maltreated or neglected, I'll make you sorry."

His eyes narrowed, chocolate brown turning stormy black in a heartbeat. Blair backed up a step. It suddenly occurred to her that she was alone on a deserted road with this man. Should she be afraid?

Probably.

He dipped his head in a mocking nod, his lips turning up in a sneer. Blair noted the dimple in what could be a handsome face if he wasn't so scruffy. And angry.

"Duly noted."

With that he led the horse down the road in the direction he'd come. Blair watched, heart racing. He had a limp, she noticed. She wondered what had happened to him.

She pressed her lips together. It was none of her business. Her only concern was for the horse. With any luck, she'd never see this man again.

Chapter Two

Blair was ten minutes late for work, despite breaking a few speed laws. She hurriedly parked her truck in the lot and sprinted into the clinic. As she opened the front door, Cole Walsh and his wife Lauren were in the reception area. Lauren greeted her with a smile.

"Good morning."

"Sorry I'm late. I found a horse wandering on the road, and by the time the owner arrived for it…" She didn't want to get into the altercation she'd had with the owner. "Anyway, I'm late. I'll stay longer to make up the time."

"There's no need, Blair," Lauren said. "It's only ten minutes. Besides, your grandfather probably expects you home soon after work."

"Yeah, he does," Blair admitted. "And I'd like to get home to check on him."

Granddad spent too much time alone as it was. His loneliness, along with his health problems, had prompted her to move her life to Masonville. That, and her desire for a fresh start.

"What did this horse look like?" Cole asked.

"It was a gray gelding with a white stripe on its forehead. The poor thing was in terrible shape. It looked as if it had been mistreated." Blair got angry all over again at the memory.

Cole frowned. "Damn."

"Do you know this horse?" Lauren asked.

"I'm afraid I do. Your brother bought it at the auction yesterday."

"Garrett? Garrett bought a horse?" Lauren sounded incredulous. "Why would he do that?"

Cole shook his head and chuckled. "I haven't got a clue. You'll have to ask him."

Garrett Saunders. So that's why he'd looked familiar. The last time she'd seen Garrett, he'd been eighteen and about to enlist in the marines. She'd been a shy, awkward, exceedingly self-conscious fifteen-year-old. Until she was sixteen, she and her brothers had spent every summer with their maternal grandparents, Everett and Anna Branson, long-time neighbors of the Saunders. Garrett had hung out with her two older brothers those summers, while she often visited with his sisters, especially Charlotte, who was closest to her in age. Being three years older, Garrett had paid little attention to her, but she'd certainly noticed him. He'd been her first serious crush.

And her first heartache. Her face heated as she remembered how she'd thrown herself at him that last summer. And how he'd gently rebuffed her.

"He's never owned a horse before. I'm not sure he even knows what to feed it. Where's he keeping it?" Lauren looked to Cole for answers.

"He talked about keeping it in your dad's garage."

"In the garage? He can't keep a horse in the garage!"

"Hey, I told him that, but he was adamant."

"This auction was yesterday?" Blair asked.

Cole nodded. "Yeah."

"So Garrett is in no way responsible for the shape the gelding is in?"

"No, not at all. In fact, I suspect the gelding's poor condition prompted him to buy it. Maybe he thinks he can save it."

Blair could relate to that sentiment. She had two rescues of her own, and if her plans worked out, she'd be able to provide homes for several more unwanted and uncared-for horses.

Damn. She'd accused Garrett of something he didn't do. That's what she got for reacting before she got all the facts.

"Where does your brother live?" Blair asked.

"He's staying with Mom and Dad on the farm," Lauren replied. "He's been there about a year and half, since he got out of the military."

"I owe Garrett an apology." Blair stared at her shoes. "I may have accused him of abusing the gelding."

"Oh," Lauren said in surprise. "You didn't recognize him?"

Blair shook her head. The man she'd met on the road this morning bore little resemblance to the handsome, carefree boy she remembered. Of course, he gave no indication that he remembered her either. She couldn't blame him. They'd both changed. In a lot of ways.

"You can't blame yourself. You had no way of knowing he was on some kind of misguided rescue mission." Lauren frowned and shook her head. "I don't understand what Garrett was thinking, buying that horse. He's been…different since he came home."

Blair wanted to ask her what she meant, but it

seemed too personal a question. It was none of her business.

Besides, she worked with Cole and Lauren, and since Cole had recently purchased a partnership in the clinic, he was also her boss. She was grateful to them for giving her a job, and she appreciated they'd hired her mostly because her grandparents had been neighbors to the Saunders family for years. Blair didn't want to give them any reason to regret their decision.

"If it makes you feel any better, Blair, I promised Garrett I'd come out and have a closer look at the horse today," Cole said. "I'll recommend a feeding regime and treat any wounds that haven't healed over."

"Thanks. That does make me feel better." But it didn't absolve her from saying she was sorry.

****

Blair pulled in front of the Saunders' farmhouse and killed the engine of her truck. She hesitated a moment before getting out. No one was in the yard and no vehicles were visible. Lauren had told her that her mother, Grace Saunders, was a teacher and often stayed late at school to prepare for the next day. Her dad, Robert, worked part-time at a hardware store in Bismarck. Perhaps neither of them was home.

Just as well. She didn't want an audience for her apology to Garrett. She'd make a quick but sincere apology and get the hell out.

Blair opened the door of the truck cab and jumped out. As she climbed the steps to the veranda of the house, she was disconcerted to discover her palms were sweating. She wiped them across her thighs, leaving a wet streak on her scrubs. *Great*.

She knocked on the front door and waited. No one

answered, so she walked back down the steps of the veranda. Frustration ate at her. All afternoon she'd psyched herself up to give her apology, her nerves on edge. But now that she was here, Garrett was nowhere to be found. The thought of having to come back to do this again made her stomach do an uncomfortable flip-flop.

With a sigh, she opened the door of her truck and got inside. She was about to turn the ignition when she saw Garrett emerge from around the side of the garage, leading the gray gelding. His limp appeared more pronounced than it had this morning, and she wondered again at its cause. Had he been hurt during his time in the military?

Not your concern, Blair.

She got out of the truck and walked toward him. He obviously recognized her because he came to a full stop, his mouth twisting with his frown.

"So you're back. Did you come here to tell me to quit beating on my horse again?"

Blair cleared her throat. "No, actually I came to apologize. Cole told me you bought the horse yesterday, so obviously you're not the one who abused him."

She had the satisfaction of seeing that she'd surprised him. "How do you know Cole?"

"I work with him at the clinic." She held out her hand, hoping it was no longer sweaty. "I'm Blair Greyson. I recently moved to Masonville."

He shook her hand, his brows knitting together. "Greyson. Why do I know that name?"

"Because I'm Everett Branson's granddaughter."

"Ah." His eyes lit with understanding. "What

brings you to Masonville?"

"My granddad. He's been alone since my grandmother died, and his health isn't great." Blair missed her grandmother fiercely. Talking about her death from a sudden, unexpected heart attack hadn't gotten any easier. "My brothers and I were worried about him, and since I have a couple of rescue horses of my own, I thought the best place for all of us was here on the farm."

With a start Blair realized she and Garrett had something in common. Neither of them had been able to turn away from a horse slated for slaughter, despite the difficulties. She'd boarded her rescue horses at a stable outside Rochester, Minnesota, where she'd been living. But the cost was brutal and had been one of the many reasons she'd approached her grandfather with the idea of moving in with him. Everett seemed happy with the arrangement, and being close to her grandfather gave Blair some peace of mind.

Garrett stroked the gelding's neck. "How are your brothers? I haven't seen them in years."

"They're fine." That wasn't the truth, but he didn't need to know. "Ben's a lawyer in Chicago, and Damon is a counselor in California." Blair cleared her throat once again. "Look, like I said, I want to apologize. I made a hasty judgment and accused you of hurting this horse. I'm sorry."

"Maybe you were right." He ran his hand along the horse's flank, avoiding her gaze. "I'm not doing Harry any favors. I have no idea what I'm going to do with him."

Blair's heart hurt for them both. "Harry? Is that what you call him?"

"Yeah. This guy is something of an escape artist. A regular Harry Houdini."

That made her smile. She stepped forward to pet the gelding's nose. "I'm acquainted with Harry's talents. I only hope he's got the smarts to stay off the Interstate next time he makes a run for it. He was heading in that direction when I found him on the road this morning."

"My dad said there was no way he wanted him inside the garage, so I tied him up behind the garage. Gave him water and feed, but he managed to pull out the stake I had him tied to. Twice. I've been chasing him all day."

She recognized the tenderness she saw on his face as he patted the horse's rump. She recognized the worry as well. It was exactly what she experienced every time she came across a horse who needed rescuing.

"I can't keep him." Garrett's voice was bleak. "It wouldn't be fair. But who's going to want a broken-down old nag like Harry? The idea of selling him to the meat buyers…"

Blair understood the bleakness, too. She couldn't save them all, and acknowledging that fact was a bitter pill to swallow.

But maybe she could do something for Harry. She hoped she wouldn't live to regret what she was about to suggest.

"I have a paddock behind the barn, where I keep my two other rescue horses. Harry can stay with us."

Garrett looked up sharply, his brown eyes boring into hers. "Are you serious? How much would it cost to board him at your place?"

Blair tapped nervous fingers against her thigh as

19

she named a figure. She wished she could take Harry in without having to charge Garrett for it, but horses tended to eat. A lot. "I think it's a fair price."

He inclined his head. "Sounds reasonable."

"We have a deal?"

He stared at her, and Blair held her breath. She'd proposed the only reasonable choice for Harry's care. She hoped he could see that. And it would help her as well, easing the cost of feeding her own two horses somewhat. Every little bit helped. But it wouldn't be enough. Not even close. Miles of fence in the pasture needed fixing. The uneven, broken concrete floor of the barn was too dangerous for horses and had to be repaired. She wouldn't be able to use the barn this winter without the floor being fixed, and she couldn't leave her horses unprotected from the cold and the wind. Maybe she could put together some kind of lean-to shelter on her own. With horse blankets and shelter from the wind, the horses would be okay. She could ask one of her brothers to come to the farm this summer to help—

"We have a deal," Garrett said.

Blair exhaled in relief as she grasped his outstretched hand in a shake. "Good. I'll bring my horse trailer after work tomorrow and take him home. I think boarding Harry at my place is the best solution."

He gripped her hand when she tried to pull away, his expression tense. "As long as you allow me to visit him."

"Of course. Anytime. He's your horse, after all."

Garrett grinned as he released her hand, and for the first time, Blair glimpsed traces of the boy she used to know.

****

Blair's grandfather was on the front porch in his rocker, his favorite spot, as she drove into the yard. She pulled into the garage and hurried to the house.

"Hi, Granddad." She dropped a kiss onto his forehead. "Sorry I'm late."

"I told you when you called you don't need to rush home for me. Take all the time you need."

"You won't believe what happened to me today."

She sat in the rocking chair beside him, the one that had been her grandmother's, and told him about finding Harry on the road that morning on her way to work.

"So it was Garrett Saunders' horse? Did I tell you I almost sold the farm to him this past winter?"

Blair blinked, surprised. "No, you didn't."

"Garrett came home from the Marine Corps about a year and a half ago. Got injured out. He was looking for a new start, and Anna and I were ready to sell. We'd even put an offer on a little house in Masonville. I would've liked to help him out, but then Anna died and I didn't have the heart to move, especially after you said you wanted to come here with your horses. This is where I want to live out my days."

Blair decided to ignore any talk of Everett's demise. "What do you mean he was injured out?"

"His leg, as I understand it."

Now his limp made sense. He was a veteran who'd served his country and paid the price. A sudden wave of guilt swept over her for starting that stupid fight with him this morning. She even felt guilty because her move here ensured her grandfather wouldn't sell the farm in the foreseeable future.

She was being ridiculous. She had no need to feel

guilty. This farm was in her blood; she'd practically grown up here. It was where she belonged right now. Everett needed her.

And if she was honest with herself, she needed him, too.

"Did you eat the lentil soup I made?"

"I had some for lunch. I figured if I didn't, I'd get another lecture about my poor eating habits."

"You figured right. Did you feed Jake?" she asked, nodding at the Labrador retriever curled up on a rug next to Everett's rocker. Jake was never far from his side.

"Yup. Gave him fresh water, too. We're both right as rain."

She grinned at the use of his favorite expression. "I'm glad to hear it."

"Heard from both your brothers today. Damon called on his lunch hour in California, which was about two o'clock here. Shot the breeze for a few minutes. He said to say hi to you."

"Next time he calls, tell him to call me and say hi himself. All I ever get from him are text messages." Blair adored both of her big brothers. Without each other to lean on, getting through their childhoods and adolescence would have been tough. "Ben called, too? How did he sound?"

Everett sighed and pushed his rocker with his foot. "Sad, though he tried to hide it. A little overwhelmed. I can relate. It's hard to lose the woman you love."

Ben's wife had died in a car crash six months ago. A drunk had sped through a red light, hitting Olivia broadside and killing her instantly. It had happened so suddenly and unexpectedly that it was hard to believe she was gone. Only a few months before the accident Blair had been celebrating with Ben and Olivia at their wedding. She could only imagine what her brother was going through.

"How are the girls?"

"Ben says they're okay. They seem to have accepted that their mother isn't coming home."

Olivia's daughters from her first marriage, Isabella, age eight, and Sophie, age five, lost their father to cancer five years ago. To now lose their mother seemed extraordinarily cruel. But Ben adored them and would raise them as his own.

"We should invite Ben and the girls to come out here this summer."

"Yup. Sounds like a good idea."

Blair rested the back of her head against the rocker and gazed out at a field of wheat, mostly green but with a golden tinge that spoke of the ripening soon to come. The sun was beginning to lower in the west. In a few hours the sunset would spread its brilliant colors across the western sky. Sunset was her favorite time of day.

"I love this spot," she said with a contented sigh.

"Your grandma loved it, too. We used to sit out here most evenings in the summer. She used to say she'd be stuck inside all winter. She wasn't going to miss one minute of summer if she could help it."

"I miss her." Anna Branson had been her favorite person in the world. Both she and Granddad had stuck by her no matter what she'd done.

"Yup, so do I. You're a lot like her, you know. Same determination, same sunny outlook on life. My Anna was a joy, and so are you."

Blair laid her hand on his arm, her throat

constricting with emotion. "That's the nicest thing you could ever say to me."

"It's only the truth." He set the rocker in motion, pushing it with his foot. "But a young woman like you should be out with other young people sometimes. It's not good for you to be stuck out here with an old goat like me."

"I'm not stuck anywhere. This is exactly where I want to be."

"Blair, girl, you need a life."

Blair rolled her eyes. "I have a life, Granddad. A really great life. I have you and the farm and my horses. And someday I'll be able to rescue even more horses." She bent to scratch Jake's ears. "And dogs, too."

Everett gave a bark of laughter. "You and your animals, my girl. You'd save them all if you could, wouldn't you?"

She laughed along with him. "I'd give it a shot."

"Another thing you have in common with your grandmother." His smile disappeared. "She'd want you to forgive yourself, you know. So do I."

Blair turned away. She could imagine where this conversation was headed, and she wasn't going there. She set her hands on the armrests. "I should get supper ready."

He laid his hand on her arm, preventing her from standing. "I want to see you happy, Blair. Quit holding onto the past. You have nothing to feel guilty about. Please—"

His face suddenly contorted, his breath coming in shallow gasps. Blair leapt to her feet.

"Granddad, is it your angina again?"

He winced as he nodded. "My nitro. On the table."

Blair raced into the house and grabbed the bottle of nitroglycerin from a basket on the kitchen table. A moment later, she removed a tablet from the bottle with shaking hands and helped her grandfather place it under his tongue, where it could dissolve slowly. In a few minutes, Everett relaxed against his rocker and his breathing returned to normal. Blair sighed in relief.

"Feeling better now?"

His eyes remained closed, but his lips curved in a smile. "Right as rain."

"Have you taken your heart medication?"

He shook his head. "Not this evening's dose."

"I'll get it for you, and then I'll make us something to eat."

His eyes opened. "You take good care of me, Blair."

She made herself smile for him. "It's my pleasure."

She entered the house and found Everett's heart pills in the same basket as the nitro. As she was running water for a glass of water, a sudden sob caught her by surprise. She put her hand over her mouth, not wanting Everett to hear her cry. He'd already had two heart attacks, and the doctors warned a third could be his last. He simply wasn't strong enough to withstand another one.

The thought of losing him, the way she'd lost her grandmother, made her more determined than ever to protect him.

Chapter Three

Garrett approached Harry cautiously with a pail of feed pellets in one hand and an antibiotic ointment in the other. Harry stepped to the end of the lead rope Garrett had tied to the tether anchored in the ground. He stamped his feet, not allowing Garrett to get too close.

"It's okay, boy. This is a good thing. Cole gave me this stuff, and he knows what a horse like you needs. This food will make you healthy and strong, and the ointment will fix those welts."

Harry shook his head as if saying he didn't believe him. Garrett was beginning to worry. The horse had eaten only sporadically the last couple of days, not counting any grass he might have consumed when he was on the lam. "Listen, buddy. If you don't cooperate, Blair's not going to want to keep you at her place."

Harry's ears pricked up as if he recognized her name. This time when Garrett stepped toward him, he didn't move away.

"Oh, so you like her, do you?" He had to admit she intrigued him. She didn't have to offer to take Harry in. She was doing him an enormous favor. He expelled a sigh.

"We both know she's not doing it for me. She thinks I'm too inept to look after you." Harry whinnied. Garrett grinned as he took another step.

"I see you agree with that statement. Can't say I

blame you, Harry. She's obviously a compassionate person. At least where animals are concerned. She probably doesn't have time for a beat-up soldier like me."

He had nothing to offer a woman like Blair.

One more step and he was standing right in front of Harry. Garrett held out the pail of pellets, and the horse sniffed at it.

"Go ahead. You know you want it."

This time Harry stuck his nose into the pail and ate. But as soon as Garrett tried to put some ointment on a welt on his hindquarters, Harry danced out of his reach. He tried again, but Harry would have none of it. The harder Garrett tried, the more agitated Harry became. He finally gave up, afraid he was simply making things worse.

"Okay, you win. But it's on you, buddy. You can't go with Blair if you won't let anyone touch you."

Harry's ears twitched once again, and Garrett laughed. "Forget it. You had your chance."

A vehicle drove into the yard. Garrett walked around the side of the garage just as Blair parked her truck and horse trailer. She jumped out of the cab.

"Hi." Blair nodded at the tube of ointment in his hand. "Any luck getting that on Harry?"

"Not much. A horse whisperer I'm not." What had ever made him think he could help Harry?

Blair tilted her head and smiled, the expression in her eyes knowing, as if she'd read his mind. "You've owned your horse for what, three days? It's not as if Harry came with an owner's manual. Horses are intelligent, compassionate, emotional creatures. I've spent years trying to get to know them and I still haven't managed to plumb their depths."

Their gazes locked. She could be talking about herself. Garrett had the feeling he could know Blair for years and discover new things about her every day.

Blair looked away first. "I'd better get Harry home. I need to make dinner for Granddad."

They made their way behind the garage.

"I want to thank you again for offering to look after Harry. The life I'm giving him here isn't much better than the one he left. The only difference is I'm not beating him."

"That's a big difference. Don't sell yourself short. If you hadn't rescued Harry…"

She didn't finish. She didn't have to.

"Hi, Harry." Blair approached the gelding slowly, her voice low and calm. Garrett stayed well back, not wanting to get in her way. "We're going to take you for a little ride, and you'll meet some friends and run around the paddock with them. You'd like that, wouldn't you, Harry?"

Harry stepped forward and nuzzled her hair as if to say he would. She pulled a carrot from her pocket and offered it to him. Harry delicately picked it from her open palm with his teeth, and Garrett was convinced the horse was doing his utmost not to hurt her. While he was distracted as he nibbled the carrot, Blair unhooked the lead rope from the tether.

"You're such a good boy, Harry," she crooned. She slid her hand down Harry's neck in a gentle stroke. "We're going to fatten you up and make you all pretty again. Don't you worry about a thing."

Harry nodded his head as if agreeing with her, and Garrett smiled. It was a relief to know he was putting

Harry in capable, compassionate hands.

What would it be like to have those hands on me?

Garrett cleared his throat. Thoughts like that had to stop. Blair wanted nothing to do with him.

Blair led Harry to her trailer, permitting the horse to set the pace. Garrett fell into step beside her.

"I've got a bag of high protein pellets that Cole recommended. I'll put it in the back of your truck."

"Good. He's probably going to need some supplements, too. I'll speak to Cole about it."

"Cole's already recommended supplements. He said Harry needs deworming and some work done on his feet, too." Cole had offered to do the work at cost, but Garrett wouldn't take charity. He'd taken on the responsibility of looking after Harry, and he would pay for it.

"Oh, if you give me the ointment, I'll make sure to treat the welts. Harry only needs some care and he'll be beautiful again. You'll see," Blair said with a smile.

"I don't care if he isn't beautiful. As long as he's healthy and happy, I'm good."

Blair turned to him and their gazes locked once more. He wondered what she saw when she looked at him. Did she see the broken soldier in need of care, or the man? This time he was the first to look away.

Blair led Harry into the horse trailer, crooning soft words to him the whole time. He balked as she led him up the ramp, tossing his head and stamping his feet. Blair waited, letting Harry sniff the trailer to get used to the new surroundings. Finally, at Blair's gentle urging, he walked up the ramp and into the trailer. Once Harry's lead was fastened inside and he was settled with his pail of pellets, Blair closed the back door. Just then, Garrett's parents came out of the house and walked toward them.

"Blair, how nice to see you again." His mother extended her hand to her. "It's been too long."

She accepted her handshake with a smile. "It's nice to see you too, Mrs. Saunders."

"Please, if we're going to be neighbors, call me Grace."

"And call me Robert," his dad said. "Makes me feel old when a young person calls me Mister."

"In that case, Robert it is," she said with a smile.

"How's your grandfather?" his mom asked.

"He's well, mostly. I'm trying to make sure he takes his pills and eats decent meals. He seems content."

"I know he's thrilled to have you at the farm, Blair," Grace told her. "He was lonely after your grandmother died. Having you here means he can stay on the farm."

"I'm sure he's happy about that," Robert said. "The farm's been Everett's home all his life."

"I'm glad to be able to help him any way I can." She pointed toward one of the flowerbeds at the front of the house. "Your flowers are gorgeous. How do you get them looking so good?"

Garrett lifted his eyebrows. Obviously, she was trying to change the subject. If his parents noted the abrupt change of topic, they didn't show it.

"That's the result of a lot of hard work on my wife's part," Robert said.

Garrett's mother shrugged. "It doesn't feel like hard work. It's more a labor of love."

"My grandmother used to have beautiful

flowerbeds." Blair's voice was wistful. "Now they're mostly full of weeds. I wish I could revive them."

"I could help you with that," his mother said.

Blair shook her head. "Oh no, I couldn't ask you to do that."

Grace waved away her objection. "Nonsense. Like I said, gardening is a labor of love for me. And you'd be helping me out. I have some plants that need dividing, and I don't have anywhere to plant them. I could put some of them in your yard."

"Mrs. Saunders—"

"It's Grace, remember?" His mother smiled brightly, and Garrett knew from experience Blair didn't have a hope of changing her mind now that it was made up. "It would be fun for me. You wouldn't want to deny me my fun, would you?"

"No, of course not, but it will be a lot of hard, physical work. Those beds haven't been worked for a while."

"I can help with the flowerbeds, Mom," Garrett said.

Both his parents turned to stare at him, clearly surprised. Garrett wiped his suddenly sweaty hands across his thighs.

"I thought I'd stop over tomorrow to see how Harry's settling in. I can work the beds while I'm there."

"Oh, I see." Grace gave him a speculative look that he did his best to ignore.

"Sounds like a great idea," Robert said.

Blair glanced at him before quickly looking away. She patted the side of the horse trailer, and Garrett got the impression she was anxious to leave. He couldn't say he blamed her. "I should get Harry back to my place and get him settled in."

"Thanks again, Blair," Garrett said.

"We'd really love to have you and Everett to dinner sometime soon. I'll give you a call in the next few days, and we can arrange a time."

"That sounds lovely. Thank you, Mrs.—Grace. Goodbye."

With that, Blair got into her truck, made a wide turn, and drove out of the yard. Grace waved at the departing truck.

"Blair's become a lovely young woman, hasn't she?"

"Yeah." He didn't like the direction of this conversation.

"She's a hard-working girl. She's taken on the responsibilities of the farm and works a full-time job. And you've got to admire her commitment to her grandfather. That shows a lot of loyalty and compassion." Grace turned speculative hazel eyes on him. "Don't you think so, Garrett?"

He had to nip this in the bud before his mother's imagination went crazy. "Mom, there's nothing going on between Blair and me, so you can put that notion out of your head right now."

She scowled at him. "There'll never be anything going on between you with that attitude."

"She doesn't want to get entangled with me."

"And yet she's boarding your horse."

"She's doing it for the horse's sake, not mine." He turned away. "She can do a hell of lot better than me."

"Don't sell yourself short, honey. You have a lot to offer. You only have to recognize that you do." Grace put her arm around his waist. "Come on. Dinner's almost ready. You can set the table for me."

"Okay."

She gave him a smile, but not before he saw the flash of sadness beneath it. Somehow, he always managed to disappoint his mother.

****

"I'm having a few people over for a barbeque on the fourth of July. Why don't you come?"

Garrett silently groaned. Lauren was only trying to include him in her social activities, but he didn't feel very social these days. In fact, he felt less social every day. He gripped his phone.

"Thanks for inviting me, sis, but I don't think so."

"Why not? Do you have some sort of pressing engagement on the fourth?"

He thought about lying but nixed the idea. Lauren would see right through him. He went with the truth.

"I don't want to come, okay? I don't want to be around a lot of people."

"Please, Garrett. I haven't seen you since Father's Day. If you come early enough, you can play with Piper until Cole's mom takes her back to her place."

As much as he loved his baby niece, he couldn't do it. "Some other time, when it's just family. I'm not fit company right now."

"Oh, Garrett."

He heard a little hiccup on the end of the line and he realized she was crying. Garrett squeezed his eyes shut. He could bear anything except Lauren's tears.

"Please don't cry."

"I can cry if I want to. I'm worried about you, you idiot. In the last few months you've turned into a recluse. Mom says you've been drinking. A lot."

He should have known trying to hide the truth from his mother was futile. All the more reason to find his own place. Grace didn't need the stress of worrying about him.

"I've got it under control."

"Do you really? Because it doesn't look that way to the rest of us."

"Don't tell me you're planning some sort of intervention. Should I book a ticket to a rehab facility?"

"Maybe you should."

He'd meant the comment to be funny, a joke. But Lauren wasn't laughing, and it scared him. Was his family really that worried about him? Was he turning into a drunk?

"All right, fine. I'll come to your barbecue. What time on Saturday?"

"Come around six o'clock and you can spend some time with Piper. Cole's mom is taking her home around seven, once the rest of the guests arrive."

Garrett scrubbed his face with his hand. "Okay. Can I bring anything?"

"No, that's fine. I've got it covered. Just come."

"I will. I promise."

She sniffed. "Good. I love you."

His throat constricted. "I love you, too."

He hit the off button on his phone, his hand shaking. His life was spiraling out of control, and he didn't know how to stop it.

Chapter Four

Garrett enjoyed playing with the baby. Piper was a beautiful child, with her mother's green eyes and her father's dark hair. He especially liked spending time with her because while she was with him, he didn't have to interact with other people. And, unlike the rest of the family, she didn't ask a lot of uncomfortable questions. But at seven, Ella, Cole's mother, took Piper to her apartment to spend the night, and Garrett had no choice but to join Lauren's guests.

Nerves danced in his stomach as he walked through the back yard. Even though he knew most of these people, had known them for years, he didn't belong. The sensation grew stronger every day. He was an alien in his own hometown.

He grabbed a can of beer from a bucket of ice and pulled back the tab. As he moved through the crowd, he nodded at a few people and even managed a few smiles before escaping to a corner of the yard where some lawn chairs had been set up under a large elm tree. He drank deeply, allowing the cool liquid to slide down his throat and quell his anxious thoughts. He emptied that can, got up, and retrieved two more.

By the time Lauren walked toward him arm in arm with a pretty young woman with long, curly hair, he had a pleasant buzz on.

"Garrett, I understand you've met Blair Greyson.

She told us about finding Harry. She recently started working with us at the vet clinic."

"Hello, Garrett."

He blinked a few times, barely recognizing her. Instead of baggy scrubs she wore a pretty red sundress with thin straps at the shoulders that showed off acres of lovely tanned skin. Her hair was unbound tonight and fell in a riot of golden-brown curls across her bare shoulders and back. But what really hit him were the long, shapely legs that seemed to go on forever. He'd always been a leg man, and Blair's legs were first class.

He sucked in a breath, trying not to be too conspicuous by how surprised he was, and how attractive he found her. He extended his hand.

"Nice to see you again, Blair."

She accepted his hand in a shake, and he held onto it, enjoying the contrast between the beautiful woman in front of him and the calluses on her palm. After a moment, she tugged on her hand and he released her.

"Garrett, do you remember when we were kids, Everett and Anna Branson's grandchildren from Minnesota used to spend every summer with them? You used to hang out with the boys."

Garrett turned to his sister, trying to keep up with her conversation, and barely succeeding. Maybe he was drunker than he thought.

"Yeah, I remember. Ben and Damon. Blair reminded me the other day."

Garrett's mind flew back in time. When was the last time he'd seen her before the other day on the gravel road? Twelve years? Fifteen? He'd mostly ignored his friends' ragamuffin little sister, even though she was forever trailing behind him and her brothers.

As a tween, she'd been skinny as a stick and sporting a full set of braces. Today, her lovely smile testified to the skill of her orthodontist.

A memory from that last summer suddenly assailed him. From one summer to the next she'd blossomed into a beautiful, desirable young woman. Fifteen-year-old Blair's long, coltish legs and gorgeous breasts had sorely tempted him. Garrett remembered his guilt at lusting after a girl so young. He swallowed and cleared his throat before speaking.

"How are you liking Masonville?"

"I love it, and I love working at the clinic. How about you? Are you glad to be back?"

He wasn't sure how to answer that question. "I'm glad to be close to my family again."

She watched him, tipping her head as if listening to the chaotic thoughts rattling around in his brain. "Starting a new life is difficult."

Especially if it's not your choice. He swallowed a mouthful of beer before answering. "It is."

"For me, moving to Masonville and the farm has been a challenge, but a rewarding one." Blair turned to his sister. "It's been great reconnecting with Lauren after all these years."

Lauren smiled fondly. "It has. Listen, I've got to run. Cole's waving at me, so I think that means the burgers are done. Why don't you two grab a seat at one of the picnic tables? I'm going to bring out the salads and we'll be ready to eat."

"Do you need any help?" Blair asked.

"No, I can handle it. Why don't you chat with Garrett?"

With a quick smile, she headed back to the house.

Garrett cringed. Lauren wasn't exactly being subtle about throwing them together.

"You don't have to hang out with me. I don't need a babysitter."

"That's good because I don't babysit." She looked him directly in the eyes, her cool gray-green gaze calm and unwavering. "I don't know about you, but I'm starved. Would you care to sit with me?"

Garrett stared at her for a moment, torn between remaining in his familiar darkness or stepping into the sunshine with her. The sun warmed, but it could also burn.

He swallowed the last of his beer before giving a negligent shrug. "Sure. I could eat."

They saw a couple of empty seats at one of the picnic tables. Garrett grabbed another can of beer from a nearby ice bucket. *How many have I had?* He couldn't remember. He pushed the unwelcome thought away.

"Can I get you a beer?" he asked.

"No, thanks, but I'd love ginger ale."

"Sure."

He found another ice bucket full of soft drinks and fished out a can of ginger ale before heading back to Blair. His sister Charlotte arrived at the table at the same time he did. He kissed her cheek.

"Did you just come from the hospital?" Charlotte was a registered nurse.

"No, I was off today. I was in Bismarck, at the pet rescue."

"Don't tell me you brought home another stray."

She gave him an indignant glare. "No, I'm between foster pets at the moment. I'm on a fundraising committee for the shelter. We're planning an event. I'll hit you up for a donation later." She touched his hand and gently smiled. "What about you? How have you been? I haven't seen you in a while."

He brushed away her concern. "I'm fine. Why don't you join us?" He'd be happy to have Charlotte act as a buffer between him and Blair, though why he felt he'd need his sister's protection, he wasn't sure.

"Charlotte, do you remember Blair Greyson? She recently moved to her grandfather Everett Branson's farm."

"Yes, of course I remember Blair." She extended her hand. "I heard from Lauren that you were working at the clinic. It's so nice to see you again."

Blair shook her hand and smiled. "It's nice to see you too. Everyone's been so welcoming. I think I'm really going to like living in Masonville."

Charlotte easily straddled the bench seat of the picnic table to slip into a space next to Blair. Garrett set his beer on the table but remained standing. Getting into tight spaces was sometimes difficult with his prosthesis.

"I'm going to grab some food from the buffet. Are you two coming?"

Blair smiled up at him. "Sure. I'm starved."

She gracefully swung her legs over the bench seat, using her hand to keep her dress in place. But not before he caught a quick glimpse of a slender, creamy thigh. A sudden hit of lust shot through his groin. For a second he closed his eyes, struggling to keep his body under control. He fought the urge to down his beer in one gulp and drown the flames of desire.

Damn it, he didn't need this. He had enough problems right now.

If Blair noticed his discomfort, she didn't show it. He followed her and Charlotte to the buffet table where they filled their paper plates with an assortment of salads, burgers, and all the fixings. They returned to their table, and Garrett set his plate beside his beer.

"Mind if I get in first? I need some room."

"Yeah, sure. Go ahead."

He sat on the bench, then swung his legs around to tuck them under the picnic table, bending his left knee but keeping his right leg straight. His prosthetic was a remarkable piece of engineering, but it wasn't a real leg and it had limitations. He hated that he needed special accommodations these days.

And he hated that he wasn't the man he used to be.

Once he was settled in, Blair and Charlotte sat as well. He was acutely aware of the woman sitting beside him, the sound of her voice, the smell of her perfume, the heat of her body. It pissed him off. He didn't want to be that aware of any woman.

"So you volunteer at a pet rescue in Bismarck?" Blair said to Charlotte.

"Yeah, it's my favorite charity. I do whatever I can for them."

"Including taking in every stray she can get her hands on," Garrett added.

"Don't listen to him," Charlotte said with a scowl in his direction. "I sometimes foster dogs until they can find a permanent home."

"Good for you," Blair said with a smile. "You take in stray dogs, I take in stray horses."

"Horses? Really?"

"Yeah, I'm afraid so. I've got two that I brought with me from Minnesota. Stormy is an Arabian. He was a racehorse, but he couldn't race anymore, so the owners were going to have him euthanized. A horse rescue I worked with housed him for a while, but they were already overfull. Rainbow is a quarter horse. She belonged to a family who bought her for their daughter, but the father went bankrupt and abandoned her at the riding stable. The stable couldn't afford to feed her any longer, so I took over her care. The horses are one of the reasons I moved to Granddad's farm. I couldn't exactly keep them in my apartment."

"So they're going to live out their lives happily at the farm."

"That's the plan. In my fantasy world, I imagine adding more abandoned horses in the future, and even putting them to work. I've been reading about how non-verbal and at-risk kids really bond with horses. Horses are very intuitive and can pick up on a person's mood. I've found myself telling my troubles to my horses on more than one occasion."

"They're like therapy dogs, only bigger," Charlotte said.

Blair laughed. "And they eat more."

The sounds of conversation at the table whirled around Garrett. He responded occasionally if asked a direct question by some of the other guests, but otherwise he sipped his beer and listened to Charlotte and Blair's conversation. He liked the sound of Blair's laugh. It was warm and feminine and very, very sexy, arousing him in a way he hadn't experienced for a long time. He shifted uncomfortably on the bench seat of the picnic table.

By the time people finished eating, darkness had fallen. Cole lit tiki torches set around the yard, and the light over the back door came on. People drifted away from the picnic tables and sat around the bonfire Cole had started in the firepit. Garrett grabbed a beer and made his way toward the firepit. He found a seat next to Charlotte and Blair. As soon as he finished his beer, he'd head home.

Someone brought out a guitar and began to play old country songs. Blair sang along with the others, and Garrett couldn't leave. He wanted to hear her voice, wanted to make believe she was singing only to him. He stumbled to the ice bucket for another beer.

Lauren addressed the crowd. "All of our neighbors got together and decided to put on a fireworks display for the fourth of July. If you'd like to watch, follow me to the empty field at the end of the block."

Blair and Charlotte got to their feet. Garrett remained in his lawn chair, nursing his beer.

"Aren't you coming?" Blair asked.

"No, you two go on ahead. I'm not in the mood for fireworks."

"Are you sure? It'll be fun," Charlotte asked. He didn't like the look of concern on her face.

"Yeah, I'm sure. I've had enough fun for one night." He brought his beer to his lips.

"Okay, we'll see you when we get back."

They walked away with the others, but he saw Blair look back at him, as if unsure she should leave. He held his breath, hoping she changed her mind about going. But she walked away, leaving him alone. Garrett drained the last of his beer.

He crushed the empty can. He should go home. He didn't belong here. He didn't belong anywhere.

He pushed himself to his feet, disconcerted by his

unsteadiness. He made a few halting steps toward the gate as Blair ran into the yard.

"I forgot my sweater," she said, grabbing the garment from the back of a chair and slipping it on. "It's cooler than I thought. Are you sure you don't want to watch the fireworks with us?"

"No, I—"

His words were cut off by a loud explosion, and his only thought was that he had to protect Blair. He grabbed her and threw her to the ground, covering her body with his. He was under attack. Why was Blair in Afghanistan? How could he keep her safe?

Through the chaos and noise he heard her muffled voice beneath him. "Garrett, you're crushing me."

He shifted his weight slightly. "Shh. I'm sorry. You have to stay down and keep quiet. I can't let them hurt you."

She stopped struggling. "Who's going to hurt me?"

"Can't you hear the mortar fire? I have to protect you."

Her hand rubbed his back in gentle circles. "It's all right, Garrett. It's only fireworks. It can't hurt us. We're safe here."

He lifted his head and looked around. He was in Cole and Lauren's back yard in Masonville. There were no bombs, no shelling, no Taliban. He looked down into Blair's face, into the pity in her eyes. He rolled off her, disgusted with himself.

Disgusted and scared. He was losing his mind.

Awkwardly, he pushed himself to his feet, and pulled his truck keys from his pocket.

"I've got to go home."

Blair snatched his keys from his hand. "You can't

drive. You've had too much to drink."

At least she didn't say he was too crazy to drive. "I can't stay here."

"I'll drive you home."

He grasped for an excuse. "No, thanks. I don't need a lecture on the evils of drink."

He tried to grab his keys, but she stepped away, easily evading him. "Don't worry. You're safe for tonight. I'll save the lecture for after you've sobered up some. Come on, let's go."

She offered him her hand. He stared at it for a moment. Her fingers were elegant and long, but he knew her hands worked hard and carried strength.

He needed some of that strength.

He put his hand in hers and allowed her to lead him to her truck. She put him in the passenger seat and reached around him to fasten the seatbelt as if he were a child. He breathed in the light, floral scent of her perfume and felt the softness of her hair as it brushed across his cheek. She pulled back and looked into his face.

"I'll be right back. I'm going to tell Lauren I'm taking you home. Don't run away, okay?"

Run? That was a joke. He hadn't run for nearly two years. "'Kay."

She disappeared into the darkness. Garrett leaned his head against the rest and closed his eyes. Fear closed his throat and threatened to suffocate him.

He was losing his mind, and there was nothing Blair or anyone else could do about it.

Chapter Five

As she drove, Blair glanced at Garrett from time to time to assure herself he was okay. He stared straight ahead, motionless and silent.

What the hell had happened in Lauren's back yard? The event had materialized out of the blue. One minute he was talking normally and the next he'd knocked the wind out of her and pinned her to the ground. Where did Garrett go in that frightening instant?

She'd been afraid at first, terrified that his intention had been to rape her, right there in his sister's yard. He was a big man, and even with an injured leg and too much to drink, he moved with the speed of a predator. If he'd wanted to force himself on her, she couldn't have stopped him.

But then she'd seen the wild look in his eyes and heard his words. *I can't let them hurt you.* Blair's heart constricted. The fireworks had caused some sort of flashback and he thought he was protecting her. She wondered what had happened in Afghanistan.

She pulled into the Saunders' farmyard and parked near the house. After killing the engine, she hopped out of the driver's side door and hurried to help Garrett get out of her truck. He leaned on her as they walked to the house, and she staggered a little under his weight.

"Home to mommy and daddy. Pretty pathetic, isn't it? A grown man living with his parents."

She could practically taste his frustration. "I guess we're two of a kind. I'm a grown woman living with my grandfather. Does that make me pathetic, too?"

She helped him up the front steps to the porch, and they stood in front of the door. She kept a steadying hand on his arm, worried he'd lose his balance.

"Hardly. You're looking after him. I only cause my parents worry."

Once more she saw the bleakness in his eyes, and she desperately wanted to ask him what had happened at Lauren's house. But that wasn't what he needed. She put a light tone in her voice.

"I don't know about that. Granddad worries about me, too. Mostly he worries that I'm more interested in horses than in men."

"Do you?"

"Do I what?"

"Like horses better than men?"

"Yeah, sometimes I do."

Garrett let out an unexpected bark of laughter. "I like you, Blair Greyson, even if you did steal Everett's farm out from under me."

"I did not steal—"

His mouth descended on hers, and for the second time that evening, he stole her breath away.

She had so not expected this, was totally unprepared for the way her body heated at his touch. His tongue swept into her mouth, stroking her tongue over and over until her knees turned to water and she had to grip his biceps to stay upright. He tasted hot, and a little desperate. Desperate for her. Her body arched toward him as he ran his hands over her buttocks and up her sides, his thumbs grazing her breasts and leaving a trail of fire in their wake.

He stopped kissing her and she wanted to whimper in protest, to beg him not to stop. He leaned his forehead against hers, breathing heavily as his hands gripped her hips.

"Don't go." His voice was a rough whisper. "Stay with me tonight."

She was far more tempted than she should have been. He'd had way too much to drink tonight, maybe even had a problem with alcohol. Though she recognized all the dangers, to her shame her biggest fear was that in the morning he'd regret sleeping with her.

She shook her head. What was she thinking? A short time ago she'd been afraid he was going to rape her. Where was her sense of self-preservation?

"I think your mother might be shocked to find me at her breakfast table in the morning."

He pulled her closer, letting her feel how much he wanted her. "Then let's go to your place."

Blair trembled in his arms. She had a bad habit of taking in strays with lots of problems, and Garrett Saunders was her biggest find yet. She instinctively understood he had the power to crush her.

"I think my grandfather might be as surprised as your mother." She lightly kissed his cheek. "Besides, I'm not that kind of girl."

"Too bad."

"Sleep well, Garrett."

She stepped away, and he dropped his hands. Blair hurried down the steps and ran to her truck before she could change her mind.

****

Garrett opened his eyes the next morning to sunshine flooding his bedroom. His first thought was relief. It was the first night in weeks he'd slept all the way through without the nightmares waking him. He felt rested, almost human again, if a little hung over.

The hangover reminded him of the events of the previous evening, and he groaned out loud. Unfortunately, he hadn't drunk enough to forget what an ass he'd been with Blair.

Once he strapped on his prosthesis and popped a couple of Ibuprofen, he pushed himself out of bed and made his way downstairs. His mother was in the kitchen, washing dishes and humming along to a song on the radio. He watched her for a moment, smiling. He truly adored Grace Saunders. If there was one thing he was certain of, it was that she loved him with the fierceness of a mother bear.

Knowing he was disappointing her hurt even more than losing his leg.

He snuck up behind her and kissed her cheek, startling her. She dropped a frying pan to the floor.

"Garrett! Look what you made me do!" But she said it with smile.

He picked up the pan. "Sorry, Mom. I couldn't resist. How are you this morning?"

"I'm good. What about you?"

"I'm good, too. I slept well."

Grace dried her hands on a dish towel. "I'm glad. I sometimes hear you walking around the house at night. Bad dreams?"

"Occasionally." He poured himself a cup of his mother's strong, black coffee, needing the hit of caffeine. Talking about his nightmares with his mother made him uncomfortable.

"You should consider talking to someone about them. I'm sure the people at the VA hospital in Fargo could refer you to a therapist."

It was the last thing he wanted to do. Some therapist sitting in an office wouldn't have a clue about how it had been out there. If he really needed help, he'd talk to one of his buddies.

"I'm fine, Mom. You don't have to worry about me."

Grace looked like she wanted to argue, but instead she expelled a deep breath and gave him a smile.

"Okay. Would you like some breakfast?"

"No, thanks. Coffee's fine. I have an errand to run."

"An errand?"

"Yeah." He finished the last of his coffee. He needed to get to the Branson farm before Blair left for work. "There's something I need to take care of. Can I borrow your car? I left my truck at Lauren and Cole's last night and caught a ride home."

Grace stared at him. She likely wanted to ask about last night and his errand this morning, but to her credit she didn't. She pulled her keys from a hook on the wall near the back door and handed them to him. "Will you be home for dinner?"

"Yeah, I should be. I'll call if I can't make it."

"Okay, honey."

Garrett went to her and enfolded her in his arms. She was tiny, no more than five foot two, but she was one of the strongest people he knew.

"I love you, Mom."

"I love you too, Garrett. I only want you to be

happy."

"I know."

He kissed her cheek once more before leaving the kitchen. To Grace, happiness meant having work he enjoyed, along with a wife and a family. But he didn't know if he could accomplish any of those goals. All those things, which he'd once assumed would be his one day, seemed an impossible dream now. Knowing his mother's happiness depended on him getting his act together overwhelmed him.

As he drove the short distance to Blair's farm, Garrett thought about what he would say to her. He decided a short apology would be best; get in, say his piece, get out.

When he pulled into the farmyard, Everett was on the front porch, sitting in his rocking chair with his dog curled on a rug beside him. Garrett lifted a hand in greeting as he descended from his truck.

"Good morning, Everett. How are you this morning?"

"Right as rain, Garrett. Haven't seen you in a while. Why don't you come sit down and tell me all your news?"

So much for making a fast apology and an even faster getaway. It would have been rude to decline Everett's invitation, and besides, he liked the old man. He'd been a neighbor, a friend, and a surrogate grandfather to him and his sisters since he was a kid. He deserved five minutes of his time.

Garrett lowered himself into the rocking chair next to Everett's. "Beautiful day, isn't it?"

"It is." Everett pushed his chair with one foot, making it rock gently back and forth. "You here to see

Blair?"

"Yes, I...um, I need to discuss something with her."

"Is that right?"

Garrett felt like a teenager meeting a potential girlfriend's father for the first time.

"Yes. Before she heads to work."

"She's working at home today. Traded shifts with one of the other girls at the clinic." Everett leaned his head against the rocker and stared out at the farmyard. "Blair's a good girl. She takes good care of an old goat like me. Always trying to save the world, that one is. Saving the world and every stray in it. She's got a kind, generous heart, and she may seem tough, but she can be easily hurt."

Garrett accepted Everett's words as the warning they were meant to be. He didn't want to hurt Blair either. That was the last thing he wanted. And he wasn't crazy about the notion that Blair felt she needed to "save" him like some stray off the street. He had some pride left.

Not much, but some.

"I'm sure Blair is a lovely person and a wonderful granddaughter. I have no intention of causing her any grief."

Everett turned to him, his blue eyes bright with intelligence. "Good to know, boy. See that you remember that."

"I will." He cleared his throat. "Where is she?"

"Out in the barn. Says she wants to reconfigure the stalls and lay some rubber matting on the floors, modernize a little. Why don't you see if you can give her a hand?"

That was his cue to leave. "Yes, sir. I will."

He pushed himself awkwardly out of the chair, using the porch railing to steady himself before walking across the yard to the large, hip-roofed barn. The old barn had to be at least seventy years old, perhaps older. He'd heard a story once that it had been built by Everett's father with help from neighboring farmers.

The sliding barn door was open, and he could hear a radio playing somewhere inside. He entered and called out.

"Blair?"

A moment later she emerged wearing denim shorts and a camo tank top, a tool belt slung low around her hips and work boots on her feet. Despite being nervous about his apology, he couldn't help but smile. She was the sexiest construction worker he'd ever seen. The remembrance of her in his arms flooded back. He hadn't been so drunk he didn't remember the taste of her, her scent, and the way she fit perfectly against him.

"Hi! What brings you here this morning?" She sounded genuinely surprised to see him.

Garrett wiped sweaty palms against his jeans. "I want to apologize for last night."

She crossed her arms and smirked. "Oh, yeah? What exactly are you apologizing for? Drinking too much, throwing me to the ground and feeling me up, or propositioning me?"

She wasn't going to make this easy. Garrett cleared his throat.

"All three?"

"I like a man who can fully admit his faults. Apology accepted." She pulled a hammer from her tool belt and handed it to him. "Here, take this. Perhaps you can redeem yourself."

He stared at the hammer in his hands. "What do you want me to do with this?"

"If you really want to make up for your bad behavior, you can help me make some repairs in the barn. Help with that would go a long way to putting you in my good books."

He folded his arms across his chest. "So how much are you paying me for this physical labor you propose?"

She grinned. "Nothing. But rest assured your effort will receive my sincere gratitude."

He wondered if her gratitude would extend all the way to her bedroom. "Well, that makes it all better then."

"I'll even throw in your meals. I'm a damned fine cook, if I say so myself. Ask my granddad."

"I will."

For the first time, her smile slipped and she looked unsure. "You do know I'm kidding, right? It's just…" She swept out her arm to encompass the vast barn. "There's so much to do, and I'm not really sure what to do, or how I'm going to get it done."

Garrett looked around the barn. "Your granddad mentioned reconfiguring some of the stalls and fixing the floor."

"Yeah. Basically, I've got to get this building fit to house the horses before winter. Once I clear out the old stalls, I'll install rubber floor mats over the concrete. The rubber is easier on the horses' feet, and not as slippery as concrete in the winter. It should smooth out any areas where the concrete is uneven. I hope." Blair narrowed her eyes at him. "Look, I was being stupid. I'm punchy because I'm feeling stressed. Whatever the truth is, I've accepted your apology, so no harm, no foul. I'll keep my end of our bargain."

Garrett didn't budge. He was by no means a carpenter, but he'd pounded a few nails in his time. He could do this. He *needed* to do this. The only chores left on his parents' acreage were cutting the grass and washing dishes. Neither of those jobs kept him occupied for long, leaving him with too much time to think. Or more accurately, to brood. He needed a diversion. Until he found his niche, maybe the best thing for him was good, old-fashioned hard work.

"So, these meals you brag about. What are we talking? Mexican, Italian, American?"

She stared at him a moment before answering. "It varies, depending on my mood. Garrett, you're not seriously considering this?"

"I've got some time on my hands these days. I'd rather be working."

"You're sure? Like I said, I don't have the money to pay you."

"I'm sure."

She puffed out a breath. "If we do this, if you're here on my farm every day, we need to set some ground rules."

"Fair enough. What do you have in mind?"

"First of all, I won't have you work for nothing. I'll board Harry for free until you can make alternative arrangements for him, or the work is done, whatever comes first."

"I agree. Anything else?"

She hesitated, biting her bottom lip before speaking. "There can be no propositioning. By either of us. If we're going to work together, it has to be strictly business."

He wasn't surprised she felt that way, considering what he'd done, but he found it interesting she included herself in that rule. "Got it."

Blair briefly averted her gaze before straightening her back and looking him directly in the eye. "Most importantly, you can't drink on the job. And you can't show up drunk or hung over. You could injure yourself, but mostly, I don't want to see you that way."

Her words shamed him. He'd fallen so far into a bottle that he was afraid he couldn't crawl out. But for Blair, he'd try.

"I promise you, I won't show up drunk or hung over. And I'll never drink on the job."

"Good. I think that covers everything. I guess we have a deal. When can you start?"

"That depends. What are you making for lunch?"

"I've got homemade chicken noodle soup on the stove."

He smiled. "In that case, now seems like a good time."

Chapter Six

The next morning before seven-thirty Garrett pulled into Blair's farmyard and turned off the ignition of his truck. As he pushed himself out of the cab, muscles protesting from yesterday's work, Blair emerged from the house and ran down the front porch steps. Her curly hair had been tamed into submission with a braid that hung halfway down her back. She wore her work clothes, a set of pink scrubs and white athletic shoes. Even in the utilitarian attire, she managed to look attractive, from her fresh-scrubbed oval face to the tips of her pink enameled fingernails.

"Good morning!" she called.

"Morning." Garrett cleared his throat, trying not to notice the way the morning sunshine brought out the copper highlights in her hair. "How's Harry doing?"

"He's settling in nicely. I just came from feeding him, and he seemed happy."

"You're sure?"

"I think Harry's happy to be with other horses again. He's calmer."

"I'll check on him later, see how he's doing." He'd brought a couple of carrots from his mother's refrigerator, hoping he could bribe his way into Harry's heart.

"You mean you want to get it straight from the horse's mouth?"

Garrett groaned at the lame joke. "Tell me you didn't say that."

Her eyes twinkled in humor. "Sorry. I couldn't resist." She lightly touched his arm. "I've got to run. Will you have dinner with Granddad and me tonight? I'm making one of his favorites. Pot roast."

"Sounds good. Have a nice day."

"Thanks. You, too."

She hopped into her truck and sped off. Garrett watched her truck and the cloud of dust it kicked up until both disappeared. Giving himself a mental shake, he headed to the barn to start his workday.

He spent the morning pulling apart the remaining stalls and partitions and stacking up the old, rotten wood near the barn door until he could haul it away. Once he was done, he surveyed the now open expanse of the barn. Garrett could see Blair's vision—the large, clean stalls, the open areas for hay, a tack room, and a washing station. Once it was completed, she could house a number of horses here, either horses she rescued or ones she boarded. Either way it would mean a lot of extra work for her on top of her full-time job at the veterinary clinic and her duties as her grandfather's caretaker.

Garrett didn't like the idea of Blair working so hard. Perhaps he could help her, lighten the load a little…

No. It wouldn't be good for either of them if he insinuated himself into her life. He'd help her with the renovations and then get out of her way.

I'm no good for her.

The thought caused an ache in his chest, so he pushed it aside and went back to work.

Garrett found a broom alongside an assortment of old, rusted tools in the corner of the barn and began pushing it across the floor. Dust flew in every direction as he swept, covering him in filth, but he ignored it, determined to finish. He pushed years of dirt and straw and bits of debris from the demolition into several mounds scattered around the barn. Then he grabbed an aluminum shovel and a garbage can fitted with a plastic trash bag and brought them to the first pile. He maneuvered as much of the dirt as he could into the shovel and dumped it into the garbage can, leaving a small ridge of dirt on the cement floor.

"Could you use a hand?"

Garrett peered through the dust motes to see Everett standing in the open barn door, one hand leaning against the frame.

"Sure. You can hold the shovel for me."

Everett approached, looking around the barn in interest. "The old place sure looks different. Much bigger."

"Yeah, for sure." Garrett handed him the shovel. "Can you hold it so I can sweep up the last of this dirt?"

"Sure thing."

Everett obediently complied. After sweeping up the dirt, Garrett handed him the broom to hold while he lifted the shovel and dumped the contents into the garbage can. No way would he allow the old man to do any kind of lifting, no matter how inconsequential. His mother had told him he almost hadn't survived his last heart attack.

Together they moved to each mound of dirt and repeated the process. Once they were done, Everett surveyed their work.

"The old barn hasn't been this clean in decades. It's been neglected for a long time. I haven't had cattle in here for at least twenty years. It'll be good to see it back in use again, but I think it's going to need a lot more work than Blair is expecting. Or can afford."

Leaning against the broom, Everett stuck the toe of his boot into a crack in the cement. "The cement is heaving and breaking up. With all the dirt and straw gone, I can see it's worse than we thought. In some places the cement is worn right through to the dirt underneath."

"Blair is planning to put rubber matting over the floor for the horses. Won't it cover up all the imperfections?"

Everett shook his head. "I don't know about that." He kicked at a piece of heaving cement. "Look at this piece sticking up here. Even if Blair lays that fancy matting over top, it's going to leave a lump that could be a tripping hazard for her and for the horses."

"Is there a way to fix it, smooth it out some?"

"Sure. We jackhammer out all the old cement and pour a new floor."

Garrett surveyed the barn. It was a huge space. Jackhammering the cement and hauling it away would be a monumental job. He couldn't even estimate how long it would take to finish. Pouring new cement had to be expensive. He wondered if Blair could afford it, or if her plans would be finished before they even started.

"You can break the news to her," he said.

"I will. Are you ready for lunch? It'll be ready as soon as I heat some leftovers in the microwave."

Garrett glanced at his watch, surprised to see it was past noon. He'd been too busy to notice the passing of time. It was good to have a job to do, a purpose.

"Sure."

They walked to the house together, Garrett slowing his steps to Everett's. On the front porch, he dusted off as much of the dirt as he could from his jeans and shirt. The old man turned to him with a grin.

"You may want to wash up before you eat."

Garrett understood Everett's amusement once he looked at himself in the bathroom mirror. His face was caked with dirt, as if he'd spent the day in the fields on the back of a tractor, like he had as a teenager. He grinned at the memory. He'd never wanted the life of a farmer, but his memories of growing up on the farm were fond.

Garrett scrubbed the dirt from his face and hands as best he could. As he entered the kitchen, Everett placed a steaming bowl of soup on the table.

"Blair left the fixings for sandwiches in the fridge," he said. "There's bread and butter and cold cuts. Go help yourself."

Garrett did as he was told. In addition to the bread and butter and meats, he found mustard and a tomato that he sliced and added to the sandwich he assembled for himself.

"Would you like me to fix you a sandwich, Everett?"

"No, the soup's enough for me, thanks."

Garrett devoured his first sandwich, along with his soup, before going for seconds. There was nothing like good honest labor to work up an appetite. For the first time in a long time, he felt good. Clearheaded and strong. It was a welcome change.

Everett poured each of them a cup of coffee and sat

across the table from Garrett once more.

"Blair tells me you're going to be boarding your horse here."

"Yeah. I don't know yet whether I'll be keeping him here permanently." Did the old man have a problem with that?

Everett nodded. "So she told me. You'll be spending a lot of time here."

It was a statement rather than a question. "Only until we get the work done on the barn."

The old man barked out a laugh. "You've seen the barn. It's going to take a while."

"I suppose so," Garrett said cautiously. "Look, if you're warning me off again, I get it. I'm no good for Blair. I'm not going to try anything with her."

"You're not paying attention, boy." Everett set his coffee cup on the table with a thud. "I said I don't want Blair to be hurt. I told you to be careful with her, not run away. She deserves some happiness. And whether you know it or not, so do you."

Garrett stared at him, stunned. "I'm not husband material, if that's what you're thinking."

Everett waved his hand, as if waving away his objections. "I'm talking about what my Anna and I had. We were partners, in every sense of the word. We loved each other fiercely and we shared everything about our lives." He leaned back in his chair and sighed, as if his little speech had exhausted him. "I'm an old man, Garrett. I don't have much time left. I want Blair to have what Anna and I had."

"I'm not that guy. I'm not what she needs."

"I've known you since you were a boy. I watched you grow up. I know you're a good man. Whatever's happened to you in the last few years, I know that good man is still inside you. All you have to do is find him again."

Garrett pushed away from the table, desperate to escape. "I need to get back to work. Thank you for lunch."

He hurried out the door and crossed the yard to the barn. Only after reaching the safety of the old building was he able to breathe again.

Everett was wrong, so wrong. He'd never be what Blair needed. He wasn't the white knight of the old man's imagination. Far from it.

It would be best if he kept his distance. Left her completely alone.

The thought served up a surprising punch to his gut.

Chapter Seven

As soon as she got home, Blair made her way to the paddock behind the barn to see the horses. Spending time with them always soothed her, no matter what happened during her day. Today she needed extra soothing. She and Jamie Garvin had had to put down a much beloved twelve-year-old cocker spaniel with cancer. The spaniel's family had been heartbroken, the ten-year-old daughter of the family inconsolable. Her mother told Blair they'd been inseparable. The child's distress had affected her profoundly, more than it should have. It had been difficult not to break into tears herself.

She eased herself between the wooden rails and entered the paddock. Harry was the first to notice her. Cautiously, he stepped forward, enticed, no doubt, by the carrots she'd brought with her.

"Hi, Harry. I'm glad to see you." Blair kept her voice low as she broke a carrot in half and put one piece in the flat-bottomed bowl she'd brought with her. "Are you happy here? I hope so. Are you making friends with Rainbow and Stormy? I hope you give them a chance, because I think you'll be here for a while."

Harry gingerly picked the carrot from the bowl. Blair stroked his mane while he chewed. It had only been a few days, but he was already looking better. His welts were beginning to heal, and Blair was sure his ribs weren't protruding as much as they had the first day she'd seen him. After finishing the carrot, Harry took a few cautious steps away from her. Blair followed him, and he allowed her to stroke him once more.

"It's all right, boy. Everything's going to be fine." A picture of the little girl crying over her cocker spaniel pushed into her memory. An unexpected sob burst from Blair's throat. "She was ten, Harry. The same age Eve would have been."

Blair leaned against Harry as the tears flowed. He stood quietly, as if trying to comfort her. Rainbow and Stormy moved toward them, forming a protective cocoon around her. She reached out to touch them.

"Sorry, guys. Stupid to break down like that. It was a long time ago…" She shivered and wiped the tears from her face with the back of her hands. "Sometimes I wonder who's rescuing who."

"Blair? You okay?"

The sound of Garrett's voice made her straighten her spine. She wiped at her cheeks, needing a moment to compose herself, to slip on her "everything's okay with me" mask. Luckily, the horses mostly shielded her from Garrett's view.

"I'm fine. Just having a moment."

She heard him step closer, and her horses whinnied nervously, not yet used to his presence.

"It sounded like you were crying."

Blair gave a shaky sigh. She couldn't bluff her way out of this one. So she went with a half-truth.

"It was a tough day. We had to put down a family's dog. They took it hard."

Rainbow and Stormy moved away as Garrett approached. Harry stayed rooted to his spot, refusing to leave her. Blair stroked his sides, grateful for his support.

"Sounds like you took it hard, too. I'm sorry."

She didn't trust herself to look into his face. "Occupational hazard. Compassion fatigue is the hardest part of the job."

"Compassion fatigue?"

Blair concentrated on breathing in and out. "Dealing with death and grief when an animal dies. Sometimes it's too much."

"I guess I thought of your job as saving animals. I never thought of the flip side."

A shiver of awareness whispered down her spine as he stepped closer, limping slightly, until he was right beside her. Blair made herself turn to him with a smile, one hand still on Harry. "Luckily for me, I have three empathetic friends here. They know what to do if I'm feeling down. Harry's proving to be a master comforter."

Garrett patted Harry's flank. "Yeah. It's like he knows what's going on in your head."

"Exactly. Horses have the ability to mirror our experiences. They pick up on nonverbal cues and can gauge a person's feelings. I've thought about opening up the farm to people who might benefit from spending time with a horse—troubled teens, people who've been abused or have PTSD."

Garrett ran his hand gently over Harry's flanks. "I know veterans who won't talk to any human therapists. Maybe they'd talk to an equine one."

Blair nodded, wondering if he included himself in that category. She sensed the turmoil inside him, the pain. The memory of Garrett knocking her to the ground and covering her with his body came suddenly to mind.

She rested her forehead against the horse's neck. What had Garrett been thinking about that night? Was it a flashback, or had the alcohol brought on some sort of hallucination? Should she ask him about it, or leave it be?

Despite her worry, she couldn't help remembering the warm weight of his body on hers, the hard muscles of his shoulders and back, the scent of his aftershave mixed with the alcohol. And later, the dizzying kiss they'd shared on the front porch of his parents' house. His lips had been surprisingly soft, his tongue hot and impatient as it swept her mouth. Blair shivered in remembrance. He'd wanted her to stay the night, to have sex with him. It had been so long. Would it really be so bad to take comfort in his arms, in his bed?

It wouldn't be bad at all. In fact, it would be very, very good.

And that's why she couldn't do it.

Harry gently nudged her shoulder with his nose, his way of saying he wanted more attention, more stroking. She complied with a scratch behind his ears. Blair was glad for an interruption to her dangerous line of thinking.

"I think Harry would be an exceptional therapy horse."

Garrett gave Harry's rump a gentle slap. "I should put him to work and make him earn his feed. He's already eaten his weight in pellets."

Blair couldn't resist some gentle teasing. "Face it, Garrett. You're a big softie when it comes to Harry. You went out of your way to rescue him and make him comfortable here."

"Just because I didn't like the idea of turning him into dog food doesn't make me a bleeding heart."

"Of course not."

Blair tried and failed to keep a straight face, while Garrett lost his battle to maintain his scowl. They both laughed, and he shook his head.

"I can't explain what came over me the first time I saw Harry. All I knew was that I had to save him."

Blair nodded, and held his gaze. He had beautiful eyes with ridiculously long lashes that women would kill for. His dark brown hair was thick and a little overlong and shaggy, but somehow it suited him. She couldn't imagine him with a military haircut. The urge to run her hand through his hair made her fingers tingle. She stepped closer to him. Would his hair feel as soft as it looked?

Her breath hitched. *What am I doing?*

She abruptly looked away, hoping Garrett hadn't guessed the direction of her thoughts. Blindly, she stroked Harry once more. Starting something with him was out of the question. She was too consumed by the past to be any kind of partner in the future. And she was certain Garrett had issues of his own.

They were quite the pair.

Garrett cleared his throat. "There's something I need to show you in the barn."

Blair nodded and followed him wordlessly inside. Her eyes needed a moment to adjust to the dull interior after the bright sunshine, but once they did, she saw the open, empty space.

"Oh, my gosh! You finished ripping out the old stalls. This place looks huge!" She'd thought he'd need a few more days to complete the job. Garrett kept surprising her.

"It *is* huge. But that presents its own problems. The bigger it is, the more it's going to cost to put it back together."

Blair's excitement instantly waned. Getting the barn in shape would eat up all her resources, and then some. "True. Where's the construction debris? I'll get changed and start loading it into my truck."

"No need. I've already hauled it to the dump."

"You should have waited for me. That was a big job." She remembered her grandfather's comment about the injury to his leg. "Is that why you're limping? Did you overdo?"

"I've already got a mother, Blair. I don't need another one."

She flinched. "I'm sorry. I only meant I didn't want you to work so hard."

"Maybe I had the same thought about you. You worked hard all day. You didn't need to come home to more work."

She stared at him, not sure what to say. He'd been worried about her? The thought inexplicably brought a lump to her throat that she covered with a shaky laugh.

"I'm not paying you enough."

He threw back his head and laughed. The sound flowed over her like a healing balm.

"You got that right," he said. "Come with me. I want to show you something."

She walked beside him into the middle of the barn. "What are we looking for?"

"Be careful. There's—"

"Oh!"

Blair's foot twisted against a piece of uneven concrete, and she felt herself going down. Strong arms clamped around her waist and prevented her fall. She found herself pressed against Garrett's chest, his lips mere inches from her upturned face. She clutched at his shoulders, unable to breathe as she stared into his dark, fathomless eyes, every nerve ending on fire as she waited for his kiss. As his mouth lowered, her eyes drifted shut, her body shuddering in anticipation.

He set her on her feet and a sudden coolness signaled his withdrawal. She opened her eyes to find him several feet away, his hands fisted at his sides.

"Are you all right?" he asked.

She told herself it was for the best. Garrett Saunders had his demons, and so did she. They were no good for each other. She had no business wanting to kiss him.

Apparently, her body had other ideas.

"I…yes, I'm fine. What happened?"

He poked his booted foot against the uneven concrete. "You lost your footing in this hole." He cleared his throat. "That's what I wanted to talk to you about. We knew the floor was uneven, but it's in much worse shape than we realized. Once I swept up the dirt and old straw, Everett and I could see it."

She walked in a circle. This was the worst area by far. In some spots the concrete had crumbled to dust, and in others it had heaved. Both situations had created deep holes that were tripping hazards for her, and more importantly for the horses. No amount of rubber matting could smooth over this problem.

Her heart plummeted. No way could she house horses in this barn. It would be dangerous for them. A broken fetlock, or ankle, on a horse could mean death. Her dream of starting a rescue farm was over. She'd be hard pressed to care for the two horses she had, not to mention Harry. They'd be fine outside for the rest of the summer and into the fall, but once the cold weather arrived, they'd need shelter from the wind and the biting cold of a North Dakota winter.

What the hell was she going to do?

Her mind started to think in practical terms. She walked around the remainder of the barn.

"The floor's not too bad over here by the back door," she said. "We could build a couple of stalls and fence the rest off."

"It's a small area. That would probably mean you only have room for two horses."

"I know." He was probably unhappy about her not being able to live up to her promise to board Harry.

"Even if you only used that small portion of the barn, the concrete is likely to crumble and heave like the rest of it in a few years."

"What else can I do? I can't afford to replace this floor."

"I know." He lightly squeezed her shoulder. "Come on. I'll walk you to the house. I think dinner is ready."

Everett was puttering around the kitchen as she entered the house with Garrett, the aroma of roast beef wafting through the room. He stood at the sink, filling the teakettle with water. Three places had been set at the table, and she was relieved to see that Garrett had accepted her dinner invitation.

Relieved? She shook her head, not understanding her own thoughts.

She went to her grandfather and kissed his cheek.

"Did you have a good day, Granddad?"

"It was interesting, I'll say that for my day."

"Yeah, mine too. But not in a good way."

He chuckled as he patted her shoulder. "We'll see if we can't fix that. Why don't you two sit down? Everything is ready."

"I can help you, Granddad."

"No. Go sit down. I may be old and feeble, but I can carry a bowl of mashed potatoes to the table."

Blair knew better than to argue with him. She obediently sat at the table across from Garrett. He cleared his throat before speaking.

"I showed Blair the barn floor."

"Good, good. I've had some thoughts about it, but I want to eat first. I like to have a full stomach before I talk business."

Everett brought the pot roast to the table, and Garrett carved it while he strained carrots and slid them into a bowl. Blair had prepared everything the night before; she'd peeled the carrots and potatoes and left instructions for her grandfather as to cooking times. But even so, it was nice to be waited on a little.

They made small talk as they ate. Blair told Everett about her day, and relayed Grace Saunders' message about having dinner with them. She kept waiting for him to bring up the subject of the barn floor, but he seemed content to make her wait. Finally, Everett was done eating and turned to her with a smile.

"Why don't you put on the kettle? We can have our tea while we figure out what to do about that barn."

Blair put the kettle on the stovetop and turned on the element. While she waited for the water to boil, she pulled a teapot from the cupboard and threw a couple of tea bags inside.

"I really can't see as there's anything to be done about that floor. I'll make do for now and save up until I can afford to replace the cement." She wondered how long that would take. She made a decent wage as a veterinary technician, and had managed to put away a few dollars, but it was nowhere near the kind of money she'd need for this project.

"You need that floor done now, for the horses you already have and the ones you want to board in the future."

"Yeah, but—"

"I'll pay for it," Everett said.

"What? No, absolutely not."

"Why not? It's not like I need anything. You take care of everything for me. And besides, the farm belongs to me, remember?"

"Granddad—"

"Don't argue with me, Blair. I've got a weak heart, remember?"

She caught the gleam of humor in his eye and couldn't help but laugh. "You devious old man. I love you, you know. But I can't take your money."

"I love you, too." He grasped her hand and squeezed with surprising strength. "You've never asked for anything from me. This is one thing I can do for you. Let me do it. It would make me very happy."

Blair got to her feet, poured boiling water into the teapot, and brought it to the table. How could she say no to that? Still, she'd be taking advantage of him if she accepted his money. She was sure her mother would see it that way.

"I don't know…"

"I'll supply the concrete and the wood for new stalls. But my plan hinges on Garrett. If he's willing to jackhammer the old concrete and haul it away, we can make this happen. What do you say, Garrett? Are you willing to supply the labor?"

"Granddad, you can't expect Garrett—"

"I can answer for myself, Blair." He gave her a cool, unsmiling nod before turning to Everett. "I'll get rid of the old broken concrete and prepare the floor for the new concrete. In exchange, you and Blair will house and feed Harry until next spring. We'll revisit Harry's arrangements at that time."

Blair blinked at him. Doing this work on her farm would mean she'd see Garrett every day, possibly for weeks. Garrett was bad for her peace of mind. Was it wise to be in such close contact with him?

"You don't have to do this. If you aren't able to find a place for Harry, you know I'd keep him here."

"I want to help." One corner of his mouth turned up in a grin that Blair found incredibly sexy. "Besides, I'm starting to like your cooking."

Blair returned his smile, then sobered. "This sounds like a lot of work. Are you really sure you want to do this?"

His gaze was steady on hers. "I'm not changing my mind."

Blair's throat tightened with emotion. Her granddad paying for such a big expense was a surprise, but not a big one. He'd always been generous with his time and money. But Garrett's contribution mystified her. The cost of boarding Harry likely wouldn't cover the cost of his labor. Why was he doing this? What did he want from her?

The possibilities that floated through her head both excited and frightened her.

"Whenever I'm not at work, I'm going to be jackhammering right alongside you," she told him. "You don't get to have all the fun."

Garrett's lips clamped together as if holding back a rebuttal, but in the end, he sighed and nodded. "I know."

"As long as we understand each other." She lifted her teacup in a toast. "To my new barn floor, and the two men making it possible."

Chapter Eight

The ringing of his cell phone woke Garrett from a deep sleep. He rolled over and groaned. Who the hell was calling in the middle of the night? Swearing, he groped blindly for the phone on his bedside table.

"Hello?"

"I woke you up. I'm sorry, I shouldn't have called. I'll go."

He recognized that voice. "Chris? Chris Redwick? Is that you? Wait, don't hang up."

"Yeah, it's me. I just…" Chris's voice cracked. "Why is everything so messed up?"

Garrett sat up, immediately awake and on high alert. "What's happened? Are you all right?"

"Why am I alive, Garrett? Tommy's dead, and your leg's gone, and I make it through three tours without a scratch. Why?"

The pain in his friend's voice grabbed him by the throat. Chris had been drinking—a lot, if he was any judge. "I don't know, buddy. All I can tell you is I'm glad you're alive. You've got a wife and a couple of kids. They need you. You've got to be strong for them."

"I know. I'm trying, but it's hard."

"Yeah, I know."

The line went silent, and for a moment Garrett thought he'd hung up. "Chris, are you there?"

"Yeah. Yeah, I'm here."

"Have you talked to anyone, you know, at the VA hospital, told them you're having trouble?"

"You know I can't do that. You're out of the military, so it doesn't matter to you, but I'm still in. If I tell them my head's messed up, my career's over. Nobody wants a head case watching their back. I'll be fine. When this leave is over, I'm going back. I'll be fine."

"Chris—"

"Sorry I woke you, man."

The hum of the dial tone told him Chris had hung up. Garrett scrubbed his face with his hand.

"Shit."

What the hell was he supposed to do? Chris had survived three tours of duty, two in Iraq and one in Afghanistan, without sustaining so much as a hangnail. But it sounded like his friend's wounds might be the kind that couldn't be fixed with the help of a skillful surgeon.

He didn't know how to help him. And even if he did, he didn't think Chris would accept help, especially if it meant jeopardizing his career.

If he wasn't reaching out for help, why did he call me?

It was pointless to try to go back to sleep. He swung his legs to the side of the bed and reached for his prosthetic and the paraphernalia that went with it. He rolled the cotton liner over his stump, and then the silicone liner, pushed his stump into the prosthetic, and stood, listening for the telltale click as the artificial leg locked into place.

Now what? What did he do at three in the morning if he wasn't sleeping?

He could go downstairs, make himself something to eat, watch TV until he got sleepy again. But he wasn't hungry, and he didn't want to wake his parents with his prowling. His mother possessed an uncanny ability to detect his insomnia, and he didn't want to worry her again. For the hundredth time he told himself he needed a place of his own.

So if he didn't go downstairs, that meant he had to stay in his room. His gaze drifted to his closed closet door. His footlocker was in there, and he'd hidden a full bottle of bourbon inside shortly before promising Blair he wouldn't show up at her place drunk or hung over.

His promise had been easy to keep to this point. After a long day of physical labor, he fell exhausted into his bed most nights and slept like the dead until morning.

Chris's words played over and over in his head. *Why am I alive, Garrett? Tommy's dead, and your leg's gone, and I make it through without a scratch. Why?*

Why am I alive?

A question he'd asked himself many times.

He fought against the bourbon's magnetic pull. He pictured Blair and the disappointment on her face if he showed up hung over and stinking of booze tomorrow morning.

All he needed was one drink and he'd be able to go back to sleep. He'd sleep off any effects of the alcohol, and Blair would never know.

He walked across his room to the closet, careful to avoid the creakiest floorboards, hating himself for acting like a thief in the night.

And hating himself for needing the bourbon.

The bottle was buried under several layers of

clothes. He pulled it from its hiding place, opened the cap, and drank deeply, savoring the fire.

One drink turned to two, then four, then six before he lost count. He set the bottle on his nightstand and stumbled into bed.

****

Sometime during the night Garrett decided that the perfect way to avoid Blair's censure was to avoid her. The next morning, instead of driving to her farm, he made a trip to Bismarck to rent a jackhammer from a tool rental shop, sending her a text to tell her what he was doing. His head pounded and his stomach roiled as he drove, which he considered penance for getting drunk. He deserved the hangover for his weakness, and especially for his cowardice in avoiding Blair.

At the tool rental shop, the clerk handed him a jackhammer so he could get the feel of it. The weight of the machine instantly brought back memories of other pieces of equipment he'd handled. He had a sudden vision of hoisting a Stinger rocket launcher to his shoulder and firing. Memories ran together. The deafening explosion, the heat, the smell.

"Mister? You okay?"

The clerk's words snapped him back to the present. Garrett set down the jackhammer and struggled to pull himself together, coughing a couple of times to cover his embarrassment.

"Yeah, I'm fine. Thing's a lot heavier than I expected."

The clerk gave him a quick tutorial on how to use the jackhammer. Included in the rental was a hard hat, eye protection, and earmuffs to deaden the considerable noise the jackhammer would make. The clerk also recommended that Garrett use heavy steel-toed boots and a dust mask. Garrett signed the papers to rent it for a week and got the hell out of the shop.

From there he went to a big box store and bought a heavy-duty wheelbarrow to move the debris from the barn into the dumpster Blair had ordered for delivery later that day. By the time he got back to Blair's farm, she was at work, as he'd planned. He loaded the jackhammer and the rest of the equipment into the wheelbarrow and pushed it to the barn.

He wondered what he'd gotten himself into. But he wasn't about to go back on his promise to Blair.

After putting on his protective gear, Garrett plugged in the electric jackhammer and began breaking up the concrete. The job was easy in areas where the concrete had already deteriorated, but miserably difficult where it was several inches thick and embedded with iron rebar for strength. The dumpster arrived shortly before noon, and it was a relief to take a break from the noise and vibration of the jackhammer to begin clearing the debris. He opened the gate at the back of the dumpster and began wheeling in loads of broken concrete. The work was heavy and dusty, and his muscles screamed in protest. He ignored the discomfort in his stump as much as he could. The silicone liner under the prosthesis got hot and incredibly sweaty in heat like today's. The moisture-wicking sock he wore inside the liner was probably working overtime.

Despite his roaring headache, despite the heat, and the sweat that ran into his eyes, he felt useful. And it sounded ridiculous to admit, even to himself, but he felt important, too. Without him, Blair's plans for the barn wouldn't be possible. He held onto that thought like a talisman. He hadn't felt important since his world had exploded in Afghanistan.

He broke for a half-hour lunch with Everett, and went back to work with the jackhammer again, alternating between breaking up the concrete and wheeling the debris into the dumpster. A couple of hours later, Everett appeared in the doorway of the barn with a thermos in his hands.

"It's time you took a break," he announced. "You'll be no good to Blair if you keel over from heat exhaustion."

Garrett set the wheelbarrow down and grinned at him. "I suppose you have a point there."

"Come on outside and get out of this dust for a while."

Garrett followed him to the side of the barn, where a couple of lawn chairs sat in the shade of a massive cottonwood. He lowered himself into a chair and gratefully accepted the thermos.

"Thanks."

He poured water into the attached cup and raised it to his lips. The water slid down his dusty throat, and he quickly drained the cup. He filled it again and again until the thermos was empty. Everett snorted.

"Looks like I'm going to have to look out for you, boy."

"I appreciate it."

He absently rubbed the spot where his leg ended and the prosthesis began. The vibration of the jackhammer and being on his feet for so long caused an irritation against his stump. For the most part, he had little pain with the stump, but if he did too much or walked too far, it reminded him that he wasn't the man he used to be. Having to admit his limitations was frustrating.

"Your leg giving you trouble?" Everett asked.

Garrett immediately stopped his massage. "It's fine."

The old man snorted again. "Sure it is, and I've got the heart of a twenty-year-old. You don't have to finish this work all in one day, you know. And you certainly don't have to prove anything to me or Blair."

"Maybe I have to prove something to myself."

Everett leaned back in his chair. "Maybe you do. See you don't kill yourself in the process. We'll need you for a while yet."

That made Garrett laugh. "Your concern is heartwarming, Everett. I promise I won't self-destruct until I've finished this job."

Everett nodded. "Good to know."

Garrett rested a few minutes longer, enjoying the cool breeze in the shade of the tree, and the sound of birds singing. Finally, he pushed himself to his feet. He couldn't sit around appreciating nature all afternoon if he was going to finish Blair's barn.

"I'd better get back to work. Thanks for the water."

Everett remained in his chair. "You're welcome. I know things aren't the same as they used to be, but that doesn't mean you're any less a man. Don't be so hard on yourself."

It wasn't exactly a secret that part of his right leg had been amputated, but he never talked about it, and no one outside of his family had seen his prosthesis. He made a point of wearing long pants, no matter how hot it was.

Even so, he shouldn't have been surprised that Everett knew. But if Everett knew, that had to mean Blair did, too, though she'd never given any indication. He hated the thought that she pitied him.

What do I want her to feel for me?

He gave Everett a brisk nod before returning to the barn. No matter what Everett said, what kind of life could he have if he couldn't do the work he loved, or live the life he wanted? And he was never going to feel like a whole man again. How could he when pity was all he could expect from any woman?

****

As soon as Blair stepped out of her truck, she heard the machine-gun-like clatter of the jackhammer coming from the barn. She headed in the direction of the noise, curious to see how much progress Garrett had made.

His naked back faced her as she entered the building. Blair's breath caught as she took in the broad shoulders, the play of muscles across his back, the straining of his biceps as they controlled the jackhammer. Garrett Saunders was quite possibly the most beautiful man she'd ever seen.

He turned off the machine and set the jackhammer on the ground. Bending with his hands on his knees, he hung his head as if he were ill or utterly exhausted. Blair hurried to his side, her heart in her throat.

"Are you hurt?"

As soon as he heard her voice, he straightened to his full height. Without looking at her, he grabbed his T-shirt from the arm of the wheelbarrow and pulled it over his head.

"I'm fine."

"Are you sure?" She touched his arm, wanting to

reassure herself that he was whole and unhurt. "You looked like you were going to be sick."

He jerked away from her touch. "I don't need you to hover over me. I said I'm fine."

His rebuff hit her like a slap on the face. And so did the smell of stale liquor that wafted from his body. He'd been drinking, and though he wasn't drunk now, he had been sometime in the recent past. She closed her eyes in anguish, the disappointment nearly bringing her to her knees. She'd believed in him, had hoped…

Don't go there, Blair.

She folded her arms across her chest, refusing to let him see how much breaking his promise hurt her. "Really? From where I'm standing, you don't look so fine, Mr. Grumpy."

"Mr. Grumpy?"

She stared him down, willing her voice not to crack. "I call them like I see them."

He put his hands on his hips and bowed his head. "I'm fine, Blair, really. Just tired."

She looked around the barn floor, searching for something to say. A large section had been jackhammered. Despite the hangover, he'd managed to get a lot accomplished.

"You've done a lot today. Are you trying to break a record or something? Most concrete smashed in a single day?"

He lifted his head to look at her, one side of his mouth turning up in a grin.

"Possibly."

"Well, cut it out. Save a little enthusiasm for the rest of the job."

"You sound like your grandfather."

"Good. He's a wise man." She headed for the door. "Dinner should be ready in about a half hour. Be there."

From the corner of her eye she saw Garrett's mock salute. "Aye, aye."

"I mean it, Garrett. If you're not in the house at exactly six, I'm feeding your dinner to Jake."

"Fine. I'll be there."

Blair hurried across the yard, torn between fury and despair. She should go back to the barn and tell him to leave right now. She would not, under any circumstances, tolerate his drinking.

She stopped at her truck to retrieve a couple of bags of groceries and slowly made her way up the front porch steps. Despite her anger, she couldn't send him away. There were practicalities to consider, the largest being her barn. No one was going to beat a path to her door to finish the work for free. She had no choice but to allow him to complete the work.

And she was honest enough to admit that even if she could afford to pay someone else to do the work, she wouldn't ask Garrett to leave. She understood he needed the purpose the renovation of her barn provided. She wouldn't take that away from him.

Perhaps she was being too soft and would live to regret her decision. But she had no choice. She cared too much about Garrett's well-being and his future to simply cut him loose.

She cared for him too much.

She didn't want to care for him. Garrett Saunders was a complex man, and she suspected he didn't share his feelings or emotions easily.

She pushed that thought aside. Whatever her feelings, she couldn't ignore what had happened. It wouldn't be good for either of them.

At ten minutes before six, Garrett walked into the house. He gave Blair a wry grin.

"I talked it over with Jake, and he said he'd be fine with his kibble."

Blair gave him a feeble smile. "That was very generous of him."

"What can I say? He's a generous dog." He avoided her gaze. "I'd better clean up before we eat."

"Dinner will be on the table when you get back."

He nodded, and then disappeared down the hallway that led to the bathroom. Blair turned her attention to setting the table. Since it was so hot, she'd made a potato salad the evening before, and picked up an assortment of cold cuts and breads at the grocery store in town after work. It wasn't much, but it was about all she had the energy for at the moment.

Why did Garrett have to ruin everything by drinking?

"That's quite the glum look on your face," Everett said. "Care to share what's on your mind?"

"Not really."

"Did you and Garrett have some kind of tiff?"

"Anyone ever tell you you're a nosy old man?"

"Only you. Are you going to tell me what's wrong?"

"No."

He folded his arms across his chest. "Hrumph."

Blair arched an eyebrow at him but said nothing more as she brought the rest of the food to the table. A minute later Garrett returned wearing a clean shirt, his face and hands freshly scrubbed. He sat at his usual spot at the table. Blair noticed his wince of discomfort as he lifted the heavy pitcher of lemonade. Her first instinct was to take the pitcher from him and pour his glass of lemonade for him, but at the last second, she decided not to draw attention to his difficulty. Garrett's pride would take a hit if she helped him with so basic a task. Unfortunately, her grandfather also saw his wince.

"If you keep pushing yourself like you did today, pretty soon you won't be able to lift a fork, much less a pitcher of lemonade."

"I'm just stiff. It's been a while since I did heavy physical labor. Once I get used to it again, I'll be fine."

"Hrumph." Everett's answer was somewhere between a grunt and a snort. "Well, I hope you get used to it before you do yourself an injury."

Garrett looked at Blair. "Is there anything you'd like to add to that? You want to let me have it, too?"

"No, thanks, I'll pass. Granddad is doing a fine job all by himself." Anything she had to say to him, she'd say in private. "Potato salad?"

"Thanks." He accepted the bowl from her and helped himself.

They ate in silence until the phone on the kitchen wall rang. Blair excused herself and got up from the table to answer.

"Hello?"

"Hello." An older gentleman's voice came on the line. "Is this Blair?"

"Yes, it is."

"Hello, Blair. This is Tom Kramer. I live about five miles down the road from your Grandpa's place. He told me you have horses, and I saw three on the road as I was coming home. I thought they might be yours. It looked like part of the fence was down."

"Oh, no. Can you tell me again exactly where you saw them?" She noticed that both her Granddad and Garrett had stopped eating to listen to her conversation.

"About four miles west of your farm at the point where your pasture meets my land. I'd hate for them to get into my wheat."

"Yes, of course. I didn't realize there was a problem with the fence in that area. I'm going to round them up right now, Mr. Kramer. Thanks for letting me know."

She hung up the phone and grabbed her truck keys from a hook near the door. "The horses got out."

"Harry too?"

"Yep. Knowing Harry, he was probably the ringleader."

Garrett rose to his feet. "I'll come with you."

"You haven't finished eating."

"Neither have you."

She didn't have time to argue, and the truth was she really could use his help. "Could you bring my trailer with your truck?"

"Sure. Where to?"

She relayed the information Tom Kramer had given her. "I'll meet you there. Hopefully they haven't wandered far from that spot."

"Tom wouldn't like it if they set foot into his wheat field," Everett said.

"Yeah, I got that distinct impression. I've got to run, Granddad."

After dashing to the garage to pick up halters and lead ropes, she hurried to her truck and raced out of the yard, gravel spitting behind her. In a few minutes she reached the horses. Blair was relieved to find them happily grazing in the tall grass in the ditch next to her pasture rather than in the ripening wheat field across the road. Aside from making a mess in the field, eating too much grain could result in colic, a potentially fatal disease for horses.

She approached them calmly, her voice quiet.

"Hi, guys. You've been very naughty, haven't you?" The barbed wire had snapped in a couple of spots and one of the fence posts had fallen over, allowing the horses to simply walk over it to graze in the lush grass of the ditch. "I hate to break up your party, but as soon as Garrett gets here with the trailer, it'll be time to go home."

Their only answer was to raise their heads and stare at her, their mouths full of grass. Blair grinned. "You could at least pretend to be sorry."

They didn't move as she slipped their halters over their heads and attached the leads. Her horses were remarkably placid and likely wouldn't have knocked the fence post down themselves, though she might not put it past Harry. But they likely found it that way and took advantage of the situation.

"Exactly what I need. More problems."

Rainbow whinnied at the distress in her voice. She patted her nose.

"Sorry, girl. There's so much going on, so many things to worry about…"

She'd checked the fences before bringing her horses into this section of the pasture, and she'd thought they were fine. Apparently, she had a lot yet to learn.

Had she taken on more than she could handle by bringing her horses here? At the boarding stable, she didn't have to worry about fences or barn floors or where to buy feed, or any of a hundred other things. She hated second guessing herself and her abilities, both physical and financial, and she hated having to rely so heavily on Garrett's help. She couldn't expect him to continue doing so much work for nothing.

Her parents had told her she was crazy to be moving to the farm. They disapproved of her career, her love of horses, and the simple, rural life. Mostly, they disapproved of her and all the mistakes she'd made.

Garrett arrived a couple of moments later. Blair led all three horses out of the ditch and eased them into the trailer without incident, though it was crowded with all three of them inside. She helped Garrett lift the ramp and secure it.

His gaze drifted to the ditch and the downed fence. "Looks like we've got some fencing to do."

"I can handle it."

"It'll go a lot faster and easier if I help you."

"I know how to fix fence. I can manage on my own."

"What's the big deal? If we work together, we can knock out this job in an hour or two."

In that moment she hit her wall. Frustration gnawed at Blair's gut. "No! Why would you volunteer for more work? I can't pay you, and I have nothing left to barter. I'm already boarding Harry, and my cooking isn't so great that it justifies everything you've done for me. I need to do this one thing on my own."

"Why? What the hell are you trying to prove?"

"That I don't need to be coddled and babysat! That I'm not a screw-up, dammit!"

Her voice rose, and she heard the desperation in it. The horses whinnied and stamped their feet in the trailer, picking up on her distress. But now that the emotions she kept so carefully hidden had pushed their way to the surface, she couldn't control them. She turned away, not wanting Garrett to see the tears that threatened to fall.

Garrett stepped in front of her and grasped her chin, forcing her to look at him. The expression on his face registered confusion and surprise. Blair squeezed her eyes closed. She hated burdening him with her problems. Of everything he'd given her, his pity would be the one unwelcome thing.

"You, a screw-up? That's crazy. You're the most together person I know. Why would you say that?"

She opened her eyes and blew out a breath, steeling herself for his reaction. "I'm not nearly as together as you think. Once, a long time ago, I tried to kill myself."

Chapter Nine

Garrett's heart stuttered at her words. He grasped her shoulders, needing to hold on to her, to touch her. His fingers pressed into her soft flesh.

"What happened?"

He felt a shudder vibrate her small shoulders. "I was sick. In my late teens. Clinical depression, they called it. A chemical imbalance. All I know is that, for a while, I didn't want to live anymore."

"Jesus." Garrett pulled her close and held her. She felt insubstantial in his arms, small and fragile. Yet she'd survived, and even thrived. Her survival spoke to her inner strength and courage. He hung onto that thought.

"First I got very drunk, and then I swallowed my mother's sleeping pills," she whispered against his chest. "I thought she was gone for the day, that no one would find me until…until it was over. But she came home, and called an ambulance, and the rest is history. I spent some time in hospital and months in therapy. But I'm all better now."

Garrett wrapped his arms a little tighter around her. "I know."

"When I recovered enough to think about a future, I told my parents I wanted to be a veterinary technician and specialize in equine medicine. They tried to talk me into something they deemed more respectable. My grandparents were the only ones who supported me."

"You made the right choice for you. Working with animals is what you're meant to do."

"I shouldn't have told you."

"I'm glad you did."

"I don't tell a lot of people because, once they find out, it changes the way they look at me. They either treat me like a freak or handle me with kid gloves. Or they feel sorry for me. Don't you dare feel sorry for me, Garrett Saunders." She fisted her hands in his T-shirt. "Don't you dare."

He grasped her shoulders and held her at arm's length so he could look into her face. So she could see the truth in his eyes. "I know what it is to struggle with that little voice in your head that tells you to give up. I know it's not easy to overcome. You're an incredibly strong woman, Blair Greyson."

She stared up at him in surprised silence, her lips parted. Had no one ever told her how amazing she was? She'd come back from the brink and was whole and strong.

Tears welled in her eyes. "Thank you."

He wiped a tear that slipped down her cheek. "Don't cry, Blair. Please don't cry."

He lost his fight to resist her. He lowered his lips to hers and drank in her sweetness, his fingers tangling in her long, silky hair. He wanted to stay with her like this forever, wanted to hear her soft sighs, feel her breasts pressing against his chest, savor the taste of her on his tongue as it danced with hers.

God, the taste of her. She was so incredibly sweet.

Too soon she broke the kiss and stepped away. She looked toward the horse trailer, avoiding his gaze.

"We can't keep them cooped up in the trailer any longer."

She obviously didn't want to talk about what had happened between them, but whether it was the confidences she'd shared or their kiss, Garrett wasn't sure. He understood how she felt. Everything they'd shared was too raw, and somehow too intimate to deal with right now.

"Right. Where are we taking them?"

"They'll have to go back into the paddock behind the barn. I'll meet you there."

With that she pulled away, and he dropped his arms. He watched her hurry to her truck and take off down the road. With a sigh, he got into his own truck. He found an approach and slowly turned the horse trailer around. Ten minutes later, he pulled the trailer behind the barn near the paddock. Blair was waiting for him. Without a word she began to unlock the gate of the trailer, her attention intent on her task. Garrett didn't want to talk about the kiss they'd shared either, but he hated feeling uneasy with her, and he didn't want her to think the confidences she'd shared meant nothing to him.

"Thank you for telling me what happened to you. I know it wasn't easy for you."

She looked up at him. "No, it wasn't, but I'm glad I told you. I hope someday you'll trust me enough to return the favor. I've been told I'm a very good listener. Anytime you want to tell me your story, I'm here."

Her generosity humbled him. "Thank you."

She turned her attention back to her work. "I haven't had a drop of alcohol since the day I tried to kill myself."

She backed the horses from the trailer one by one and set them free in the paddock. Following a leisurely drink at the trough, they ambled off. Blair leaned against a fence post and watched them until they disappeared in a copse of trees. She turned to him, her eyes not quite meeting his.

"I know you've been drinking again. I smelled it on you earlier, in the barn."

Garrett stared at a broken window on the barn. Shame filled him, making him feel small and weak. Losing his leg didn't hurt half as much as losing Blair's respect.

"I'm going back to the house," she said. "Why don't you come with me? You can finish your dinner."

"I think I'm going to head home."

"Okay." She swallowed and gave him a wobbly smile. "I'm off work tomorrow, so you can show me how to use the jackhammer. I told you you couldn't have all the fun."

"Won't you be busy fixing fence in the pasture? All by yourself?"

Her smile waned. "Right. Thanks for reminding me."

"No problem." He hesitated, then swallowed. "Are you sure you want me to come back tomorrow?"

"Yes, I want you to come back. I'm hoping this was a one-time thing and it won't happen again. You won't make me regret my decision, will you?"

He'd die before disappointing her again. "You won't regret it."

She smiled, and he saw relief in her eyes. "Good. I'll see you tomorrow."

"Bye."

Blair headed back to the house. Once she rounded the corner of the barn and was out of sight, Garrett expelled a pent-up breath and unhitched the horse trailer from his truck. She was nothing if not honest. He respected her for it. He was a man who drank, and she was a woman who couldn't tolerate drinking. End of story. She could have tossed him out on his ass, but she'd given him another chance. He'd known a relationship with her wouldn't work even before she spelled it out, however subtly. Not that he'd been looking for a relationship.

So if he knew all this, why did he feel so goddamn empty?

****

Blair attached the fence stretcher to each end of the broken barbed wire and, using the ratchet on the stretcher, pulled the wires between the two posts taut. With her pliers, she bent a small loop in each broken end, and using another piece of wire a bit longer than the gap she was trying to mend, looped the two broken ends together. A few twists more and the wire strand was mended. Only three more strands to go.

Finishing, she surveyed her work. Not bad, perhaps not as neat as her granddad would have done in his day, but it got the job done. At least for now.

But not in the long run. Most of the fencing in her one-hundred-and-sixty-acre pasture was old and had been originally constructed for cattle. That meant the majority of it was made of barbed wire, which had a lot of disadvantages for horses. They couldn't see it well and could run into it, injuring themselves. Fortunately, the fence was so old that it would fall over before causing any injury. An ideal fence for the horses would have all wood posts and rails that would be highly visible for the horses, and tall and strong enough to keep them securely inside the pasture.

Unfortunately, she couldn't afford such a fence for the entire pasture. Only the area nearest the barn had a post-and-rail fence. The rest would have to be barbed wire, or maybe electric rope in a couple of places. One problem at a time.

She gathered her tools and stowed them in the back of her truck, pleased that it had only taken her a couple of hours to mend the barbed wire and replace the rotten fence post. She'd have time before lunch to help Garrett with the barn floor.

Garrett. Blair swallowed past the lump in her throat. The intimacies they'd shared yesterday—the conversation and the kiss—had left her feeling raw and vulnerable. She rarely talked about the suicide attempt that had nearly killed her. His reaction to her confession, that she'd been strong enough to overcome her demons, had warmed her heart. But he didn't know the whole story. If he did, perhaps he wouldn't be so quick to forgive.

She pushed the troubling thought from her mind, unwilling to go there.

Instead, she considered their other problem. He'd broken his promise to her and showed up hung over. The incident at his sister's party began to look less like a one-off and more like a chronic problem. Blair didn't know if that was the case, but her gut told her that where there was smoke, there was fire.

Alcohol was a problem in her family. She understood what a devastating addiction it could be. And yet here she was, entering into a business agreement with Garrett.

Despite knowing her for such a short length of time, Garrett understood her in a way her family, with the exception of her granddad, had trouble with. His instinct was to help her with the fence, but he'd given her space to handle it on her own because he realized how important it was for her to know she could do it. He trusted her abilities.

It hurt to know they could never be more than friends. Especially after yesterday's kiss.

Yesterday's kiss. She'd never known a kiss could be so sweet, yet so erotic at the same time. She loved the way he'd held her close, as if she was something precious, and the way his tongue swept her mouth, possessing her, mastering her, yet so gentle it made her want to weep. The first kiss they'd shared had been all fire and urgency, and it had tempted her beyond reason. But yesterday's kiss had broken her heart with its quiet tenderness.

She drove back to the farm and parked in front of the house. As she walked toward the barn, she saw Garrett push the wheelbarrow up a wooden ramp and into the dumpster. He emptied the contents and pushed the barrow back down the ramp. As soon as he saw her, he set the barrow down. His smile appeared tentative, as if he wasn't certain he had any right to smile at her. Blair's heart ached for him. She had no wish to make him feel ill at ease with her.

"Hey. Did you get your fence mended?"

"Yeah, all done. Until the next time it falls apart."

"Harry tells me he and his friends promise not to wander away again as long as you keep the carrots coming."

"I'll make sure to lay in a fresh supply."

Conversation stalled. Blair didn't know what to say, or even where to look. Yesterday's shared intimacies had left both of them feeling their way. She didn't want to be awkward with Garrett. They had to work together, and even after it was all over, she hoped they could remain friends. Or at least a reasonable facsimile to friendship.

"It won't happen again. I won't show up hung over again."

Blair blinked at Garrett. He lifted his chin, and she saw a glimpse of the proud man who had taken several blows but wasn't ready to be counted out.

"I screwed up and got drunk the other night. As long as I'm working on your farm, it won't happen again. If it does, I won't bother showing up."

Blair swallowed, and nodded, her heart beating so hard she was sure he could hear it. She stared at the ground, at her scuffed and dirty sneakers, and at his dusty work boots. She wanted to ask him what had happened to cause him to break his promise to her, but their relationship was hardly intimate enough for such confidences. For a split second she wished it were.

She lifted her gaze to his. "Thank you for being so honest with me."

He nodded curtly and backed away, but not before Blair saw what looked like relief on his face. "I'd better get back to work."

"I'm going to the house to fix lunch, but later you need to show me how to use that jackhammer."

A slow smile spread across his face. "Are you still obsessed with that thing? Trust me, it's heavy and loud and kicks up a hell of a pile of dust."

"Tell the truth. You don't want to share."

His grin grew wider. "Seriously, what's with the fascination for jackhammers?"

"I just…" She tried to find the words to explain. "This is my home now, and I want to be a part of it all. I want to know that I've had a hand in everything that happens here. That I can handle whatever comes up."

His expression gave no hint as to his thoughts. "I see."

"I know it must sound silly to you—"

"No, not at all. I'm sure I'll feel the same way with my own place. After lunch, I'll show you what you need to know, and you can break up all the concrete you want. Try not to hurt yourself."

"Thanks."

As she walked back to the house, Blair couldn't stop smiling. A corner had been turned in their relationship, she could feel it.

For one crazy moment, she wished their relationship could be something more. Then she thrust away her wishes. There could never be anything between them, because whatever problems Garrett might have, whatever sins he may have committed, hers were far greater.

She could never forget it.

Chapter Ten

"There's no way you're going to maneuver that thing."

Blair raised her chin, her eyes bright with purpose. "Watch me."

She grasped the handles of the wheelbarrow, bent her knees for leverage, and lifted it onto its front wheel. The barrow was loaded with chunks of concrete and probably weighed twice as much as she did, but Blair was nothing if not determined. The barrow wandered a little from side to side as she pushed it out of the barn and toward the dumpster, but she was doing it. Garrett admired her grit, and the spark inside her that wouldn't say no to a challenge. He'd made an offhand remark about the full load of concrete debris in the wheelbarrow being too heavy for her to lift.

This was one time he was happy to be proven wrong.

With a grunt, she pushed the wheelbarrow up the low ramp leading into the dumpster. Suddenly she lost control and the barrow tipped to one side, dumping its contents to the ground. She let fly with an impressive string of cuss words.

Garrett couldn't stop his chuckle. "Close, but no cigar. Too bad, Greyson."

"Nobody likes a smartass, Saunders."

Her words were tough but spoken without venom.

Her smart mouth was one of the things he liked most about Blair. That and her quick laugh, and even quicker wit. All of it was wrapped in a pretty package and tied together with a beautiful smile and ever-changing gray-green eyes.

But he couldn't forget what she'd confessed to him. It was hard to believe the beautiful, confident woman he saw now could have tried to kill herself.

"I'll get a shovel and help you clean up your mess."

He laughed when she stuck her tongue out at him.

He returned a couple of minutes later with two shovels. It didn't take long to scoop up the broken chunks of concrete and throw them into the dumpster.

"Do you think I need to call for another dumpster?" Blair asked as she leaned against her shovel. "They said not to fill it more than half full with concrete waste or it would be too heavy to lift back onto the truck. We're nearly at the halfway point now."

"I think we should have enough room. We're almost done with the demolition."

"Thank goodness! I'm not too proud to tell you that I'm exhausted. If I never see another wheelbarrow it'll be too soon."

He wasn't surprised she was tired. For the past week, she'd joined him every day after work, either operating the jackhammer or shoveling the debris into the wheelbarrow and hauling it to the dumpster. She'd worked every bit as hard as he had, maybe harder.

He was proud of her. But that didn't stop him from teasing her.

"You can't quit yet. We have to prepare the floor and pour the concrete. Of course, if it's too much for you, you can always stay in the house where it's nice and cool."

Her chin jutted defiantly. "Tell me if it's too much for *you*. I'm not going anywhere."

He laughed. "I could use a break. Let's take five and get a drink of water."

She puffed out a tired breath. "Yeah, good idea."

They walked to the front porch of the house together. When he was working on his own, he'd have a quick drink and get back to work. But if Blair was with him, he made sure they sat down and rested for a while.

Everett sat in his rocking chair, with Jake at his feet. A tray with a pitcher of ice water and three glasses had been placed on the small table next to him. Blair poured herself a glass and dropped into the rocking chair beside him.

"You look all done in, girl," Everett chided.

"I'm fine, Granddad. A little break will do me wonders."

"It's eight in the evening. Isn't it time you called it a day?"

"There's a lot of work to do."

"Hrumph. Garrett, didn't you tell me you had something to do this evening? That you had to leave early?"

Everett raised his eyebrows. Garrett blinked at the old man for a moment, not sure what he was talking about, until he suddenly understood Everett's intent. Blair wouldn't stop working until he did. That meant he had to go.

"Ah, yes, that's right. I almost forgot," he said. "I should get home. I promised my mom I'd do something for her. I need to help her with some gardening stuff."

"Some gardening stuff?"

"Yeah, you know." He didn't know anything about gardening and said the first thing that came to mind. "Digging in the dirt."

Blair frowned. "Really? That's your pressing engagement?"

"Hey, it's for my mom." He made his way down the steps. Maybe if he left, she'd call it an evening, too. "I'll see you tomorrow."

She followed him to his truck, her smile telling him that she was onto him. "Make sure you're here extra early tomorrow. Unless you've got more digging to do?"

He couldn't help his answering grin. "I'm sure I'll finish helping my mom tonight. Get some rest, okay?"

"You and Granddad are a couple of manipulators. I should be mad at both of you."

"But you're not, right? I mean, how could you stay mad at charmers like us?"

She laughed up at him, her eyes a warm green in the early evening light. "You're full of crap, but you're right. I can't stay mad at either of you."

An overpowering need to touch her assailed him. Garrett gently tucked a wayward lock of curly hair behind her ear, his thumb caressing the impossibly soft skin of her cheek. All traces of laughter left her face, replaced by a hunger in her turbulent gray-green eyes that mirrored the desire roaring through him. In that moment he wanted to crush her against his body, feel her arms enfold him, taste the sweetness of her kiss. He wanted to bury himself inside her, deep and long and complete.

But he wasn't what she needed, especially after

what she'd told him. He was too messed up to be of any use to her. Aside from the sweat of his labor, he had nothing to offer her. He had no job and no prospects for one. No future.

Blair deserved so much more. She deserved a better man.

Dropping his hand, he stepped back and forced himself to look away.

"I'll see you tomorrow."

He didn't look at her again until he was safely inside his truck. She remained standing in the same spot, watching him. Garrett hit the ignition, afraid if he didn't leave now, he wouldn't be able to stop himself from going to her and taking her in his arms, despite Everett watching their every move. He put the truck in gear and sped out of the yard.

As soon as the work on Blair's barn was finished, he had to get out of her life. And then he had to figure out what the hell to do with the rest of his.

****

The next day was Saturday, and Blair worked the entire morning on what was left of the concrete demolition. She wheeled the final load of debris into the dumpster and, using her last ounce of strength, overturned the wheelbarrow to discard the contents. The bits of broken concrete and iron rebar made a satisfying thud. She blew out a relieved breath and massaged her aching left shoulder, glad this part of the job was over. She'd never worked so hard in her life.

Or sweated so much. She distracted herself with thoughts of the bath she was going to run for herself this evening. Hot water, lavender oil, and bubbles. *Heaven.*

But her heavenly bath had to wait. In a couple of hours, a load of gravel would arrive. The gravel needed to be spread over the barn floor to form a solid base for the new concrete. Where the old concrete had been removed, Garrett had spent hours already, smoothing and compacting the dirt floor to make it as even as possible.

Garrett. She closed her eyes, and the look on his face last night immediately flew into her mind's eye. She sensed his touch on her cheek once more, so gentle, yet so powerful. That simple touch, that look, conveyed his elemental desire for her. He wanted her. She'd experienced it in every cell of her body. And despite all the logical reasons that told her to stay away, she wanted him, too.

With that touch, she'd lost her will to resist him. She'd never been happier to lose a fight. Or more frightened.

She'd never known such overwhelming desire for a man before, like she might spontaneously combust from one of his heated looks. Might break into a million pieces if he didn't kiss her, didn't make love to her.

Though his touch may have been simple, Garrett Saunders was anything but. He was complex in ways she didn't yet fully understand. But one thing she did comprehend: the demons he fought had the potential to break her along with him.

"Blair, are you okay?"

Garrett's voice abruptly tore her out of her reverie. She turned toward him and opened her eyes, surprised by the worry that furrowed his brow. She made herself smile.

"Yes, of course. I was saying a prayer of thanks to

the construction gods."

His mouth quirked in a grin. "The construction gods?"

"Sure. I was giving thanks for managing to live through the demolition stage."

"Amen to that. I hope your gods stick around for the rest of the work. We could use their help."

"I'll give them a call."

He laughed. "Come on, let's go to the house. What did you make me for lunch? I'm starved."

She stepped out of the dumpster. "You're a walking stomach, Saunders."

"I'm a hardworking man. I need fuel to sustain me."

She turned to him. "You work too hard. Why are you doing this?"

"Because you need my help."

"I can't pay you back. I'll never be able to pay you back."

"I'm not asking you to."

"I feel like I'm taking advantage of you."

"You're not."

"But—"

He grabbed her by the shoulders. "Shut up, Blair. Just shut up."

He crushed her against his chest, his mouth descending on hers in a hot, demanding kiss. She opened willingly to him, sliding her tongue boldly against his. His big hands clutched her hips and pulled her hard against his erection. She groaned, loving the evidence of his desire for her, wanting him so much she nearly orgasmed right there in the middle of her yard. She needed to touch him, skin to skin. She fumbled with the buckle of his belt, and the zipper of his jeans. His hand stopped hers.

"Wait. Stop. We can't."

"Why?" She heard the desperation in her voice. "Please, Garrett. You want me. I know you want me."

He leaned his forehead against hers, his breathing harsh and rapid. "For a start, your grandfather is sitting on the front porch."

Blair couldn't believe she'd forgotten her granddad was close by. Only a row of hedges shielded them from his view. "Oh."

"God knows I want to make love to you right now. But I'd hate myself if I took advantage of you."

"I'm a big girl. You wouldn't be taking advantage of me."

He put his hands on her shoulders and squeezed once before putting some distance between them. "Go to the house. I'll be along in a few minutes."

"Garrett—"

He closed his eyes in anguish. "Go. Please."

She wanted to touch him, hold him, make him change his mind. But Garrett was ruled by honor. If he lost control and had sex with her now, no matter how amazing it might be, he'd hate himself, and maybe end up hating her.

When they made love, she wanted them both to receive nothing but pleasure from the act. She wanted no regrets.

The thought brought her up short. Had she really decided she wanted a physical relationship with Garrett? It seemed her body had made the decision without fully consulting her brain. Only a short time ago she had some serious doubts about getting involved with him. Was it really the best decision?

She made herself take a step away. And another, and another, until she made it to the house. Everett eyed her critically as she walked up the front porch stairs.

"What happened to you?"

She looked up in alarm, wondering if Everett had suddenly become psychic.

"Nothing happened. Everything's fine."

"Hrumph. Just wondering why your face is streaked with dirt."

"It's a dirty job." She swiped a hand across her face and brushed at her T-shirt, sending dust motes dancing. Had Garrett left dirty handprints on her ass? In case he had, she turned sideways as she passed her grandfather on her way into the house. "I'm going to clean up and start lunch. I'll call you in a few minutes."

Everett grabbed her hand with surprising quickness, preventing her from making her escape.

"Don't allow the past to stop you from making a family of your own, Blair girl. What happened is in the past, and none of it was your fault. Before I die I want to see you happy. I want to live long enough to see you with a family of your own, or at least the start of one."

It alarmed her to hear him speak of his own death, so she made a joke. "In that case, you'll be around for a long time."

Everett squeezed her fingers. "I want you to be happy."

"I *am* happy."

"You know what I mean. I want you to be settled, with a family of your own, and a man who loves you. Garrett could be that man."

Blair couldn't stop herself from glancing toward

the barn. Garrett was nowhere in sight. Could Garrett make her happy?

Her gut told her no one could do that for her. She had to find happiness for herself.

They had passion, and enough heat between them to burn down the barn. But maybe that was all they'd ever have.

Blair gently pulled her hand from Everett's grasp. "I should go in and start lunch."

"Will you remember what I said?"

She kissed his balding head, loving him so much her heart nearly burst. Everett and Anna had always been there for her, no matter what she'd done.

Even if she hadn't deserved their love.

"Of course I'll remember."

Though she smiled for her grandfather, she had no idea what to do about his assertion that Garrett was the one. They were a long way from coming to that sort of decision about each other. She had serious concerns about his drinking. And she was sure her past suicide attempt gave him pause, too.

Yet something had shifted in the last few days, and especially in the last few minutes. The soul-shattering, heat-inducing kiss they'd shared had changed everything for her.

What if she was falling in love with Garrett? What if he could never feel the same way about her?

Maybe I'm not worthy of his love. Of anyone's love. The thought robbed her of breath. Though fear twisted her heart, she nearly laughed out loud at the cruelty of fate. It would be her luck to fall for a guy who couldn't, or wouldn't, return her love.

And maybe it would be exactly what she deserved.

Chapter Eleven

In the afternoon, a truck arrived and hauled away the dumpster. A short time later, another truck showed up with a load of gravel. The driver dumped it as close to the barn as he was able. Blair nearly groaned out loud at the sight of the massive pile of gravel, knowing that every last pebble would have to be hauled into the barn. By hand. With the blessed wheelbarrow.

She considered actually praying to the construction gods for help.

With a sigh, she grabbed her shovel and began throwing gravel into the wheelbarrow. Garrett brought over a second wheelbarrow that he'd borrowed from his dad and began doing the same. As soon as the wheelbarrow was full, or as full as she could make it while still being able to control it, Blair wheeled it into the barn and dumped it into the farthest corner. Garrett was right behind her and dumped his load a short distance away.

"Only thirteen million more loads to go," she said with a sigh.

"If that's your attitude, I guess I won't tell you there's another load of gravel coming later today."

She groaned. "You're kidding me, right?"

"Sorry, no. Look on the bright side. Soon the floor will be finished, and you'll be able to start your boarding business and your rescue."

"Right." She lifted her empty wheelbarrow and prepared to fill it once more. "Keep your eyes on the prize, Blair."

"That's the spirit."

She flashed him a grateful smile, not only for the encouraging words, but for resuming their easy relationship with its teasing banter once more. Lunch had been awkward. Neither of them had known what to say or even where to look. Blair hadn't been able to look at Garrett's mouth without thinking about the way he'd kissed her.

She still couldn't. But in the interests of moving forward she was going to fake it.

She maneuvered the wheelbarrow to the gravel pile, filled it once more, wheeled it into the barn, and dumped it.

Shampoo. Rinse. Repeat.

They continued the process over and over until the gravel pile began to shrink, and Blair's arms begged for mercy. She dumped her latest load, then rubbed her aching shoulder.

"You okay?"

She couldn't help smiling at him. "Has anyone ever told you that you have an overdeveloped sense of protectiveness?"

A hint of a smile curled his lips. "Only you. How about we switch gears for a while? We need to spread the gravel evenly over the floor."

Anything had to be better than hauling the wheelbarrow. "Sure."

Garrett went to the garage and returned with two rakes and a couple of pairs of leather work gloves. He handed her one of each. "Here. Knock yourself out."

They worked in silence for a while. After raking the gravel for about a half hour, Blair stopped and stretched her back, surveying the progress they'd made.

"If I'd known what I was getting into, I might have set a match to this barn instead of trying to repair it."

Garrett stopped raking to grin at her. "No way you would have done that. You know what you want, and you go after it, no matter what. I admire that about you. And I envy it, too."

That surprised her. "Really? What do you envy most? My aching back or the impressive calluses I'm developing on my hands?"

"You know who you're supposed to be."

That was true in the work part of her life. But in the personal, not so much. "And you don't?"

He shrugged. "I used to. But since I've been home…"

His words trailed off. Blair stepped closer. "You said you wanted to buy land. Have you thought about raising cattle?"

"I don't know anything about cattle. I can't even look after Harry properly." He turned away from her and started raking again.

"Okay, what would you like to do? In your heart of hearts, what would you really like to do with your life?"

He was slow in responding. For a long time, he pushed gravel around with his rake, until Blair thought he wasn't going to answer her question. With a sigh, she started working again, almost missing his soft-spoken words.

"I always thought after my military career was over, I'd come back to civilian life and begin a career in policing or firefighting."

"Those both sound like good options. So why haven't you applied to some police forces or fire departments?"

The anger in his eyes took her breath away. "Are you deliberately trying to be cruel?"

Blair stepped back, shocked by his words. "No, of course not! What are you talking about?"

"I'm not exactly a prime candidate for either one."

"Why would you say that?" Was he worried about his drinking as well? Did he think he'd be unable to handle the rigors of policing or firefighting because of it?

He tilted his head. "You don't know, do you?"

"Know what?"

He bent at the waist and rolled up his right pant leg till it was above his knee, revealing a device made of metal and plastic where flesh and bone should have been. He rose to his full height and looked her straight in the eye, as if daring her to pity him.

"As you can see, I'd have a tough time acing the physical."

Blair wanted to cry. She wanted to run into Garrett's arms and hold him forever, to make all the hurt go away. She wanted to scream and yell and rail against war and all the stupidity and intolerance in the world.

But Garrett wouldn't appreciate her tears, and crying wouldn't solve anything.

So she sucked them back and raised her gaze to his, willing her chin not to tremble.

"I hope you're not going to use your leg, or lack thereof, as an excuse to get out of work. There's still plenty to be done here."

He rolled his pant leg over his prosthesis once more, straightened, and grinned at her.

"I wouldn't dream of it."

Somehow Blair managed to smile back at him. "Good answer."

****

Monday morning at the clinic, Blair pounced on Lauren as soon as she entered the building.

"Can I talk to you? In private?"

Lauren blinked in surprise. "Yes, of course. We can use one of the examining rooms."

Blair followed her into examining room three and shut the door behind them. Lauren turned to her in concern.

"What's going on? Are you okay?"

"Yes, I'm fine. I… Why didn't you tell me about Garrett's leg? He showed me his prosthesis for the first time on Saturday. I didn't know…"

The tears that she'd been holding inside since Saturday filled her eyes. "Granddad said he'd been injured, and I saw his limp, but I didn't realize…"

She couldn't speak. Every time she thought about what he'd gone through, what he continued to go through, she wanted to weep. The pain he must have endured. Did he have pain now? The thought of Garrett suffering made the tears flow faster.

"I thought you already knew. Does it make a difference to you?" Lauren asked quietly.

Blair grabbed a tissue and blew her nose. "What do you mean?"

"You two have been working together all summer. You've become close. I hoped that your relationship would grow into something more meaningful. But if you're…uncomfortable with Garrett's injury…perhaps it's best if you end things between you now."

"Are you asking me if I think his amputation is ugly?"

Lauren's gaze was steady. "Do you?"

"No! I want to understand. Why didn't he tell me? Is he in any pain? How did it happen?"

"Did you ask him?"

Blair wiped her eyes. "I was afraid to. I don't want him to think I'm pitying him. I know he'd hate that."

"He would, but I think he'd hate knowing that we were talking about him behind his back even more." She caught Blair's hands. "If you ask him what you need to know in an honest, straightforward way, he'll be okay telling you."

Lauren was right. If she had questions, she needed to ask him for answers, not his sister. She only hoped she could talk to him without crying.

She nodded. "I'm sorry about this."

"Don't worry about it. It's nice to know you care so much about my brother."

Alarm bells went off in Blair's head. She didn't want Lauren and the rest of her family to think there was something going on between her and Garrett. He'd hate having his private life talked about and speculated on. "We're not… I mean, I like Garrett, of course, but we're not…involved. We're friends."

"I'd hoped that there was more to your relationship." Lauren paused, tilting her head as she looked at her. "Do you want there to be something more?"

"I don't know." Blair chose her words carefully. "I care about him. I want him to be healthy and happy, and not feel like there's something wrong with him because of his injury."

"I sense a 'but' coming."

Blair wasn't sure how much Lauren already knew about Garrett's drinking, or how much she should tell. "But I'm not sure it's wise for me and Garrett to be any more than friends."

"Because of his drinking?"

"You know?"

Lauren sighed. "Yes. I'm more worried about the scars we can't see. My mom says he often has trouble sleeping. And he self-medicates with alcohol."

"He's really working on his drinking." She told her about the deal they'd made. "Once he finds his place in the civilian world, things will turn around for him."

"You're good for him," Lauren said with a squeeze to her hands. "Garrett is the best brother in the world, and I adore him. He's always been there for me. Don't give up on him, Blair."

She couldn't help smiling. "You sound like my grandfather."

"A wise man, your grandfather." Lauren smiled before letting go of her hands. "I'd better get back to work before there's a pile-up of clients at the reception desk."

"Thanks for listening. I…I needed to talk, you know?"

"Yeah, I know. He's going to be okay, Blair. Aside from Cole, Garrett is the strongest person I know. He'll find his way, and if he needs help, he always has his family. And his friends."

Blair nodded, not trusting herself to speak. Lauren left the room and closed the door behind her. Blair grabbed another tissue and sank into one of the chairs, taking deep breaths to get herself under control. She had a full day of work ahead of her and she needed to focus.

But no matter how busy she was, Garrett wouldn't be far from her thoughts.

****

Grace Saunders showed up on the farm after work, the trunk of her car held open with bungee cords. Blair ran down the front porch steps to greet her.

"Mrs. Saunders—Grace. It's nice to see you."

Grace grasped her hand in a warm shake. "It's nice to see you, too, Blair. I didn't forget about the flowers I said I'd give you."

She removed the bungee cords to open the trunk all the way. It was full of containers filled with dirt and plants that Blair couldn't identify.

"I know this looks a little intimidating. My intention is not to make more work for you. These are all hardy perennials that require little fuss. We'll plant them in your flowerbeds, give them water, and they'll take care of themselves."

"This is very kind of you."

Grace waved away her thanks. "It's nothing. Like I told you, I needed to divide some of my plants, and I had no flower beds left to plant them in. So you're helping me out."

Blair didn't believe it for a minute, but she smiled anyway. "Even so, I appreciate it."

Grace reached into the trunk and lifted out a container. "Garrett said he worked a couple of your flowerbeds. With any luck, we can simply pop these plants right in."

Blair helped Grace move the plant containers from the trunk of her car to the flowerbeds at the front of the house. Garrett had indeed worked the soil, probably by hand with a hoe.

Like he wasn't working hard enough on her farm.

Grace helped to arrange where the plants should go and to identify any existing plants that were worth keeping. After retrieving some garden tools, they dug appropriately sized holes, popped the plants out of their containers, and stuck them into the ground. By the time Blair brought the garden hose to the front of the house to water the plants, her grandfather and Garrett had emerged from the barn and were speaking to Grace in front of the house.

"Looks good, Mom," Garrett said.

"Thanks, but Blair did most of the work. Thanks for working the bed. That saved us a lot of time."

"No problem."

Grace instructed Blair on how much water to give the plants in the next few days. She patiently explained how big the plants would eventually get, and told her that if these plants didn't survive, given the lateness in the season for transplanting, they could always try again before freeze-up.

How different Grace Saunders was from her own mother. She couldn't imagine Victoria Greyson digging in the dirt, or patiently explaining the differences between various perennials to her. If Victoria wanted a flowerbed, she hired someone to create it and tend it for her.

All Blair ever wanted was a mother who would make time for her. Care for her with kindness. Her parents had always been more interested in maintaining appearances than in actually parenting. They showed off their children to their wealthy, powerful friends like trophies they trotted out whenever it suited them. She remembered attending political rallies with her parents and brothers as a little girl. Her mother would dress her in fancy clothes, and she'd be expected to sit still through long, boring speeches. If she fidgeted, she'd receive a painful pinch to her knee. God help her if she cried out. Blair could still hear Victoria's voice hissing in her ear, *"For God's sake, smile!"*

She pushed away the hurtful memories and the longing. She couldn't change anything about the past, and she couldn't change her parents.

"Grace, would you like some lemonade?" Everett asked.

"I'd love some, Everett, but I've got to run. I left Robert's dinner in the oven, and I'd better go take it out before it's burnt to a crisp. But I'll be back to check on the plants in a few days and take you up on your offer."

Everett extended his hand to her in a shake, and she accepted it. "Thank you, Grace. Anna would be pleased to see her beds brought back to life."

"It's my pleasure."

Blair held out her hand, intending to shake Grace's hand, too. "Thank you for all the gardening information."

"You're so welcome, dear."

She ignored Blair's hand and went in for a hug. Grace was tiny, and Blair had to stoop to hug her. She breathed in the older woman's scent, a combination of soap and shampoo and earth. What would her life have been like, and the lives of her brothers, if they'd had a mother like Grace?

Don't go there, Blair.

Blair ended their embrace, and a moment later, Grace was driving out of the yard with a honk and a wave. Longing swamped her. How she wished her grandmother was alive. With her wit and humor and kindness, Anna Branson had made many things bearable.

But some things even her grandmother couldn't fix.

****

"You better stop and have a drink of water before you keel over."

At the sound of the old man's voice, Garrett glanced up from the iron rebar grid he was building that would be embedded in the barn's concrete floor to give it strength. He grinned at Everett as he approached, straightening his back and stretching.

"What would I do without you looking after me?"

"I shudder to think. Come sit in the shade. Morley and I have something we want to give you."

He'd seen Morley's old Cadillac pull into the yard. Morley Walker had been a lawyer in Masonville for longer than Garrett had been alive. He and Everett had been close friends for years. For the past week or so, he'd seen Morley's car in the yard almost every day.

Intrigued, Garrett followed him outside where he'd once more set up lawn chairs in the shade of the cottonwood trees. But this time there were three chairs. Morley already occupied one. He sat comfortably with a tall glass of something in his hand.

After Garrett shook hands with Morley, Everett opened a thermos and poured a glass of water, which Garrett accepted gratefully.

"At least this job isn't as dirty as the demolition," Everett said, as he sat in one of the lawn chairs.

Garrett dropped into the other chair. "No, but in some ways it's harder."

"Because of your leg?" Morley asked.

"Yeah."

Under normal circumstances, he would have laid the rebar directly on top of the bed of gravel that he and Blair had finished preparing on Sunday. He would have worked on the grid pattern on the ground, tying the rebar together with bits of wire. But these were not normal circumstances. Kneeling for long periods was uncomfortable and difficult, so he devised a way to get around his disability. He laid lengths of rebar in a checkerboard pattern on top of several sawhorses. Once he tied a section of rebar together, he carried it to a spot on the floor, dropped it into place, and connected it with wire to sections already laid.

He slowly drank the cool water. It felt odd to think of himself as having a disability. He'd always been the strongest, the most capable, the most athletic. He'd counted on his body, got used to its strength. If nothing else, working on Blair's barn had shown him he could be useful. He only had to find new ways to do things.

"How soon does the concrete truck come?" Everett asked.

"In two days. I've got to get the rebar ready by then."

Once he was done with the rebar, his job was essentially done. A truck, or likely two, would bring pre-mixed concrete that would be poured directly over the prepared floor. Men from the concrete company would screed and float the newly poured cement until it was smooth and perfect.

He'd no longer be needed here.

It was for the best. How long could he resist Blair? The day she'd asked him to make love to her, he'd almost given in. But she didn't know what his amputation looked like.

"You're doing a great job. Blair is lucky to have had your help. You've worked really hard."

"Thank you."

The praise from Everett came as a surprise, and gave him an inordinate amount of satisfaction, knowing the old man didn't readily throw around a lot of compliments.

"Even though part of your leg is gone, it doesn't mean you can't contribute. You've proved that here. Sometimes you need to use your head a little more, that's all."

"I appreciate you saying that, Everett."

He waved away his thanks with a sweep of his bony arm. "Hrumph. Just stating the truth."

"Maybe I needed to hear it."

Everett's blue eyes narrowed as he gazed at him. "Maybe you did." He turned to Morley. "Give it to him."

Morley reached for a large manila envelope tucked beside him on the chair and handed it to Garrett. "We need you to look after this."

"Sure. What is it?"

"It's Everett's Last Will and Testament. He'd like you to be one of the executors, along with me."

Garrett shifted uncomfortably in his chair and turned to Everett. "I'm happy to help you in any way I can, but wouldn't you be more comfortable having a member of your family handling your estate? What about Blair, or your daughter?"

"I don't want to burden Blair with this. I trust you. I know you'll do the right thing. Once I die, I want you to give copies of my Will to my grandson Ben, the lawyer. He'll know what to do."

Garrett didn't understand why he wouldn't send Ben a copy of the Will himself. But if Everett wanted him to act as an intermediary, he wasn't going to argue.

"I appreciate your trust. It means a lot to me. I'll find a nice, safe place to keep your Will. I'm sure it'll be years till I need to look at it again."

"We'll see," Everett said with a smile.

Chapter Twelve

Garrett's phone rang at exactly ten-forty-five p.m. Chris's number came up on the screen. He was in bed, but at least this time he wasn't sleeping.

"Chris, buddy. How are you doing?"

"I've been better." Garrett heard the drunken slur in his voice. "Alison left me. Took the kids and went to live with her sister. Said she couldn't handle living with me anymore."

"Jeez, I'm sorry."

"Said I was scaring the kids. Too many erratic moods, too much drinking. She didn't want to hang around and watch me kill myself, she said." Chris's voice cracked with pain. "They were all I had, and now they're gone. I've got nothing left."

Garrett pushed himself to a sitting position and gripped his cell phone. "Hang in there, buddy. I can be in Minneapolis in a few hours. I'll bring you back here to North Dakota. There's a great VA hospital in Fargo. There are people there who can help you."

"No, no, I don't want to go away. I want to stay close to my kids."

"But your wife—"

"As long as I'm sober, she says, I can see them. I need to be here to put my family back together."

"You need help, man. Go to the VA hospital in Minneapolis. Talk to someone there. You can't go on like this."

"I will," Chris answered quickly.

"Really? You promise?"

"Yeah, I'll go. I promise."

"I want you to phone me every day so I know how you're doing." Would it be enough to keep tabs on him by phone? He wracked his brain to think of someone he could call on in the Minneapolis area to check in on him.

"I will," Chris said.

"Good, that's good."

Garrett's gut told him it wasn't that simple, that Chris had given in far too easily. Maybe he should make the six-hour drive regardless of what he said. He swung his legs to the side of the bed and checked his bedside clock. If he hurried, he could be there before five a.m., earlier if he pushed it.

"I'm not going to kill myself, if that's what you're thinking," Chris said suddenly. "I wouldn't do that to Alison, to my kids. They need me."

Garrett expelled a relieved breath. "I'm glad to hear you say that."

"It's hard, you know. Sometimes I'm more scared here than I ever was in Afghanistan."

"Yeah, I know what you mean." The transition to civilian life had been far more difficult than he'd ever imagined it would be. But Chris's problems were far worse. "Anytime you want to talk, really talk, call me and I'll be there. Okay?"

Chris's breath hitched. "Okay."

"Phone me tomorrow."

"Okay. Goodnight."

"Goodnight."

Garrett blew out his breath. He couldn't force Chris to accept his help. And even if he did, what did he know about helping someone with what he suspected was a serious case of PTSD? He had a hard enough time dealing with his own problems. What use would he be to Chris?

Talk about the blind leading the blind.

The best thing he could do for his friend would be to convince him to talk to someone at the VA, someone who knew what they were doing.

****

As soon as Blair got home from work, she jumped from the cab of her truck and headed to the barn, eager to see how the new cement floor had turned out. She couldn't stop her squeal of delight as she peeked through the open barn door. Beside her, Garrett chuckled.

"It looks pretty good, doesn't it?"

"Good? It's freaking awesome! I never thought a cement floor could be beautiful, but this is absolutely stunning! You did an amazing job."

"I can't take credit for the finishing work. The professionals handled that."

"Yeah, but you did all the demolition and prep work. None of this would have been possible without your hard work."

"I seem to recall you pushing a wheelbarrow or two. You did your share."

"I suppose I did, but I wouldn't have had a clue on my own. Thank you."

"You're welcome."

He smiled at her, and Blair's heart thumped painfully. Seeing the finished floor was wonderful, but it reminded her that the work on the barn would soon be done and she wouldn't see Garrett every day. Would he stop by the farm sometimes, or would he simply move on?

Perhaps it would be best if he did. Especially for Garrett.

She swallowed and looked away, not wanting to think about the future. Instead, she knelt in front of the open barn door.

"We need to mark this momentous occasion."

"We do?"

"Of course, we do." She pressed her right hand into the wet cement. After a few seconds she lifted her hand and was pleased with the perfect impression it made. She reached for his hand.

"Now it's your turn."

"Seriously? How old are you? Twelve?"

"Don't be such a party pooper. Think of it as leaving your mark for posterity."

With a shake of his head, he knelt on his good leg and allowed her to push his hand onto the cement in the spot next to her handprint. She liked the shape of his hands, the square nails, the long fingers. His big hands could work hard yet hold her with infinite tenderness. She lifted her hand from on top of his.

"That should be enough."

He removed his hand to reveal a perfect replica captured in cement, right down to the heart line across his palm.

Their gazes met and held. Blair saw longing in his eyes and knew the same emotion was probably reflected in her eyes. Would he miss her?

Not as much as she'd miss him.

Garrett cleared his throat and pushed himself to his feet. "The floor will need twenty-eight days to cure, so don't use it till then."

Blair rose as well, disconcerted by her shaking legs. "Don't worry. I'll guard this floor with my life." She started to head to the house, then stopped and turned when he didn't follow her. "Aren't you staying for dinner? It's nothing fancy, chicken salad sandwiches, with ice cream for dessert. It's too hot to cook much."

Garrett hesitated, and she saw his throat work as he swallowed. "Thanks, but no, I should head home."

Disappointment swamped her. She'd become used to sharing meals with Garrett, but it looked like she'd have to get used to his absence. Emptiness filled her at the prospect.

"Right, okay."

"Now that the floor's done, there's no reason for me to stay," he said quietly.

"I still have a lot of fence to fix. You could help with that."

The words surprised Blair almost as much as they surprised Garrett. She hadn't known she was going to say them until they blurted from her mouth.

"I thought you wanted to do the fencing on your own. As I recall, the last time I tried to help you with it, you brushed me off."

"I managed a small section on my own, but I can't fence the entire pasture myself." She injected a light note into her tone. "I don't have the time. I have to work for a living, you know. And sleep."

Garrett's lip curled in a smile. "Sleep's overrated."

Some of the tension began to ease from her

shoulders. "Perhaps, but I do enjoy a few hours of shuteye now and again. What do you say? Can you help me out with the fence? I'll teach you everything I know."

"What are you going to pay me?"

Blair hid her smile, knowing he was going to say yes. "Same as with the barn. My everlasting thankfulness."

Garrett's grin broadened. "How can I say no to terms like that?"

"I don't see how you can. Why don't we go have dinner with Granddad?"

Garrett nodded and followed her to the house. Blair's relief at his staying was tempered by the knowledge that once the fencing was done, there'd be no more excuses for him to stay.

****

Blair's phone rang as she finished drying the supper dishes. She was surprised to see her brother Damon's name on her phone since they usually communicated in text messages. She clicked the talk button.

"Hey! Why didn't someone tell me hell froze over? You never phone me."

Damon chuckled. "I wanted to hear your voice."

"I'm not sure whether I should be flattered or concerned by that statement."

"Be flattered. I had a few moments between appointments, and I wanted to check in with you, see how Granddad's doing."

Blair peeked out the window. Granddad was in his usual spot in his rocking chair on the front porch, Jake at his feet, and Garrett in the chair beside him. "He's doing well."

"That's good."

Blair waited a beat. "Is there anything else you'd like to talk about, Damon? Are you moving again or something?"

Damon was a restless soul. She couldn't count the number of times he'd moved in the last ten years. Some of the moves were due to his time in the army, but mostly he couldn't stay in one place for long before needing to move on.

She heard him expel a breath. "Victor Campbell is up for parole."

"Oh, Damon. I'm sorry."

Victor Campbell. One of her parents' wealthy, powerful friends. Assistant to a senator, son of a congressman. Pedophile.

"I'm going to the parole hearing."

Blair heard the determination in Damon's voice. It would be useless to try to talk him out of going. This was something he had to do.

"Where is it?"

"In St. Paul. I fly out in a few days."

"I could drive to St. Paul, come to the hearing with you. It's only about a five- or six-hour drive from here."

"No. I want you to stay with Granddad. He needs you. I'll be fine."

Maybe Ben could attend the hearing with him. Blair rejected the idea immediately, knowing it was impossible. Now that Olivia was gone, the girls needed him at home.

But Damon shouldn't be alone.

"I'm sure Morley would stay with Granddad for a couple of days. And Garrett is here. He'll keep an eye on him."

"Garrett? You mean Garrett Saunders?"

"Yeah." She told him about Garrett's injury and his retirement from the military. About how he was helping to get the barn and the fences back in shape.

"So, you and Garrett Saunders, huh?" There was a teasing note in his voice.

"What? No! You're deliberately misunderstanding me, you idiot."

He chuckled. "Methinks she doth protest too much."

"Listen, Shakespeare. There's nothing going on between us. So stop it. Really." She *was* protesting too much. "Do you want me to come to St. Paul or not?"

The amusement left his voice. "As much as I'd love to see you, I'd feel better if you stayed with Granddad. And, to be honest, it would be easier for me to go to this hearing if you're not there to listen to the testimony."

Oh, Damon. Blair squeezed her eyes shut. "Okay. Promise you'll call once it's over, or if you need to talk. Please?"

"I will. I knew I could count on you, Blair." He cleared his throat, all business once more. "I've got to run. My next client is here. See you, Sugarplum."

She smiled at the use of her grandmother's childhood nickname for her. She could almost hear Anna's voice: *Because you're so sweet.* "Bye, Damon."

Blair ended the call. She wished she could help her brothers. Even if she was able to go to them, what could she do? She couldn't take away the pain of the past for Damon or bring back Ben's wife.

She stuck her phone in her back pocket. All she

could do was listen if they wanted to talk.

It was totally inadequate, but all she had.

****

Garrett pounded a staple into the new fence post, securing a string of barbed wire to the wood. The work was physical and a little tedious, but he found it satisfying to see the long, straight line of fencing he'd already finished. The fence posts stood tall and proud, like soldiers on parade. Somehow, he found them comforting.

Four days ago, Blair had started him off, showing him how to set the fence posts, string the barbed wire, and repair broken pieces of wire that could be salvaged. And then she'd left him on his own. It was good to know she trusted him to handle the work.

Blair's trust and regard had become very important to him this summer. *Blair* had become very important to him. He pushed the unwelcome thought from his mind and kept on working. She deserved much more than he could give her.

At five o'clock, Garrett packed his tools into his truck and headed back to the Branson farmhouse. He tried to convince himself he was calling it a day because he'd run out of fence posts, but truthfully it was because Blair was due home soon. A part of him longed to see her, to bask in her smile.

Would she smile if she saw the full impact of his amputation? She'd been surprised when he'd shown her his prosthesis, but she hadn't appeared repulsed. It still jarred him sometimes to see the stump where his lower right leg used to be, so he had no idea how she'd react.

Would she think him less a man? His gut knotted.

Perhaps he was. He hadn't been with a woman

since he'd lost his leg. He didn't think he could bear any looks of revulsion. Or pity.

Especially from Blair.

She was so perfect, so beautiful. He'd never known a woman with such creamy, touchable skin. The light dusting of freckles across her nose only made her more appealing.

And it wasn't simply her looks. There was a strength inside her, and a warmth that lightened his heart to be near. But sometimes he detected a sadness in her that made him wonder about the forces that had shaped her life. Was she truly over the desperation that had led to an attempt on her life?

He didn't like to think about it. With a sigh, he put the truck in gear and made his way across the pasture and back to the farmhouse.

Blair's truck was in the yard, and his heart rate kicked up in anticipation. Garrett shook his head in disgust and told himself to quit acting like a hormonal teenager. He blew out a breath and climbed from the cab.

Raised voices greeted him through the open windows as he climbed the front porch steps. Garrett hung back, not wanting to eavesdrop but unable to avoid hearing their conversation.

"Stop fussing so, Blair girl," Everett grumbled. "You're worse than your grandmother was."

"Grandma was looking out for you, and so am I. We have to because you're too stubborn to look out for yourself. Why didn't you take your heart pills today? I laid them out for you this morning."

"Forgot, that's all. Those pills don't help much anyway. My heart's gonna give out, and the extra day or two they might give me won't matter much."

"It matters to me!" Garrett heard tears in Blair's voice. "Don't talk like that! Don't even joke about it."

"Aw, don't cry, Blair girl. I'm sorry. I'm a stupid, forgetful old man with a big mouth. Can you forgive me?"

He heard Blair sniff, as if trying to hold back her tears. "I'm sorry, too, Granddad. I shouldn't have yelled at you."

"It's all right. Everything's gonna be all right, Blair. You're not responsible for what happens to me any more than you could have prevented what happened to Eve."

"I know."

"Do you? Do you really understand in your heart that you did nothing wrong?"

She didn't answer, and the next thing Garrett heard was the sound of pots and pans clanging. Questions whirled in his head. Who was Eve, and what had happened to her?

Guilt swamped Garrett. It was none of his business. He couldn't stand here listening any longer. He opened the door, making as much noise as possible, before entering the kitchen.

"Hi." He nodded at Everett before turning his attention to Blair, who kept her back to him as she worked at the stove, shoulders rigid with tension. Garrett struggled for something to say. "Did you have a good day at work?"

She cleared her throat but didn't look at him. "Yeah, it was fine."

He glanced at Everett, but the old man's expression revealed nothing. "I'm going to wash up before dinner."

He left the kitchen and headed for the bathroom. As he ran water in the sink, he contemplated his options. He could head home and give Blair her privacy. But something told him she wanted him to stay, even needed him. It seemed ridiculous. In what universe would Blair need him for anything other than hard labor? He stared at his reflection in the mirror and hoped he wasn't misreading the situation.

Garrett took his time in the washroom. After drying his hands, he headed back to the kitchen, hoping he'd given Blair enough time to compose herself. She was at the table, sitting at her usual spot beside Everett as he entered the room. Their gazes met and held. Garrett searched her face, looking for some clue about what had caused her earlier upset, but she appeared calm. She quickly looked away as he sat down.

"I bought a couple of salads at the grocery store deli," she said, handing him a Greek salad with pieces of cucumber, sweet peppers, bits of feta cheese, and black olives. "And a dessert."

"Looks delicious." Garrett wondered if his continued presence at her farm was causing her stress, even though she'd been the one who'd asked him to stay. He was certainly causing her to cook or purchase extra meals. He could go home for dinner, spare her the extra work. But he couldn't make himself do it.

"How's the fencing going?" Blair asked.

"It's going good. I finished a section of the east side of the big pasture before I came in for dinner."

Everett had kept one hundred and sixty acres of pasture and had rented the rest of his land to area farmers. Twenty years ago, he'd kept cattle in the pasture, but for the last several years it had been seeded to alfalfa, which he'd then sold to cattle farmers for feed. Blair's plan was to divide the hundred and sixty acres into three sections; two sections closest to the farmyard would be used for the horses to graze in. The largest section would continue to be harvested for hay that would feed the horses in the winter.

She gave a fleeting smile. "You're making good progress."

"Thanks. I had a good teacher."

Their eyes met again before Blair looked down at her plate. Garrett noticed she wasn't eating. It seemed her argument with Everett had caused her appetite to desert her.

"Ben phoned today," Everett said. "I invited him to come out to the farm with the girls for a week or two this summer, like we talked about, but he said he thought his children needed to be close to home right now."

"I'm sorry they won't be coming, but I guess I can understand." Blair turned to him, and he could see the disappointment in her eyes. And the sadness. "Ben lost his wife Olivia in a car accident a few months ago."

That was a shock. "I'm sorry to hear that. He has children?"

Blair gave him a fleeting smile. "Yes, his two stepdaughters from Olivia's first marriage. They're great kids."

Conversation lagged after that, and the rest of the meal passed mostly in silence. Everett pushed away from the table once he was done eating.

"I believe I'll sit on the porch a while."

He squeezed Blair's shoulder as he walked by, and she covered his hand with hers. Though nothing was said, Garrett recognized that a whole conversation of understanding had passed between them.

Everett shuffled out of the room, with Jake following closely behind. At the sound of the door shutting, Blair got to her feet.

"I'd better clean up."

"I'll help."

"There's not much to do. I can handle it."

"I know you can. But you don't need to handle everything on your own."

Their gazes locked once more, and Garrett thought she might ask him to leave. Instead, she shrugged one shoulder. "Suit yourself. You want to wash or dry?"

"I'll wash."

They worked in silence. Questions whirled in Garrett's head. Why had the mention of this Eve person made Blair cry? How close had she been to her? Why did she think she could have prevented whatever happened to her?

"Blair, who's Eve?"

She turned sharply to face him, her face alarmingly pale. With careful precision she set the stainless steel pot she'd been drying on the counter. "Were you listening to my conversation with my grandfather?"

"I'm sorry, I didn't mean to." He turned to face her. "If you want to talk, if there's anything I can do—"

"There isn't."

Her tone more than her words cut off any further conversation. Garrett finished washing the remaining dishes in silence, calling himself all kinds of stupid. He was sticking his nose into places where he had no business being. Blair had every right to be pissed.

He finished washing and dried his hands before

daring a look at her.

"I'll be back tomorrow to work on the fence."

She nodded, her eyes not meeting his. "Okay. Good."

Garrett made his way to the door and stood with his hand on the knob. "I'm sorry."

With that, he opened the door, nodded at Everett, and rushed to his truck as quickly as his prosthetic leg would carry him.

Chapter Thirteen

Blair stood in the doorway and watched Garrett leave, her heart heavy. His question had shocked her, coming out of the blue the way it had. Despite the heat of the July day she shivered, feeling as if her insides had turned to ice.

If only her heart would turn to ice and stop bleeding all over the place.

She dropped into Grandma Anna's rocker. Everett rested his head against the back of his rocker and raised one eyebrow.

"Garrett left in a hurry."

"Yeah." She looked away and swallowed. "He heard our conversation and asked about Eve."

"What did you tell him?"

"Nothing."

He'd taken her by surprise. She didn't talk about Eve, ever, with anyone. To have Garrett say her name…

Her gut twisted, the old memories playing over and over in her head, until she was dizzy.

"You *should* tell him, Blair. Him or somebody else. You've been holding this inside for too long. It's eating you up."

Blair couldn't answer. Granddad was right, but the thought of baring her soul to anyone, especially Garrett, was unthinkable.

She jumped to her feet. "I have to feed the horses, Granddad."

Blair hurried across the yard to the paddock behind the barn. The three horses were on their way to forming a close bond. Perhaps they could sense the trauma that each of them had been through.

She put feed in their bowls and made sure they had water, then climbed to the top rail of the wooden paddock and watched them eat. In the weeks Harry had been on her farm, he'd filled out and his coat had become healthier looking. He looked almost sleek now. With a little more TLC, he'd be quite handsome.

Garrett had said he'd looked into Harry's eyes and something inside the horse spoke to him. All the pain shone through, and Garrett realized he had to save him.

Now that he'd saved Harry, he had to find something, or someone, else to save. And she happened to be handy. That's why he asked about Eve. He sensed she needed saving, too.

No. She didn't need saving, and she didn't need Garrett.

That's what she told herself, but she couldn't quite make herself believe it.

****

Blair's red satin ball gown swirled around their legs as they glided effortlessly across a dance floor. The music of a waltz filled the vast room, though Garrett couldn't say where it was coming from. There was no orchestra, no dee-jay, no crowd of other dancers.

It didn't matter. Nothing mattered except Blair. He'd never seen her more beautiful. She smiled up at him, her eyes full of joy. He couldn't believe she was here, in his arms, that she wanted to be with him.

He wanted her with a fierceness that nearly brought him to his knees. Slowing their dance steps, he brought her closer. The scent of her perfume intoxicated him as he lowered his lips to hers and kissed her lightly.

"Come home with me, Blair."

She wound her arms around his neck, her breasts pressing against his tuxedo jacket and igniting a flame of desire that threatened to consume him. Giving up all pretense of dancing, she stretched up to meet his lips.

"Yes." Her whispered breath was warm against his face. "I'll come home with you."

Her lips touched his softly, tentatively at first. Gradually her kisses grew bolder, her hands growing restless as they clutched at his shoulders. He shifted his stance to bring her hard against his erection, to let her know how much he wanted her, needed her. Blair moaned and opened her mouth to him, her tongue dancing with his. She tasted of sunshine and honey, so sweet his head swam with the sensation. No liquor had ever made him feel so high.

He was drunk on Blair, and he never wanted to be sober again.

A sudden explosion rocked the dance floor. Glass shards rained down around them as windows shattered and walls shook. He threw Blair to the floor and covered her with his body. The wooden dance floor disappeared, replaced by sand and rocks. The oppressive sun beat down on his back, making him sweat inside his heavy gear and uniform.

He lifted his head to look into Blair's face. "Are you okay? Are you hurt?"

She stared at him but her eyes were empty and unseeing. A trickle of blood oozed out of the corner of her mouth.

"You can't help me," she whispered. "You never could."

Her eyes slowly closed as the life seeped out of her body. Garrett shook her limp body, fear screaming in his ears.

"No! Don't leave me. You can't leave me!"

Garrett woke with a start, his breathing heavy and his heart racing. He sat up, trying to catch his breath, his head in his hands.

He'd hoped he'd beaten the nightmares, that they'd finally left him alone.

Wrong.

You can't help me. You never could. The words haunted him. Blair didn't trust him enough to share her secrets with him. And why should she? He wasn't good enough.

He'd never be good enough. He wasn't even a whole man.

I need a drink.

After sliding his prosthesis onto his stump with trembling hands, he crept to his closet and found the partially empty bottle of Jack Daniels at the bottom of his locker. Why hadn't he tossed out the bottle to remove the temptation? Had his subconscious known he couldn't go without the booze? Was he testing himself?

Garrett hesitated for a moment, the bottle trembling in his hands. He had a choice. He could choose the bourbon, or he could choose life.

A vision from his nightmare flashed into his memory. He saw Blair's face, her beautiful eyes closing in death.

She didn't trust him. The pain of that knowledge was unbearably harsh, though why it should hurt so much, he couldn't say. Why was it so important that she open up to him?

He opened the bottle, held it to his lips. And stopped.

If he drank, he couldn't go back to the Branson farm. He'd promised Blair he'd stay away if he got drunk one more time. He could see the look of disappointment on her face.

He'd disappoint himself, too. He was better than this. He was a United States Marine, for God's sake. He could beat this.

Quietly, he made his way down the stairs, holding the bottle in one hand. Once in the kitchen, he set the bottle on the table. What he needed to do now was empty the contents down the sink and throw away the evidence. To throw away the temptation.

He wiped his sweaty palm across his mouth. He was hot and cold at the same time, sweating and shivering and shaking with tremors. The need to pick up the bottle, hold it to his lips, and drink deeply called to him in a seductive siren voice. It would be so easy and make him feel so much better. He needed the bourbon in that bottle.

That stopped him cold. *Dear God*. He *needed* the bourbon?

No. What he needed was to stand on his own two feet. He needed to build a life for himself. He couldn't do that if he was stuck at the bottom of a bottle.

Garrett grabbed the bottle and dumped the contents down the sink. Relief flooded over him as the amber contents disappeared. *I can do this.*

As he reentered his bedroom, his cell phone rang. Garrett's stomach swooped at the sight of Chris's name on the screen. He hit the talk button.

"Chris? Hi, buddy. How are you?"

"I'm just calling to say you're a good friend, Dakota. Real good friend."

Chris hadn't called him by his old nickname since Tommy's death. His words were slurred. He'd been drinking. A lot. Garrett sat up straighter, his senses on high alert.

Something was very, very wrong.

"Where are you, buddy?"

"Motel." There was a muffled sob. "I just want it to stop. I can't make it stop."

"What do you want to stop?"

"The pain. Everything hurts. You know? Every time I close my eyes, I hear Tommy screaming. I see your mangled leg, and there's not a damn thing I can do about it. Not a bloody thing."

"It's not your fault, Chris. None of it. You couldn't have saved Tommy, and you couldn't have saved my leg."

"It's not right! Why am I alive?"

The pain in Chris's voice grabbed him by the throat. "You can't blame yourself. It was war."

"I want it to end." Chris's voice was tired and flat. "Tonight. I called because I want to say goodbye."

"No! Don't say that!" Panic bubbled in Garrett's chest. He forced himself to calm down, to think. He had to think, to make a plan.

"It's no good, Garrett. I can't do this anymore. It hurts too much."

"I know it does, buddy. But we're going to find a

way to help you. You don't...you don't have to kill yourself to make the pain stop."

Garrett pushed himself to his feet, grateful he hadn't drunk himself into oblivion. He'd need his wits about him if he was going to help Chris. He put his phone on speaker and grabbed his jeans from the floor. "I'm coming to you. Do you hear me? We're going to talk this out. Your wife and your kids need you. *I* need you, dammit! I'm not going to let you die."

"She said I was scaring the kids." Chris gave an anguished sob. "My own kids are scared of me. I'm no good for them."

"We're going to find a way to help you so you can be the dad you want to be again." He zipped his jeans and pulled a T-shirt over his head. "Tell me where you are. Exactly where is your motel?"

Chris's sigh sounded tired. Defeated. "It's no use, Dakota. I've made up my mind."

"I'm not giving up on you and neither should you." Panic made his tone harsher than he'd intended. He was afraid Chris would kill himself right now while he was on the phone. "Where are you, Chris?"

There was another sigh, followed by silence. Garrett threw a few clothes into a duffle bag, grabbed the keys for his truck from his dresser, and opened his bedroom door. To his surprise, his parents were in the hallway, no doubt woken by his intense conversation. He mouthed an "I'm sorry" and headed down the stairs. Grace and Robert followed him to the kitchen.

The silence on the line dragged on. "Chris? Are you there?"

"I'm here."

"You didn't call me to say goodbye. You're

reaching out for help. You don't want to die, not really. Tell me where you are."

Garrett stared at his parents. His mother's face was white with fear. Had she been afraid he might contemplate suicide, too?

Chris's voice trembled across the air. "I'm in a motel on the outskirts of Minneapolis." He gave the name and address. Grace raced to a drawer and pulled out a pen and a pad of paper and scribbled it down. She tore the paper off the pad and handed it to him. Garrett gave her a brief smile, grateful for her understanding.

"I'm going to stay on the line the whole time I'm driving to Minneapolis. Do you hear me? I'm going to be with you all the way."

He hugged his mother in thanks and hurried out the door. Robert followed him to his truck and hopped into the passenger side. For a surprised moment Garrett thought he meant to come with him. He watched as his dad rummaged through the console between the front seats and pulled out a charge cord for his phone. He plugged it into the dash and then into Garrett's phone. Garrett started his truck and punched the address Chris had given him into the navigation system. Robert clapped a hand on his shoulder, nodded, and left the truck, closing the door firmly behind him. Garrett lifted his hand in goodbye before putting the truck in gear and driving off.

****

Blair stared out the kitchen window, knowing she was stalling. She checked her watch. Garrett was usually at the farm by this time of the morning.

They'd parted yesterday under a cloud of tension. He'd probably decided they both needed a day or two to cool off, even though he'd said he'd work on the fence today. Or maybe he'd decided she was too much trouble and had simply chosen to end their association.

Her heart had nearly stopped at the sound of Eve's name on his lips. Emotions had swept through her like a prairie fire—anger, surprise, panic, fear.

She knew Garrett well enough to know he'd offered to listen because he wanted to help. But Garrett was the last person she wanted to talk to about Eve.

Blair set down her cup, the coffee curdling in her stomach. If Garrett didn't know, there was a chance he'd still like her. Maybe even respect her.

In her head she accepted that she wasn't solely responsible for her child's death, but in her heart...

She checked her watch one more time. She couldn't wait around any longer or she'd be late for work.

"He'll show up. Or if he doesn't, there's a good reason why."

Everett sipped his coffee, his outward calm belying the shrewd speculation in his eyes. She should have known she couldn't hide anything from her grandfather.

Blair got to her feet and put her coffee cup in the dishwasher. "Probably, but right now I don't have time to speculate about Garrett Saunders' motives. I have to run."

"Gonna be a hot one today."

"It is. Spend some time in the air conditioning instead of out on the porch." She kissed his cheek. "Bye, Granddad. I'll see you after work."

"Love you, Blair girl."

She smiled wistfully at him. How she wished she could say the words back to him. She only hoped he knew how much she loved him.

Once Blair got to work, she was too busy to speculate if Garrett would ever show up on her farm again. But it didn't stop her from thinking about the way he'd kissed her. And as she talked with Lauren about a medication for a client's dog, she couldn't help thinking about the fourth of July party and the way he'd thrown her to the ground and covered her with his body. She couldn't stop *feeling* him.

What the hell was wrong with her?

Her phone rang in the pocket of her uniform while she was out on a farm call with Cole in the afternoon, vaccinating some calves. She checked the phone right away, always concerned that her grandfather needed her. Garrett's name on her screen sent her stomach into a nervous nosedive.

Cole looked up at her, one eyebrow raised, as the phone in her hand continued to ring. "Are you going to answer that?"

"I…yes, okay." Blair swallowed and hit the talk button. "Hello?"

"Blair. I'm glad I reached you." Garrett sounded tired. "Sorry I didn't call you earlier, but things are pretty crazy here."

Blair turned and stepped away from Cole. "Where are you?"

"Minneapolis. My friend Chris called me last night. He needed help." Garrett hesitated, and Blair could almost feel the tension in him. "I got him to the VA hospital here. He's on suicide watch."

"Oh, Garrett. I'm so sorry."

"I didn't want you to think I bailed on you. As soon as I get back, I'll finish the fence."

"There's no hurry. The horses can wait a few days. The important thing is to help your friend."

"Yeah." He sighed wearily. "I wish there was more I could do for him."

"He reached out for help and you went to him. That's everything, Garrett."

"But he needs more, and I don't know what to do." There was a long silence. Blair gripped her phone and held her breath as she waited for him to speak again. "He saved my life. He pulled me from the Humvee, risked his life so I wouldn't be incinerated. Like our friend."

Oh, God. An unwanted picture formed in her head. Garrett trapped in an overturned army vehicle, flames licking dangerously close. She put her hand over her mouth to muffle the cries that threatened to escape.

"It's my turn to pull him back from the abyss."

Blair breathed deeply, willing herself to be strong. "Of course."

Garrett cleared his throat. "How's Everett?"

"He's fine. He said if you didn't show up, you'd have a good reason. He's never going to let me forget he was right."

"You were waiting for me this morning?"

Yes. I've been waiting for you all my life.

Blair cleared her throat. "Well, that fence isn't going to fix itself. Good help is hard to find."

"Especially good free help." She heard the smile in his voice.

"Exactly."

For a moment, neither of them spoke. The sounds of the VA hospital hummed in the background; people talking, announcements on a PA system, the beep of machines. Finally, Garrett sighed. "I'd better go back and check on Chris."

"He's in the best place he could be, Garrett. They'll know what to do for him. You did the right thing taking him there."

"I hope so." Garrett sounded tired and unsure, and it broke her heart.

"How long will you be staying there?"

"I don't know, a few days. I won't leave until I know Chris is out of danger."

"Take care of yourself. Get some sleep."

"I will. And Blair?"

"Yes?"

"Thank you."

"For what?"

"For listening, I guess."

Blair's throat clogged with tears, and for a moment she couldn't speak. Once she recovered, she made herself inject a light tone into her voice.

"Anytime. I'm always around whenever you want to talk. And I don't charge near as much as a shrink."

He chuckled. "I'll remember that. Bye, Blair."

"Bye."

She hit the Off button and tucked the phone back into her pocket as she walked toward Cole. Avoiding his gaze, she prepared another vaccination syringe.

"That was Garrett. He's in Minneapolis. A friend of his is in a bad way and Garrett had to take him to the VA hospital." Her hands shook a little as she pushed the air out of the syringe. "He's suicidal."

Cole blew out a breath. "That's rough. It must be hard for Garrett. I know Lauren's worried about him. How'd he sound?"

"Worried, but mostly tired. He drove half the night to get to his friend." She dared a glance at Cole. "Why is Lauren worried about him?"

He shrugged. "He's not the same as he was before he deployed, especially since he lost his leg."

Blair nodded. She hadn't known Garrett well as a teenager, but she remembered a confident, energetic young man who saw exactly what he wanted and where he was going. The Garrett she knew now was far less certain.

"I'm going to say something, and after that I'm going to forever keep my mouth shut. Garrett is a good man, the best. But he's been through a lot. If you plan to get involved with him, make sure you're serious. Garrett needs someone who can accept him for the man he is now, emotionally and physically."

With that, Cole went back to work, leaving Blair breathless. Did she want to get involved like that with Garrett?

It was too late for second thoughts. On an emotional level, she was already involved.

Jana Richards

Chapter Fourteen

Garrett stared into the dregs of his coffee at the bottom of his Styrofoam cup. The stuff they served in the hospital cafeteria could double as paint remover. He didn't want to think of what it was doing to the inside of his stomach.

Since he'd arrived at the hospital with Chris yesterday morning, he'd drunk enough bad hospital coffee to give himself an ulcer. But if bringing Chris here helped, it would be worth it.

He got to his feet, needing to stand and stretch. He'd spent most of the day sitting in uncomfortable chairs. He had to get up and move before he took root.

"I'm going to the cafeteria, Alison. Would you like to come with me?" Garrett kept his voice low so as not to wake Chris. After a tumultuous day and a half, he'd finally crashed fifteen minutes ago, and Garrett wanted to make sure he slept a while longer. He suspected it was the first sleep his friend had had in some time.

Chris's wife Alison looked up at him, her smile tired. "No, I think I'll stay here. I have to leave soon to pick up the kids from my sister's house."

"Can I bring you anything?" he whispered.

"No, I'm fine, thank you." She reached for his hand. "Thank you, Garrett. Chris needed you, and you were there for him."

He squeezed her hand. She'd been there for him,

152

too, responding immediately to Garrett's call that he'd brought Chris to the hospital. She'd been at Chris's side ever since.

"I could say the same to you."

Alison's smile faded. "If I hadn't left, Chris wouldn't have fallen so far. But the way he was…the kids were scared."

"You did what you had to do for your kids. Don't blame yourself."

Alison swallowed and looked away. Of course she blamed herself.

"I love him. I never *stopped* loving him. I only want things to be the way they used to be."

Garrett understood that sentiment better than she could imagine. He'd give anything to have things the way they used to be.

To have his leg back. To be the man he used to be.

He squeezed her hand one last time. "If I don't see you before you go, have a good evening. Give your kids a hug for me."

"I will."

Garrett left the room and quietly closed the door behind him. Once out in the hallway, he was at loose ends. He nixed his plan to go to the cafeteria. He wasn't hungry, and he definitely didn't want more terrible coffee.

So he walked. The place brought back bad memories of a similar hospital in Fargo. After the amputation at the military hospital in Germany, he'd been brought to Fargo to recuperate and to be fitted with his new prosthesis.

And to figure out what his new normal was.

He'd gone to counseling, said the right things about

accepting what had happened. But deep down, it wasn't the truth. He hadn't accepted that his leg was gone, not really. He hadn't accepted being unable to do the things he'd done before, and he hadn't accepted the end of his military career. He wasn't sure he'd ever be able to accept what his life was now.

Down a hallway he heard shouts and hoots of laughter and headed toward it, needing a diversion from his own thoughts. In a large gymnasium, men in wheelchairs were playing a cut-throat game of basketball, one side shirts, the other skins. The wheelchairs were different from any he'd seen before, appearing smaller and lighter with wheels that slanted outwards. His counselor in Fargo had tried to get him interested in wheelchair basketball, but Garrett hadn't been able to dredge up any enthusiasm. He loved basketball, but if he couldn't play on two good legs, he didn't want to play at all.

He slipped inside the gym and watched, riveted. None of the men held back as they attempted to score and keep their opponents from doing the same. One man's chair tipped over, clattering to its side on the floor. Garrett stepped onto the floor to help him, but before he could reach him, the player used his upper body strength to right himself, landing with a *plop* back on his wheels. With a start, Garrett realized the player had only two stumps above the knees where his legs should have been.

After about fifteen minutes, the game broke up and the men started to wheel out of the gym. Garrett pushed away from the wall he'd been leaning against. He should head back to Chris's room. Alison had to leave, and he didn't want Chris to be alone.

"Hey, are you interested in playing?" The man who'd taken a tumble in his chair pushed toward him. He was older than Garrett had realized from watching him play, probably in his fifties.

"No, thanks. Just watching. A friend of mine's been admitted, and I was killing time while he slept."

"You a vet?"

"Yeah. First Battalion, First Marines. You?"

"Army, Second Brigade, First Armored Division. I've been working here at the Minneapolis VA for the last twenty years."

"What do you do?"

"I'm a counselor." He patted his legs. "After I lost my legs in Desert Storm, I had to find a new line of work."

"Was it hard? Starting over, I mean?"

"It took me a while to get over feeling sorry for myself. I finally decided I could keep on hating the world or I could live." He met Garrett's eyes. "What's your amputation?"

Garrett wondered how he knew. He worked hard to conceal the fact from the world. "Right leg, below the knee."

The man nodded and extended his hand. "I'm Hank Dawson, by the way."

Garrett shook his hand. "Garrett Saunders. Do you work with vets with PTSD?"

"Yeah. Your friend, the one who was admitted, is that what's going on with him?"

Garrett nodded, and gave Hank a brief account of the day his world, and the world of his friends, changed forever. "I feel so useless. I can't help Chris. I can't even help myself."

"What do you mean?"

"I'm thirty-one years old. These should be the best, most productive years of my life. But productive at what? I have no idea what to do with the rest of my life."

"Tell me, what was your first instinct, your first reaction, when your friend called asking for help?"

He answered without having to think. "To get to him. To help. I drove half the night from North Dakota."

"Then that's your answer."

Garrett stared at him. "What are you talking about?"

"You wanted to help. You drove five hours in the middle of the night to keep your friend from killing himself. That says a lot about you."

"Anyone would have done the same thing."

"Maybe, maybe not. The point is, you did it." Hank reached into a pocket in his shorts and pulled out a business card. "If you're going to be around for a while, give me a call. We can talk some more."

Hank turned his chair around and headed to the locker room. Garrett stared at the card. What was Hank trying to tell him? That he should be a counselor like him? There was no way. He didn't have the education. He didn't know if he wanted to get that involved in other vets' problems.

Even so, now that the seed had been planted, he couldn't let it go.

****

Garrett's phone call came shortly before nine in the evening. Everett had already gone inside the house, saying he was going to watch the news before heading to bed. Blair stayed out on the front porch watching the sun sink into the horizon, enjoying the view along with a few quiet moments of solitude. She answered on the first ring.

"Hello?"

"Hi. I hope I'm not disturbing you."

"Not at all. I'm just sitting out on the front porch." *Waiting for your call.* He hadn't promised to call, but somehow she'd known he would.

"Is your granddad with you?"

"No, he's gone inside."

"How's he been?"

"He's good. How's your friend?"

Garrett hesitated. "I'm not sure how to answer. His wife Alison has been at his side the last couple of days. She left him a few weeks ago because his behavior became erratic."

"Do you think they'll be able to patch things up?"

"I don't know. I hope so. I know they love each other, but I'm not sure love is enough."

"I could be naive, but perhaps this crisis is the best thing that could have happened to them. If they get the help they need, they've got a chance of getting back together."

"I hope you're right." She heard him sigh. "So tell me what's going on at the farm."

For a moment, Blair was at a loss, unsure what he wanted to hear. "Not much, really. Living here on the farm is life in the slow lane. Glaciers move faster than we do."

He sighed. "I know. But I need...I need to hear something normal. Something good."

If he wanted normal, that's what she'd give him.

"Granddad ordered lumber for the new stalls in the barn. It's supposed to be delivered tomorrow. Harry's fine. He's eating well and filling out nicely. Actually, he's become something of a glutton. You might even say he's eating like a horse."

Garrett groaned and then laughed. "You didn't just say that."

It was good to hear him laugh. "Hey, this is what you get for asking me for normal. But seriously, Harry is doing great. He and my horses have made themselves into a tight little family."

"That's good. What's Jake been up to?"

"Jake? Well, as usual, he's Granddad's shadow, though the other day, he got into some mischief. I baked some cookies and left them cooling on the counter while I went outside to work in the flower garden. By the time I came back to the kitchen, Jake had scarfed down a half dozen oatmeal cookies."

"I can't blame him for that. Your cookies are pretty good."

"Pretty good? My cookies are world class, Saunders."

He laughed again, the sound creating a bubble of happiness in her heart. "I stand corrected. Your cookies are top notch."

"That's better."

"What else is going on?"

She told him about vaccinating calves with Cole, about the cat who took exception to the distemper shot she'd administered and scratched her arm from wrist to elbow. About the new puppy his sister Charlotte was fostering.

"How much you want to bet Charlotte won't be

able to give up that pup when the time comes?" he asked.

"I'm not going to take that bet. She brought him in for a checkup yesterday, and he's adorable. She's totally smitten."

"How's Daisy taking to the new pup?" Garrett asked, referring to Charlotte's beagle.

"According to Charlotte, she's taken to him like a mother hen. She's treating him like he was her own pup. I'm not sure how well Daisy's going to like him once he gets bigger and starts bossing her around. We figure he's a German Shepherd/Lab cross of some kind, so he'll likely be pretty big."

"Can't wait to see him. Does Char have a name for him yet?"

"Last I heard, she'd narrowed down the choices to three but hasn't made a final decision yet."

"Sounds like Char." He had a smile in his voice. "She has a soft heart. Like you."

Blair kept her voice light even though her heart was pounding. "We both have a thing for strays, I guess."

"Yeah."

"Lucky for Charlotte, her strays don't eat as much as mine."

"You mean, they don't eat like horses."

Blair groaned. "That is such a bad joke."

"Hey, you started it." His voice sobered. "I miss the farm. Sometimes while I'm working out in the pasture, fixing fence, I stop and listen. I can hear frogs croaking in the creek and the birds singing. The tall grass makes a rustling sound as the wind blows through it, and I can smell wild sage in the air. I never realized how much I missed North Dakota until I came back. It's good to be home."

Blair put her hand over her mouth. Tears stung her eyes and her throat felt tight, but she wouldn't cry. She didn't even know why she wanted to. Garrett needed her to be strong right now, so she would.

"If you're getting that much enjoyment out of fixing my fence, I'm feeling a lot better about not paying you."

He laughed, the sound warm. "I'm really glad I called you, Blair."

"I'm glad, too." She hesitated. "Will you…will you call again?"

"Would you like me to?"

Oh, yes, please. I need to hear your voice. To know you're okay. "Well, somebody has to keep you up to date on what's happening in Masonville."

"That's true. I wouldn't want to get behind on the gossip."

"I wasn't gossiping," Blair said indignantly.

"Well, next time, you should."

This time she laughed. "Okay. I'll keep my ear to the ground and listen for something juicy."

"That's my girl. I'll talk to you tomorrow night. About this time okay for you?"

"It's perfect. Goodnight, Garrett."

"Goodnight, Blair. Sleep well."

"You, too."

She disconnected the call and set her phone carefully on the table between the two rocking chairs. Her heart was beating too fast. She inhaled deep breaths and slowly expelled them until her mind and body calmed.

What was she doing? Was she inviting trouble by asking Garrett to call her? Should she call him back and tell him she couldn't speak to him tomorrow night after all? Should she call him back and tell him…

Tell him what, Blair?

Tell him she was afraid she was falling in love with him, and she was terrified at the thought. Her heart began to pound wildly again.

She picked up her phone and stared at it, clutching it so hard her knuckles turned white. With one last deep breath, she got to her feet, stuck the phone in her back pocket, and walked into the house.

****

"King me."

Garrett groaned loudly as he topped one of Chris's checkers with another to make the king, but his heart lightened at the gleeful note in his friend's voice. "You've got a ruthless streak, man."

"Unlike you, I take these games seriously. What's your next move, buddy?"

Garrett didn't have a clue. He was saved from further humiliation when Alison walked into Chris's room, holding the hands of two little girls. Chris's eyes lit up, but Garrett saw apprehension there as well.

"I told you Daddy was here, girls," Alison said. "Come say hello."

The younger of the two, no more than five, clung to her mother's leg and stuck a thumb in her mouth. The older one, Hannah, almost eight, walked up to Chris with a wary expression on her face.

"Mommy said you were sick. Are you better now?"

"I'm getting better, sweetheart. Every day."

"Are you going to come live with us again?"

161

Chris glanced at Alison. "I hope so. Some day."

"As soon as you're all better, you mean?"

"Yeah."

"What if you get sick again?"

Garrett swallowed. *Out of the mouths of babes*. It was the question that haunted him, too. Chris was doing well now and seemed to be responding to treatment, but would it last? Would the pressures of everyday life prove too much for him again, once he left the relative safety and security of the VA hospital?

Chris got down on one knee in front of his daughter. He lifted a hand and gently smoothed her hair from her face. "I know what to do now if I get sick again. I'll come here to the hospital. I know they can help me. I promise I won't let things get as bad as they did before."

She gazed at him solemnly before finally nodding. "Okay. Can I play checkers with you?"

"Sure, as soon as Garrett and I finish our game."

Garrett cleared his throat. "You can take my place, Hannah. I have to be going, anyway."

"Don't leave on our account, Garrett," Alison said.

"Actually, there's someone I have to meet," he lied. Chris needed to reconnect with his children, and he was only in the way. He squeezed Alison's shoulder on the way out. "Have a good visit."

"We will." Her smile was more genuine than it had been a couple of days ago. With a nod, Garrett left the room.

He headed down the hall, not sure where he was going and feeling at loose ends. He and Chris had already eaten dinner in the hospital cafeteria, so he wasn't hungry. He could go back to his motel room and watch TV, but the idea of being alone for the rest of the evening didn't appeal to him. He could find a sports bar someplace and watch a game. He nixed the idea as soon as it formed. Putting himself in such close proximity to alcohol was tempting fate. He wouldn't disappoint Blair even though she wasn't there to see it.

Blair. Longing hit him hard. It was only seven p.m., too early to call her. She'd likely be spending some time with Everett right now, looking after his needs before he went off to bed. He'd have to be patient and call her in a couple of hours.

He stuck his hand in his pocket and felt the edge of a business card. He pulled out the card and stared at it, like he'd done several times since Hank had given it to him.

This time he had to do more than look at the card. An overwhelming need to talk to someone, someone in a similar situation, struck him. Garrett pulled out his phone and punched in Hank's number.

"Hank Dawson speaking."

"Hank, it's Garrett Saunders. I don't know if you remember me. We met in the gym a few days ago and you gave me your card."

"Sure, I remember you. What can I do for you, Garrett?"

Panic rippled through his chest, but he tamped it down. "I was wondering if you have a few minutes. To talk."

"No problem. I'm in my office right now. Why don't you come over?"

Hank gave him directions, and within a few minutes Garrett was knocking on his office door. At Hank's "Come in," he closed his eyes briefly and steeled himself before opening the door.

Hank wheeled his chair around his desk. "Good to see you again. How's your friend?"

At Hank's gesture, he sat in the chair in front of the desk. "Better."

"Does that mean you'll be heading home soon? You said you were from North Dakota, right?"

"Yeah, from a place called Masonville, near Bismarck. I'm not sure when I'm going home." He thought of Blair once more, and longing swamped him. "How did you get back to your life after your injury?"

"You mean occupation-wise?"

"Yeah, but also for other things, more personal things."

"Like what?"

Garrett had the feeling Hank knew exactly what he was asking but wanted him to say the words. "There's a woman back home."

"So you want to know what sex and intimacy is like with an amputation."

"Yeah." His face heated, and he felt like a schoolboy having "the talk." But he needed to know.

"This woman, did you know her before your amputation?"

"No. Well, yes, but we were kids. Most of the time I didn't notice her."

"But you're noticing her now."

"Yeah." He couldn't stop thinking about Blair. She occupied his waking thoughts. He almost resented her for the space she was taking up in his head.

And in his heart.

He didn't want to feel that way about anyone. Not yet, anyway. Not till he figured some things out.

"How long's it been since your amputation?"

"Almost two years."

"Have you been intimate with anyone since your surgery?"

Garrett shook his head. Since his amputation, the stirrings of desire had abandoned him. He'd begun to believe that part of his life was over. The possibility made him feel even less a man than the amputation had.

And then he'd met Blair, and his body had roared back to life. But he was afraid to act on those feelings.

"How does this woman feel about your amputation?"

Hank's question gave him pause. "I don't know. I've shown her my prosthesis but not the stump. We haven't talked about it."

"How do *you* feel about your amputation?"

Garrett sat back in his chair. The question caught him off guard, though he should have known Hank would ask it.

You wanted to talk, Saunders. So talk.

His hands fisted in his lap. "I'm angry about it. Angrier than I've ever been about anything. I can't have the career I want because of it. I can't play the sports I used to." He closed his eyes briefly and gulped in a breath to calm himself. "I don't know why she'd want to have sex with me."

"Why do you think that?"

Garrett glared at Hank. "Why the hell do you think? Because I'm not whole. Because I'm ugly!"

"Is that how you see yourself? Ugly?" Hank gestured toward his missing legs. "Is that how you see me?"

"No!" Garrett turned his face away from Hank's

knowing eyes. "Yes. It's how I see myself. I've been lying since I got out of the hospital. I said all the right things, made it sound like I'd accepted the way my body looks now. But the truth is, I can't look at myself in a mirror without feeling repulsed. I can't help thinking no woman would want me the way I am now."

"Those beliefs are pretty normal," Hank said. "I certainly had them, and I'm sure there aren't many amputees out there who haven't experienced at least some distress about the way their body looks after the loss of a limb."

"Did you get over it?" Garrett asked.

"Eventually, with time, and love. My situation was different from yours because I was married before my amputation." A smile quirked Hank's lip. "My wife wouldn't permit me to wallow in self-pity. And she convinced me she still found me sexually attractive."

"She sounds like an amazing woman."

"She is. I'm one lucky bastard." Hank's grin faded. "What about your girl? Do you think she could look past the missing leg to see the man?"

Garrett didn't have a clue. He wasn't sure if *he* could look past his missing leg. He had no idea if he could be the man he used to be. The confident man, so sure of himself and his abilities. The man women wanted to be with.

He was afraid that guy was gone and was never coming back.

Chapter Fifteen

Garrett drove his truck back to the motel after his meeting with Hank but didn't go inside his room. Instead he paced outside. He was itchy with restlessness, too keyed up to sit around. Before his amputation, he would have gone for a run whenever restless energy hit him like this. Now, he had to content himself with a leisurely walk.

A fucking walk.

Frustration made him want to put his fist through the window of his motel room. Taking a deep breath, he made himself walk away. He headed to a park he'd seen a couple of blocks from the motel.

He should consider himself lucky, he supposed. His injury could have been far worse. He could have lost both his legs the way Hank had, or suffered traumatic brain injury. He'd seen men with brain injuries at the hospital in Fargo, men no longer the people they'd once been. If that had happened to him, he'd rather be dead.

No, he didn't feel lucky at all. But he couldn't go on living this half-life. He hated the anger and self-loathing inside him. It had to stop. But how?

He walked the square block perimeter of the park three times before moving to the center of the park to sit on a bench. Absently, he rubbed his right knee. What was Blair doing now? He checked his watch and saw that it was eight-thirty p.m. Only thirty more minutes till he could speak to her. His breathing calmed at the thought.

In the distance, Garrett watched a half dozen kids enjoying themselves on a play structure. Their excited laughter made him smile. He'd always thought that someday he'd have kids. At least two, a boy and a girl. He thought of Chris's little girls and what they'd been through with their dad. Unless he learned to live with his disability, Garrett couldn't inflict himself on a child.

Did Blair want children?

He blew out a breath. He was getting way ahead of himself.

The parents seated on the benches next to the play structure got to their feet and called to their kids. Reluctantly, they climbed off the structure, took their parents' hands, and waved goodbye to their friends. Soon the park was empty and quiet. Garrett retrieved his phone from his pocket and saw that it was nine p.m. Relief filled him now that he could finally call Blair.

She answered on the first ring, as if she'd been waiting for him. "Hi."

"Hi. How was your day?"

"Pretty good. I assisted on two feline neutering surgeries, tattooed and microchipped a Standard Poodle, and cleaned three sets of canine teeth."

Hearing her made him smile. "Busy day."

"It was. How about you?"

"I hung out with Chris most of the day. Alison was at work, so I didn't want him to be alone. She came tonight with their kids. It's the first time they've seen their dad since she kicked him out a few weeks ago."

"How did they react to him?"

"They were cautious initially, especially the younger one. I didn't stay to see if she warmed up any. I didn't want to get in their way."

"What have you been doing this evening?"

"I hung out with another veteran for a while." She didn't have to know that Hank was a counselor, and she certainly didn't need to know what they talked about. "And I walked. I'm in a park close to my motel right now. How about you? Where are you?"

"I'm on the front porch again. I like it here this time of evening, with the sun going down. Granddad usually goes to bed around now, so I have a few moments to myself. It's always nice to have a little solitude."

"I'm disturbing you."

"No, never. I wanted to hear from you."

They were both silent for a beat. Garrett cleared his throat to dispel the sense of intimacy the silence brought.

"So you promised me some juicy gossip. What've you got?"

She laughed. "I was hoping you'd forgotten."

"No way. Spill it. What do you know?"

"Isabelle has added Boston Cream to the list of pies at the Harvest Restaurant."

"That's not gossip."

"Mr. Jenkins down the road is getting a hip replacement."

"I'm sorry for Mr. Jenkins, but that's not gossip either."

"What can I say? I'm not the gossipy kind."

"You're no fun," he said on a laugh. "I'm going to have to quiz my parents once I get home."

"Yeah, I guess you'll have to. Do you have any idea how soon that might be? When you're coming home, I mean."

"I'm not sure. I think Chris is out of danger, but they're watching him closely. His wife is here to support him, and now his kids. I need to know he's okay before I leave. If I left and then something happened—"

"Nothing's going to happen, Garrett. Your friend reached out for help and you were there. His family and the people at the VA hospital will take it from here."

"Yeah." She was right. There wasn't anything more he could do, aside from playing checkers with Chris. He wished there was.

"Granddad asked me how you were doing, at supper tonight. I think he misses having you around."

"Yeah? Tell him I miss him, too."

"I'll do that. It'll make his day."

He heard the smile in her voice, and it made him throw caution to the wind. "What about you? Do you miss me too?"

"I…I—"

What had he been thinking? "I'm sorry, Blair. You don't have to answer that."

"I miss you." Her voice was barely above a whisper. "I shouldn't, but I do."

Energy crackled over the air waves between them. "Why shouldn't you?"

"Because I have nothing to give you. You deserve better."

Her answer stunned him. "I could say the same. You deserve better than a broken-down soldier with no prospects."

"Garrett." She was silent for several long beats. Only the sound of her labored breathing, as if she were holding back a torrent of emotions, told him she was still on the line. Finally, he heard her sigh. "There are things about me you don't know."

"You already told me about your suicide attempt."

"Yes."

"If there's something more, you can tell me."

"I can't." Her voice was taut with strain. "If I told you, you'd hate me."

"Blair, there's nothing you could tell me that would make me hate you." He breathed in a ragged breath. "I was a soldier. I killed people. There's nothing you could say that could be worse than that."

"You were doing your duty."

"I suppose." He had killed to save his life, or the lives of his friends or innocent civilians. But taking a life was not something he bore lightly. Or got over easily.

He wouldn't push her to talk if she didn't want to. He'd hated counselors who urged him to spill his guts so his confessions could fit neatly into a one-hour session. It was especially galling if the counselor had never seen battle. He didn't talk unless he was ready. He'd give Blair the same consideration.

"I won't push you, but if you ever want to talk, I'm here. Okay?"

"Okay." Her whispered reply sounded relieved. "Garrett…"

He waited a beat, but she didn't continue. "Yeah?"

"Thank you. Whatever has happened to you, whatever physical scars you bear now, that hasn't changed who you are deep down. You'll always be the best man I know. Aside from my granddad, of course."

"Of course." Blair never ceased to surprise him. Hell, she turned him upside down and inside out with only a few whispered words.

"Will you...will you call again tomorrow night?" she asked.

"Yeah. I'll call." Nothing would stop him from calling her. He realized with a start that he needed to hear Blair's voice like he needed his next breath. "I should go. Goodnight, Blair."

"Goodnight, Garrett."

He hit the Off button on his phone. As he looked up, he realized the sun had set and the street lights had come on. Garrett pushed himself to a standing position. Time to go back to the motel.

As he walked back, a nagging worry wouldn't leave him alone. What did Blair think she'd done that was so horrible? The woman he knew, the woman who loved animals and treated her grandfather with such care, wasn't capable of hurting anyone or anything. Whatever she thought she'd done, she must have blown up the significance in her head.

Those self-inflicted wounds were often the deepest.

****

Garrett shifted his position on the park bench so he could stretch out his prosthetic leg. Chris sat beside him, quietly taking in the beautiful afternoon in the hospital's courtyard. The last couple of days, the VA staff had allowed Chris to visit the courtyard as long as he wasn't alone. Garrett hoped that meant they thought he was making progress. And was no longer a threat to himself.

Chris cleared his throat. "I've been thinking. It's

time you headed home."

Garrett stared at his friend, surprised. "You're kicking me out? Are you sick of me?"

"You've been here five days. You must be ready to get back to your own life."

He nodded at his friend, the sudden lump in his throat making it hard to speak. Chris was in good hands now and was getting the treatment he needed. Alison visited every day, and she and Chris appeared to be forging strong bonds once more. He wasn't needed here any longer.

So why did he feel like he should be doing something more?

Garrett cleared his throat. "Yeah, I guess I am."

He'd been staying in a motel near the VA hospital, and after five days the costs were adding up. But aside from that, he wanted to go home. At one time he couldn't wait to leave home and see the world, but now he missed Masonville.

And if he was honest with himself, he wanted—no, needed—to see Blair. He missed her, too, missed her smile, even missed the way she teased him. He missed everything about her.

They'd spoken every night since he'd been away. He wondered if she thought of him at all during the day, the way he thought of her.

Chris lifted his face to the late afternoon sun and closed his eyes. "It's peaceful here. Gives me a chance to think without the noise in my head drowning out my thoughts."

"That's good."

"I want to thank you." Chris opened his eyes and turned to him once more. "If you hadn't dropped everything to come to me…thank you."

"I'm glad I could help." Garrett didn't want to think about what might have happened if Chris hadn't called him.

Chris sighed. "I have a long way to go to be the husband and the father I want to be."

"You'll get there."

"I hope so. I'm going to work damn hard." Chris leaned forward and rested his elbows on his knees. "What about you? For the last year, every time we talk it's been about me and my problems. It's suddenly occurred to me that I've never asked how you're doing." He turned to him. "So, how are you doing?"

The question caught Garrett off guard. He sat up straighter. "I'm fine."

"You're living with your folks, aren't you?"

"Yeah. I'm looking to buy a place of my own, but so far the right property hasn't come up."

"I've never asked how it's been for you." Chris nodded toward his right leg and his prosthesis. "I mean, without your leg."

Talking about his problems made him uncomfortable. He told himself it was because he didn't want to burden his friend, but the truth was he didn't have any answers about where his life was going, and it scared him. "Still trying to find my place in the world, but I'm doing all right."

"You're not sure what you're meant to do now because of your amputation. Is that what you mean?"

"Yeah, but it's fine. I'll figure it out." Garrett pushed himself to his feet. "You ready to go? It's almost time for your counseling session."

"I'm ready." Chris rose from the bench. "When do

you think you'll head back?"

Garrett hesitated before speaking. Alison planned to bring the kids again tonight. Chris wouldn't be alone. He'd have his family with him, so there'd be no reason for Garrett to hang around.

He checked his watch; nearly four. If he hurried back to the motel, he could check out and be on the road within an hour. That would get him back to Masonville around ten p.m. Suddenly, he couldn't wait.

"I think I'd like to leave right away. Tonight."

They walked back into the hospital. As they stood outside the therapist's office, Chris extended his hand.

"Don't forget to look after yourself. You deserve to find a place in the world. A good place."

Garrett was touched by his friend's concern. "Thanks, buddy."

"Call me?"

"Sure. You can't get rid of me that easily."

They embraced, and for a moment Garrett clung to Chris, afraid to let him go. But he wasn't sure if he was afraid for Chris or for himself.

Chris was first to pull away. "Have a safe drive home."

"I will. Take care."

With one last nod, Chris opened the door of his therapist's office and stepped inside. For a moment Garrett stood immobile and stared at the door. He prayed Chris would be okay. He'd done what he could for him. The rest was up to him.

Hard on the heels of that realization came another thought. *I'm going to see Blair soon.*

Garrett made his way out of the hospital, his heart lighter with every step.

He was going home.

****

By the time Garrett reached the western outskirts of Minneapolis, traffic had thinned out some. He used the Bluetooth in his truck to call Hank's number. The counselor picked up on the second ring.

"Hank Dawson here."

"Hi, Hank. It's Garrett Saunders. I'm on my way back to North Dakota."

"That's good. Your friend is better?"

"I think he's going to be okay. He's the one who said I should get back to my own life."

"Then he's as good a friend to you as you are to him. As long as you were looking out for him, you didn't have to deal with your own stuff."

Hank was probably right, but he wasn't going to tell him so. "So, anyway, I'm on the road. Should be home in five or six hours."

"Drive carefully. And Garrett?"

"Yeah?"

"Have you ever thought about counseling other vets?"

He went with honesty. "I've been thinking about it since you put your business card in my hand. But I don't have the education for that kind of thing." He wasn't sure he had the temperament, either.

"There are different kinds of counselors, different ways to serve. All that's required is a desire to help. You dropped everything to go to your friend. That says something about your character."

"All it says is that he's a friend. We went through a lot together. I'm not some kind of saint."

Hank chuckled. "Don't worry. Sainthood's not one

of the job requirements. Give the idea some thought. If you want more information, call me. We can discuss it further."

"I'll think about it, but I'm not promising anything."

"That's fine. I only want you to think about your strengths and your goals and what you really want going forward. What you need out of life and a career." Hank paused before continuing. "If you want to talk more about your girl, and intimacy with her, you've got my number. Don't hesitate to use it."

Garrett tried to swallow, but his mouth had gone dry. He'd done little else in the last few days but think about what intimacy with Blair would be like. "Thanks for everything, Hank."

"You're welcome. And listen, Saunders. If you don't call me, I'll be calling you. Don't make me go all therapist on your ass."

"Okay, okay. I'll call."

"Good. Have a safe trip."

Garrett disconnected the call, and with a grin, shook his head. Hank was one of a kind. Where did his optimism, his drive, his desire to help fellow vets come from? If he'd lost both of his legs the way Hank had, he wasn't sure he'd want to go on.

The thought shamed him. His family would have been devastated if he'd died. Especially if he died at his own hands. He was lucky. He had people who loved him and a community that had welcomed him home.

It's time to quit feeling sorry for myself.

His thoughts immediately flew to Blair. Could she be one of the people who loved him? Did he want her to be?

The answer came to him on swift wings. *Absolutely.*

There were things they didn't know about each other yet, details they hadn't shared, but Garrett *knew* her, knew her heart. She was kind and sweet but turned into a tiger when defending someone, or something, she loved. He hoped one day he could put himself in that category.

He couldn't wait to hear her voice. He searched for her number in the truck's Bluetooth and hit the button. She answered after a couple of rings.

"Garrett? Hi. I wasn't expecting to hear from you until later tonight. Is everything all right?"

His body relaxed at the sound of her voice, and the concern he heard in it. Knowing she cared was a balm to his soul. Ironically, he also came to life. It was as if he wasn't quite alive until he connected with her.

"Everything's fine. I'm on the road, on my way home."

"Oh, that's great. Your friend is okay?"

"He has a way to go, but yeah, he's okay." Garrett checked the clock on the dashboard; five-thirty-five p.m. "Are you at work?"

"I'm in my truck on my way home. Where are you?"

"West of Minneapolis, past St. Cloud. I should be home around ten."

"That's good."

Blair went silent. Garrett waited, an instinct telling him there was more she wanted to say. Instead the silence continued, and he couldn't wait any longer.

"Blair?"

"I'm here." He heard her shaky intake of breath.

"Garrett, once you get back to Masonville…when you get home tonight, will you come here to my farm?"

His breath caught in his throat. "What are you asking, Blair?"

"I'm asking you to spend the night with me." Her voice was barely a whisper. "I'm asking you to make love with me."

Garrett gripped the steering wheel. He was glad traffic had thinned out on the four-lane Interstate, because his focus was riveted on Blair's voice and not on the road.

"I want that, too, sweetheart."

"That's good." She gave a hiccupping laugh that came out as a sob. "I'm glad."

The tears in her voice alarmed him. "If you're glad, why are you crying? If you're not sure about this, we don't have to do anything. We'll still be friends."

It would kill him, but he'd never push himself on her. She had to want him as much as he wanted her.

"No, I *am* sure. I want to make love with you. More than you can imagine. But I'm scared of disappointing you. It's…it's been a long time for me."

"You could never disappoint me, Blair. No matter what happens." He owed her some honesty, too. "I'm afraid of disappointing you, too."

"What do you mean?" She sounded genuinely perplexed.

"I'm not the man I used to be," he said hesitantly. "Because of my leg."

"Your leg?"

"Yeah." He concentrated on keeping the truck between the lines of the highway. "You haven't seen the stump. It's not pretty."

179

"I think you're beautiful, Garrett. Your leg doesn't matter to me."

"You might feel differently once you saw the stump."

"I don't think so. Your amputation is only a small fragment of who you are. And besides…" Her voice lowered to a seductive, sultry whisper. "I'm more interested in other parts of your anatomy."

His libido went from zero to sixty in two point five nanoseconds. For a moment he couldn't form words.

Finally, he laughed. "You're killing me, Blair."

"I swear that wasn't my intention." She laughed. "Or maybe it was, I don't know. All I know is that I want you and I'm tired of fighting it."

Dear God, he wanted her, too. His body thrummed with want. And deep, driving need.

"Yeah. I'm tired of fighting it, too."

"I'm glad you feel the same way." He heard her breathe in deeply and slowly let it out. "If we do this, we have to go in knowing this is about sex, about a physical relationship. We're friends, but it can't go any further than that."

Disappointment swamped him. *What had you expected, Saunders?* He'd take whatever she was able to give. "Understood."

"Good." She sounded relieved. Unexpected longing hit him in the solar plexus, but he pushed it away.

"Where should we meet? If your grandfather wakes up, he won't like finding me in your house in the middle of the night."

"Drive around to the side of the barn and meet me inside. I'll improvise something."

"That's my girl."

Garrett stepped on the gas pedal. Despite the limitations she'd put on this arrangement, he couldn't wait to get home to her.

Chapter Sixteen

After her grandfather went to bed around nine, Blair dragged an old mattress she found in the attic down the stairs and out onto the front porch. Unless Everett was a remarkably sound sleeper, he couldn't have missed the thumping of the double mattress hitting each stair on the way down, or the slamming of the screen door that she couldn't catch before it closed. She leaned the mattress against the wall and went back inside the house. This time Blair eased open the screen door and quietly closed it, tiptoeing past the kitchen to peek down the hall. Everett's bedroom door remained closed and all was quiet. She didn't know whether he was actually asleep or if he'd figured out what she was doing and chose to ignore it. Either way she was grateful.

Blair retrieved the wheelbarrow from the garage and pushed it to the front porch. Memories of using this wheelbarrow to haul the broken concrete out of the barn flashed through her head. The strongest memory was of Garrett lifting his pant leg and showing her his prosthetic leg. She remembered his pride and pain, and his defiance. He'd expected revulsion from her, or perhaps pity. With his stubborn, angry glare he'd dared her to feel sorry for him. At the time, she'd only felt sorrow for the pain he must have gone through. She'd managed to hide her distress from him, or at least she hoped she had.

This would be the first time she'd see his amputation, if he chose to show her. She'd be wise not to reveal how much it hurt her to imagine his pain, both physical and emotional.

Laying the mattress across the wheelbarrow, she made her way to her grandmother's potting shed behind the garage, stopping every few feet to adjust the mattress so it wouldn't slide to the ground. Blair hadn't been in the potting shed since she'd moved to the farm, but on earlier inspection that evening, she'd been pleased to see that Grandma had left it neat and organized. Aside from flowerpots stacked under the wooden counter and a few gardening tools hanging on the walls, the shed was empty. The south-facing windows over the counter had brightly patterned curtains that could be closed to block the sun or give privacy, and the floor space was large enough to accommodate the double mattress. It even had electricity. All she'd needed to do was sweep the floor and brush away a few cobwebs.

Finally, she reached the shed with her awkward bundle. After wrestling the mattress through the door, Blair surveyed the room. The shed was small but cozy. Of all the buildings on the farm, this was where she felt her grandmother most. Anna had spent a lot of time here, starting flowers and vegetables from seed and repotting plants. Granddad had built the shed to give her pleasure and had maintained it with care. For Blair, the shed symbolized their love for each other. She sensed her grandmother would approve of what she intended to use the shed for tonight.

Nervous energy rippled through her at the thought

of making love with Garrett.

Over the next hour Blair fetched sheets and blankets and pillows, a battery-powered lantern and, most importantly, the box of condoms she'd hidden in her truck. After Garrett's phone call, she'd made a quick run into Bismarck to pick them up. Even though she wanted Garrett with every fiber of her being, she had to be smart about this.

She couldn't afford another unplanned pregnancy.

As she tucked the fitted sheet around the mattress and smoothed a blanket over it, she heard a vehicle drive into the yard. She listened as it pulled around the side of the barn and stopped. Blair's heart slammed against her ribs, and nerves danced in her stomach. *I want this,* she reminded herself. *I want him. I've always wanted him.* Expelling an indrawn breath, Blair hurried out of the shed and ran to the barn.

Blair watched as Garrett descended from the cab and walked around the front of his truck. He stopped when he saw her. Neither of them moved or spoke. Seconds ticked away, and Blair wondered if he'd changed his mind. But to her relief, with a few tentative steps, he came closer. She saw his throat work and she realized he was as nervous as she was. Perhaps more so.

It was all the encouragement she needed. Blair ran to him and threw her arms around his neck. His arms came around her, holding her so tight she could barely breathe. But it was so good to be in his arms. So *right.*

Blair leaned back to look at him. In the dim moonlight, his face was all sharp angles. Only his eyes were soft as they gazed into hers.

"Hi." She lifted her hand to touch his cheek and run her fingers through his thick hair. "I'm glad you're home."

"Yeah. So am I."

He kissed her, his mouth urgently descending on hers with hot need. She responded with need of her own, and all the pieces of her life clicked into place. This was where she was meant to be. This was the man she was meant to be with.

"Come." She caught his hand in hers and led him to the shed.

She'd left the lantern burning on the floor next to the mattress, and it gave a soft glow to the room. With the colorful curtains drawn and the door closed, the space was intimate, blocking out the world and all its distractions. Blair turned to face Garrett.

"I hope this is all right." She clutched her hands together to keep them from shaking.

"It's perfect, Blair." He gently pried one of her hands loose and tugged her against him. "And so are you. Perfect."

He kissed her, softly, gently, a mere brushing of his lips against hers. Somehow, he understood she had to do this slowly, and she was grateful he was willing to let her set the pace. It had been so long, and she'd been an inexperienced teenager. Her memories of sex were uncomfortable—fumbling hands, hurried, sometimes painful coupling, a swift adjustment of clothing, a quick goodbye. No words of love or even affection, only a release of sexual need.

This was different. For the first time she would be making love, not merely having sex.

Blair relaxed into Garrett's kiss and wound her arms around his neck. *Yes*, she decided. *This is my first time*.

Still kissing him, she began unbuttoning his shirt. He broke the kiss and began to do the same, a smile on his face.

"Do you remember the last summer I saw you, just before I joined the Marines? Your brothers were both working for the summer, so you came out to your grandparents' farm on your own."

Blair's face grew hot at the memory. She pulled his shirt from his jeans and laid her palm against the warm, hard muscles of his abdomen. "You mean the summer I threw myself at you and you totally rejected me? No, I barely remember that at all."

He chuckled as he pushed her shirt off her shoulders. "I was sorely tempted that summer. There you were, prancing around in your short shorts and bikini top, working in your grandmother's garden while I mowed the lawns. You must have known you were driving me crazy."

Actually, she hadn't known. He'd done a great job of ignoring her and making her believe she was nothing but a nuisance. She looked up at him, tilting her head to one side. "If you were so tempted, why did you tell me to take a hike when I tried to seduce you?"

"You were fifteen, Blair. Three years younger than me and just a kid. If you'd known what I wanted to do with you..." His unfinished sentence shimmered between them.

He was such an honorable man. He hadn't wanted to take advantage of a young girl with a case of raging hormones and too little sense. A girl who believed her only worth was in what her body could give to a boy.

"Perhaps you can show me now." Blair slowly lowered the zipper of his pants. "I'm not a kid anymore."

"Yes, I can see that."

He claimed her mouth in a searing kiss that left her breathless, and suddenly Blair no longer wanted to take things slow. She answered his kiss with need of her own, touching her tongue to the seam of his lips and begging entry. Garrett immediately opened to her, devouring her with a hunger that matched her own. Their tongues danced and twisted together, warm flesh sliding over warm flesh.

Garrett unfastened the hooks at the back of her bra, and it fell to the floor. The feel of her naked breasts against his hard chest with its light dusting of hair sent shivers rippling through her body. Garrett rubbed her upper arms.

"Cold?"

She gulped in a breath. Why was it so hard to breathe? "No. Exactly the opposite. You make me burn, Garrett."

Instead of laughing the way she thought he might, he cupped her face between his two big hands.

"Sweet, beautiful Blair."

His words brought a lump to her throat and an ache to her heart, especially accompanied as they were by the tenderness in his eyes. No one had ever looked at her that way, like she was something special. Something precious.

Garrett kissed her once again, then knelt in front of her on his good knee, his leg with the prosthesis at a right angle. Slowly, he unzipped her jeans and pulled them, along with her panties, down her legs to the floor. She stepped out of them and pushed them aside with her bare foot, suddenly aware she was standing in front of him naked. Vulnerable. But she wasn't embarrassed. This was Garrett, and the way he looked up at her in wonder, even joy, made her feel beautiful.

And loved?

She tossed the thought from her mind, not wanting to go there. This night was about want and need of the physical kind. There was no room for anything else.

Blair ran her fingers through his hair. She loved the texture of it, thick yet silky and smooth, the curls winding themselves around her fingers.

"I know women who would kill for hair like yours."

He laughed. "There's nothing special about my hair."

Blair only smiled. He was wrong, of course. There was something special about every part of him. *He* was special.

She patted his hair to smooth it once more and extended her hand to him. "Come to bed, Garrett."

He shook his head, a whisper of a smile playing on his lips. "Not yet."

With that, he placed his hands on her ass and drew her forward. Blair's heart pounded.

"Garrett, I've never—"

"Shh, sweetheart. Let me love you."

His warm breath whispered across her thighs. He parted her sex with his fingers and licked the exposed knot of nerves in a slow, languorous motion. Her knees buckled. She would have collapsed if he hadn't held her upright.

"Oh!" Somehow it was the only word she could form.

He brought her even closer, working her with

tongue and fingers, sucking gently until the pleasure was almost too much, on the edge of something wonderful she couldn't quite reach.

But then she did.

Blair orgasmed with a gasp. She clutched at Garrett's shoulders while spasms wracked her body with waves of pleasure. *Dear God, it felt so good. He felt so good.*

She rested her cheek against the top of his head while she caught her breath. She didn't know it could be like this. Her previous fumbling experiences with sex hadn't prepared her. The wonder of it brought tears to her eyes.

Garrett reached his hand out to her. "Come lie down, sweetheart."

She seized his hand and did as he asked, pulling back the blanket to snuggle inside. Garrett stood beside the mattress, his hands on the waistband of his jeans, the zipper already down.

"Turn off the light, Blair."

For a second she thought about arguing. She wanted to see him, all of him, the way he'd seen her. But the look on his face told her that wasn't going to happen. She wondered if this was a first for Garrett, too. The first time he'd made love since his amputation. Some intuition told her it was. She reached for the switch on the lantern and turned it off.

The shed was thrown into darkness. Blair heard the rustle of clothes as Garrett finished undressing, and she could see the outline of his body in the darkness but couldn't make out any details. Which was the point, she supposed. It made her sad that he didn't trust her enough to show her his amputation.

Soon he was on the mattress, lying next to her. He rubbed her hip with his calloused hand.

"I'm afraid this is going to be over very quickly," he said sheepishly. "It's been a while."

"It's all right, Garrett." She smoothed his hair from his forehead. "But condom first, okay? The box is beside the lantern."

"Right."

He reached for the box, grabbed one plastic pouch from inside, and then tossed the box in the direction of the lantern. Blair could hear the sound of the pouch opening and saw Garrett looming over her as he affixed the condom. She wished she could see him doing it.

He moved over her, one leg on either side of her hips. "I don't want to hurt you. If I hurt you with my prosthesis—"

"You won't." She ran her hand over his back and buttocks in what she hoped was a soothing motion. "I'm a tough country girl, remember?"

He chuckled. "I remember."

He lowered his hips to hers, his erection poised at the opening to her body, most of his weight resting on his forearms. Slowly, he began to push inside, tentatively. Blair wrapped her legs around his waist, forcing him deeper. Needing him there.

"Please, Garrett." She pushed her hips against his, meeting his rhythm stroke for stroke. "You're not going to hurt me. I swear. I need you."

Her words broke his last restraint. He pounded into her, and she welcomed him, loving the weight of him on her, the feel of him inside her body, even the sounds of their lovemaking. In a few moments, his body went rigid and with a shout of triumph, his release came. He collapsed on top of her, and she held him tightly.

"I told you it was going to be quick," he murmured.

"It was perfect." It *was* perfect.

Absolutely perfect.

****

Garrett woke with Blair snuggled against his side, the scent of lavender surrounding him. A strand of her curly hair tickled his nose, making him smile. Contentment washed over him.

She shivered in her sleep and he pulled the blankets over them, tucking them around her shoulders. Blair sighed and buried her nose against his chest. Longing overwhelmed him.

If only...

He couldn't think about what-ifs or it would drive him nuts. He could only deal with the here and now. And the reality of what his body now was.

He wished he knew what her feelings were for him. But she wouldn't be lying with him now if she didn't care at least a little about him; one thing he was sure of was that Blair didn't do casual sex.

Doubt crept into his thoughts. Why was she here? Why had she asked him to meet her here? He tightened his grip around her shoulders. Did she feel sorry for him? He couldn't bear her pity.

Blair stirred in his arms as she slowly woke. She looked up at him, her eyes heavy with sleep.

"What time is it?" she asked.

He reached around her to flick on the lantern. The shed was instantly bathed in soft light. He glanced at his wristwatch.

"It's twelve-thirty-five."

Blair sighed. "I guess you should probably leave soon. I should go back to the house."

"Yeah." The last thing he wanted to do was leave her.

She smiled up at him. "But I don't want to."

He smiled back, smoothing the hair from her face. "Me neither."

He kissed her and his body flamed to life once more. He smoothed his hands over the silky skin of her back, her hips, her thighs. She arched into him, silently asking for more. Garrett was more than willing to comply. She rolled on top of him, straddling him. As she leaned over him for a kiss, her breasts grazed his chest.

"I need to turn off the light, Blair."

"Leave it. I want to see you. You're beautiful, Garrett," she whispered.

He stilled, his hands gripping her hips. "No, I'm not."

"You are." Her expression was fierce. "You *are*."

Garrett stared into her eyes. She thought she believed what she was saying. But he hadn't taken off his prosthesis, hadn't allowed her to see what was left of his leg. He wasn't ready for that, and he wasn't sure he'd ever be.

"I don't want you to see it. Not yet."

"Why would you think your stump would bother me? It's not a big deal."

"It's a big deal to me!"

She tilted her head. "Yes, I can see that." She laid her hand on his cheek. "I'm sorry. I won't push."

The relief was immense. "Thank you. I'm sorry—"

She laid her finger over his lips. "Shhh. Don't

apologize. When you're ready, you'll show me and you'll see everything is all right. It really is, Garrett."

God, he loved this woman.

He loved her commitment to her grandfather and the horses she rescued. He loved her kind heart, her sweetness, her toughness. He loved everything about her.

"I appreciate you giving me some time."

"No problem." She grinned at him suddenly. "But don't think you're getting off easy. I'm not done with you yet."

Garrett's body stirred to life, and he discovered he wasn't done either.

"Is that a fact?"

"It is."

She grabbed the box of condoms, pulled out a pouch, and tore it open. She rolled the condom over his erection, and he nearly lost it. There was something utterly erotic about the way she touched him, though he guessed she'd never done it before.

Blair turned off the lantern and climbed into his lap. "How about you forget everything else and make love to me again?"

He grasped her hips and settled her against his erection. "Anything for the little lady."

She swatted his shoulder and laughed. "Little lady, my ass."

He laughed with her, his heart lighter than it had been for a very long time. And when she leaned forward to kiss him, her hands clutching his shoulders and her breasts grazing his chest, all he could think was that she was his and he wanted her in his life. Forever.

Chapter Seventeen

Garrett left for home around two a.m. after a long, luxurious goodnight kiss. Once he drove out of the yard, Blair pulled on her clothes, turned off the lantern, and headed for the house. She crept up the stairs to her room, being careful to avoid the creakiest stairs. She didn't want to disturb her grandfather's rest, but even more, she didn't want to answer his curious questions, or see his smug smile.

Once she made it to her room, she closed the door softly behind her and rested her forehead against the solid wood. She could still feel Garrett's hands on her, feel his lips touching hers. She shivered at the memory of his lips blazing a trail down her belly, his mouth finding the sensitive nub of nerves at the apex of her thighs, and with lips and tongue and questing fingers bringing her to climax over and over again. Blair nearly orgasmed again as she relived the sensation.

With a shaky breath she pushed away from the door. She didn't bother turning on a light as she undressed and crawled under her covers. Moonlight cast shadows across her ceiling as she lay wide awake trying to process her feelings. And her actions.

There was no doubt she found Garrett attractive. Always had. Losing part of his leg hadn't dimmed his attractiveness for her. She'd wanted to be with him since she was fifteen years old, even before she understood what that meant.

But things were different now. She was different. What did she have to offer Garrett aside from sex? Had it been a mistake to invite him to meet her tonight? All she knew was that she'd longed for him while he was gone. She'd been shocked by how much she'd missed him. How much she'd wanted him.

Blair rolled over, tossing the blankets to one side. Why shouldn't she and Garrett have a simple sexual relationship? They were unattached adults with healthy sexual needs. There didn't have to be any deeper meaning. Why did she have to analyze it to death?

She rolled over again, this time punching her pillow until it molded into a comfortable shape. Exhausted, she lowered her head to the pillow and closed her eyes.

Having a sexual relationship with Garrett didn't have to mean anything. They could have some fun. God help them, they could both use some fun in their lives.

Would everything change if Garrett found out about Eve?

Her eyes popped open once more. She couldn't bear to see the disgust in his eyes once he discovered she hadn't kept her baby safe.

She wouldn't tell him. He didn't have to know the sordid details of her past any more than she needed to hear about the trauma of him losing his leg. After all, this was to be a simple sexual relationship. Neither of them needed to rip the Band-Aids off those wounds.

Blair breathed a sigh of relief and relaxed against her pillow, satisfied she'd worked things out. She only needed to be careful about birth control and everything would be fine. As soon as she could, she'd book an appointment with a doctor in Bismarck and get a prescription for the pill. It wouldn't hurt to be doubly sure there were no surprises.

As Blair drifted between sleep and wakefulness, she remembered Garrett pulling her against him as they slept. She remembered his warm, smooth skin, the scent of their lovemaking surrounding them.

She remembered how safe she'd felt with him. How perfect it was to be with him. She'd never been more content. Happy. How she longed to lie with him every night and wake in his arms every morning—

No, no, no. She couldn't think like that or she'd go insane. Letting herself feel something deep for Garrett, something lasting, was a sure-fire way of getting hurt. He wouldn't mean to hurt her; he had a good heart. But it would inevitably happen if she forgot they couldn't be more than friends.

Friends with benefits.

With a groan, Blair rolled over once again. She was afraid it was already too late not to feel something deep for Garrett.

****

Garrett pulled his truck in front of Blair's house at seven a.m. like he had every morning in the three days since he got back from Minneapolis. He'd dragged his ass out of bed because he had work to do on the fence. But mostly, he got up extra early because he wanted to see Blair before she left for work.

Every evening around ten Garrett met Blair in the potting shed. He arrived in her yard with lights out, driving around the side of the barn so his truck couldn't be seen by Everett from the house, or by anyone who happened to drive down the main road and glance into the yard. Blair was adamant.

The clandestine measures made him feel like a thief in the night. Like Blair believed what they were doing was wrong.

But all the doubts and worries disappeared when they were alone together in the shed. The ardent way she responded to his kisses, his lovemaking, gave him hope she cared for him.

Would she ever love him the way he loved her?

He couldn't get a read on her. She was the one who first asked him to meet her, asked him to make love with her. And she held back nothing as she made love to him. Yet every morning at two a.m. she woke him so he could go home. She wasn't ready for Everett to know they'd been sleeping together, she said. And she didn't want his parents to realize he was gone during the night. Though he didn't tell them he was meeting Blair, they knew he was leaving the house, and they likely had their suspicions as to why. Unlike Everett, they were awake at ten as he left the house.

All day while he worked, he couldn't stop thinking about her, couldn't stop feeling her soft skin beneath his rough hands. Each time he breathed, her scent filled his head, reminding him of their nights together.

Did she not want to be seen with him? Was she ashamed of him because of his amputation? Was that the reason she didn't want anyone to know they were sleeping together? His gut turned at the thought.

Garrett blew out a breath and got out of the truck. He knocked on the front door before going inside.

"Good morning, Garrett." Everett lifted his coffee cup in greeting. "Need some coffee?"

"Sure." He raised his hand as Everett struggled to

his feet. "No, sit. I can help myself."

He grabbed a mug from the cupboard and poured himself coffee from the pot already made. For the first time, he dared a look at Blair.

"Good morning."

She gave him a hint of a smile. "Good morning. Granddad wanted scrambled eggs with bacon and toast. That okay with you?"

"Sounds good. Thank you."

She filled a plate for him, adding a generous portion of bacon. As she handed the plate to him, their eyes met. Electricity sparked around them and heat rushed through his body, filling his world with color and bringing him to vivid life.

Blair appeared dazed as well. She continued to hold one side of the plate, her eyes wide and her lips parted slightly. Finally, she released her grip on his plate and stepped away, ducking her head so he could no longer see her expression. He wished to hell he understood what was going on in her head.

The three of them ate breakfast together, making small talk about the weather and the thunderstorm that was forecast to hit the area by evening. After finishing her juice, Blair excused herself to get ready for work. Everett set down his coffee cup as soon as Blair was out of the room.

"My granddaughter is a good girl. She deserves to be treated right."

Where was this coming from? "You won't get any argument from me."

"If you want to see her, see her. There's no reason to sneak around like you're doing something wrong."

"That's my feeling exactly, but your granddaughter

has different ideas." He averted his gaze, busying his hands by folding a paper napkin into squares. "I guess she doesn't want to be seen with me."

Everett's brow wrinkled. "That doesn't make sense. She cares about you."

Did she? So far, she was staying true to her promise that their relationship would be strictly about sex.

Garrett finished the last of his coffee and pushed himself to his feet. He cleared and wiped the table, putting the dishes they'd used into the dishwasher. As he started running water in the sink to wash a couple of pans, Everett got to his feet.

"Step aside, son. I can wash a few dishes in my own kitchen."

Garrett held up his hands in surrender. "They're all yours."

The old man hobbled to the sink, rolled up his sleeves, and dipped his hands into the hot, soapy water. "She cares for you. I know it as surely as I know my own name. She has...she has a hard time telling people how she feels."

Before Garrett could respond, Blair entered the kitchen, her face freshly washed, and her hair pulled back into a ponytail. Her pink scrub top, emblazoned with cartoon depictions of panda bears, made him smile.

She kissed Everett's cheek. "Bye, Granddad. I'll see you after work. There's a stew cooking in the slow cooker for supper and the fixings for sandwiches in the fridge for lunch."

"I'm going to turn into a porker if you keep feeding me like this." Everett's voice complained, but Garrett saw the half-grin on his face.

Blair laughed as she picked up her purse and headed to the door. "I don't think there's much danger of that. See you this afternoon."

"Bye, Blair girl." Everett turned back to the task of washing dishes. "Garrett, will you be joining me for lunch today?"

"Not today. I told my mom I'd have lunch with her. I'd better get to work, too. I'll see you later, Everett."

The old man lifted one wet hand in goodbye. Garrett held the door open for Blair, falling into step beside her as they walked to the garage where her truck was parked. Garrett waited until they were inside the garage before he spoke.

"Your granddad knows we're sleeping together. He thinks I'm not doing right by you by sneaking around."

She stared at him in surprise, then looked away. "I'll talk to him later. I have to go or I'll be late for work."

Before she could get in her truck, Garrett set his hand on her arm, stopping her. "Would it be so terrible if people knew we were together? Could we at least tell our families?"

Panic flared in her eyes. "I…I'm not ready. Please, don't push."

Would she ever be ready? "Are you ashamed of us, of me?"

"No! No, I'm not ashamed. I could never…I need some time, that's all. Please? Don't be angry."

He dragged her into his arms and held on tight. "I'm not angry, sweetheart." He sighed. "If you need to take it slow, that's what we'll do."

She relaxed against him, her cheek against his chest and her arms hugging his waist. "Thank you. Will you...will you come by tonight?"

He held her a little tighter. "Do you want me to?"

"Yes. I...I want to be with you, Garrett."

"Then I'll be here."

He heard her expel a breath before she stepped away from him, her gaze not quite meeting his. "I have to go. I'll see you tonight, Garrett."

"See you tonight."

She climbed into the cab of her truck and backed out of the garage. Garrett stood watching until she drove out of the yard and disappeared down the main road. With a sigh, he loaded barbed wire and fence posts into the back of his truck before heading out into the pasture.

As he worked, one thought wouldn't leave him alone. Would Blair feel the need to hide their relationship if he wasn't an amputee?

****

Garrett didn't show up for supper that night. As soon as Blair got home from work, Everett informed her that Garrett had dropped by earlier to say his sisters, brother-in-law, and baby niece were gathering at his parents' place for a family dinner since it was his dad's birthday.

The news punched Blair in the gut. She told herself she was being ridiculous. Of course Garrett would want to spend his father's birthday with him and the rest of his family. But coming after their conversation this morning, Blair wondered if this was the beginning of the end. Perhaps Garrett was using this family dinner as an excuse to start pulling away from her. He'd said he'd drop by later, but she wondered if he would.

Blair pushed away her disquieting thoughts and made herself smile for her grandfather.

"How was your day, Granddad?"

Everett chuckled. "Good as all the rest, I suppose. Jake and I sat out on the front porch, and we watched some TV. Morley dropped by, and we shot the breeze for a while. A friend from my days on Masonville town council telephoned. But the day went by a little slower because Garrett ate lunch with Grace and Robert instead of with us."

Blair ladled stew from the slow cooker into bowls, her back to her grandfather. "So did Garrett mention whether he'd be eating with you tomorrow at lunch? I'm wondering if we'll have enough leftovers."

"He didn't mention anything about tomorrow." Everett put down his coffee cup as she brought the bowls to the table. "Is it true it's your idea to meet with Garrett on the down low?"

Her face flamed and her appetite deserted her. "I'm not ready for anyone to know."

"I know it's none of my business, but there's no reason you have to hide your relationship with Garrett, especially not from me or Garrett's family."

Blair noted he didn't include her parents in that circle. "I don't even know if we have a relationship, or how long it will last. So what would be the point?" For all she knew, it might be over already.

Everett grabbed her hand and squeezed, the strength in his bony, arthritic fingers surprising her. "I'm not so old and blind that I can't see Garrett cares for you. Don't push him away because you don't think you deserve him."

She pulled back her hand and folded it in her lap. "I'm not doing that."

"Aren't you?" He gave a sigh and sank back against his chair. "You're a beautiful, loving soul, and you deserve everything good. You deserve to be loved and to feel good about it. What happened with Eve was not your fault."

His impassioned speech left him looking drained, and his face ashen. Blair dredged up a smile, not wanting to upset him further. She reached across the kitchen table to touch his hand. "Thank you for saying that. It means a lot to me."

Instead of smiling, he only looked sadder. "I wish you could believe it."

She nodded as she pulled her hand away. "Eat your stew, Granddad."

Neither of them said much else during the meal. The stew was probably very good, but it tasted like sawdust in her mouth. She only ate so her grandfather wouldn't worry.

After dinner, Blair cleaned up the dishes. She made a lunch to take to work the following day and laid out a clean uniform. For a while she watched TV with Everett, until he announced he was ready for bed shortly after nine. She got to her feet and kissed his cheek.

"I'm going to put the horses in the barn before the storm hits, so I'll say goodnight now, Granddad."

"I love you, Blair girl." His voice was gruff. "Remember what I said. You deserve to be happy."

She kissed him again. "Thanks, Grandad."

With a nod, he headed to his room. Blair watched him go, her throat stinging with tears.

No matter what he said, she couldn't make herself believe she deserved to be loved.

Chapter Eighteen

Garrett arrived at Blair's place around ten-thirty. As usual, he parked around the side of the barn and killed the engine. Instead of immediately getting out of the truck, he sat staring straight ahead, watching lightning flash in the distance through the rain-obscured windshield.

Would Blair be waiting for him inside the shed? She'd said she wanted him to come, but he wasn't sure. He wasn't sure about anything where Blair was concerned except that he loved her.

He glanced toward the barn and noticed light filtering through the small windows. She was inside, waiting for him here. Or perhaps that was wishful thinking. Maybe she'd decided he wasn't worth the trouble.

There was only one way to find out. Garrett pulled the keys from the ignition and opened his door. The rain was coming down heavier now, and by the time he made it inside the barn he was soaked. He closed the door behind him and ran a hand through his wet hair as his eyes adjusted to the dim light. The smell of fresh hay greeted him, and the soft whinny of the horses told him he wasn't alone.

"Garrett?"

His heart beat faster at the sound of Blair's voice.

"I'm here."

She came toward him carrying the lantern. "I wasn't sure you'd come."

"I said I would."

"I know." She stood in front of him, her tense face illuminated by the light. "I should have more faith in you."

"Yeah, you should." He reached out to cup her face. "I'd never lie to you, Blair."

She closed her eyes and leaned into his hand, her free hand resting against his heart. "You're wet."

"The storm's moving in."

A clap of thunder put an exclamation point on his words. She shivered at the sudden explosion of noise. "It is. You must be cold."

"I'm fine."

He was burning up. The effort of holding back, of being this close to her and yet not quite sure of his welcome, spiked his temperature. He wondered if she could feel the unsteady pounding of his heart beneath her hand.

Blair opened her eyes and lifted her gaze to his.

"I hope it's all right that I brought the horses in here even though the concrete isn't completely cured. I didn't want them out in the storm."

"I'm sure the concrete will be fine."

"I brought extra blankets to the shed. So we'd be warm. And I have an umbrella."

"Why don't you take me there?"

She interlaced his fingers with hers and pulled lightly on his hand, leading him to the back door of the barn, which was closer to the shed. The rain beat heavily on the roof of the barn, matching the staccato rhythm of his heart.

Blair handed him the lantern and opened the umbrella. "Let's make a run for it."

Though it was a short distance and they had the umbrella, they were both wet by the time they got inside the shed. Blair closed the umbrella and set it by the door. She stared at the makeshift bed and clutched her hands together. "I should have brought a heavier blanket. Or a heater."

She looked unsure and nervous, as if she didn't know that making love with her was the only thing he'd thought about all day. He'd thought about her, about this, the whole time he'd been with his family celebrating his dad's birthday. He'd thought about her as he played with his baby niece and wondered if Blair ever considered having children. Since Piper's birth a few months ago, he'd realized children were important to him.

He was getting way ahead of himself. Right now, as she stood staring in trepidation at the mattress, he was sure that having a baby with him was the last thing on her mind. How did he make her understand how much he wanted her? Loved her?

"Sweetheart." He reached out his hand to her. "As long as I have you to keep me warm, I'll be fine. You're all I need."

That made her smile. She clasped his hand. "Same goes. You're a regular little furnace."

Garrett wrapped his arms around her and grinned. "All the better to keep my baby warm."

She laughed as her arms went around his neck. "So I'm your baby, am I?"

"Yeah." He kept his tone light. He wished he could tell her the depth of his feelings, but if he spoke about love and forever, he was sure she'd bolt. "You are."

She smiled up at him. "I think I like that."

"Good."

He lowered his head to kiss her. As soon as her lips touched his, a prairie fire raced to life inside him. He needed every ounce of his self-control not to rip off her clothes and push hard and deep into her body until she screamed out his name. Garrett willed himself to slow down, afraid he'd scare her. He broke the kiss and rested his forehead against hers. Blair pulled at his clothes.

"Easy, baby. We've got lots of time."

With a growl of frustration, Blair unbuttoned his wet shirt. "I'm through with waiting."

She pushed the shirt off his shoulders with impatient hands and ran questing fingers over his chest.

"You're beautiful, Garrett." She kissed each nipple in turn. "I love the feel of your skin. So smooth and hot."

"Blair." He heard the tremble in his voice. "I'm not anywhere near beautiful."

She looked up at him in surprise. "Because of your leg? I thought we were past that."

"You don't have to say things to make me feel better." He averted his gaze, not wanting to see pity in her eyes. "I'd rather you be honest."

"All right. I will." With her eyes on his, she grabbed the hem of her T-shirt and pulled it over her head. "You make me want to do this."

Garrett blinked. "Blair—"

"Shhh." She put one finger over his lips. "You asked me to be honest. The least you could do is listen while I'm telling you the truth."

Where was she going with this? The woman never ceased to surprise him. The thought made him grin.

With a flick of each ankle, her flip-flops flew into a corner of the room. With slow deliberation, she pulled down the zipper of her jeans. "I told you before, I don't even notice your prosthesis. I don't care about your leg."

She shimmied out of her jeans, then reached behind her to unclasp her bra. "All I see is a beautiful, sexy man."

The bra joined her jeans on the floor. Garrett stepped toward her, but Blair held out her hand to stop him. "I'm not finished yet."

He groaned, his erection pushing painfully at the zipper of his jeans. "You're killing me, Blair."

"Good. I hope then you'll believe I don't care about your leg. It's part of you, but it doesn't define you." She pulled her panties down her hips and let them slide down her legs. Standing naked in front of him, her eyes betrayed a touch of vulnerability, but she didn't attempt to cover herself. "Even if you had two good legs, I couldn't possibly be more attracted to you. I couldn't possibly want you more."

Garrett drank in the sight of her. Long slender legs, generous curves, luscious breasts. She'd opened herself physically for him, but even more importantly, she'd laid bare her heart. He believed her. His amputation didn't matter to her.

The least he could do was to be open and honest with her.

He unzipped his jeans and pushed them down his legs. He did the same with his underwear. Garrett lowered himself to the mattress and stretched his legs out in front of him. His hands trembled as he removed the prosthesis and set it aside. He glanced into Blair's face, but all he could detect was curiosity.

She touched the cotton liner covering his stump. "So does this act as kind of a sock to keep your prosthesis from chafing against your skin?"

"Yeah."

She looked into his face. "Would you take it off for me?"

Sweat broke out on his brow despite the cool night air. But she had to see it, and he had to know. No matter what.

He pulled off the liner, exposing his stump. Blair touched it, running gentle fingers around it. She looked up at him. "Does it ever hurt you?"

"Not so much anymore. Only if I bang hard into something solid."

"So I don't have to worry about hurting you when we make love?"

He stared at her. Was she serious? Was that the only thing she was worried about?

"Look at it, Blair. Really look. This is me now, and there's nothing I can do to change it. So if the stump bothers you, tell me. It's best we know now." Anger and frustration made his voice harsher than he'd intended.

"Why would you think your stump would bother me? Like you said, this is you now. You could have a paunch. I told you, it's not a big deal."

"It's a big deal to me!"

She tilted her head. "Yes, I can see that." She laid her hand on his stump and gently stroked. "If something happened to me, say I lost a breast to cancer, would you think I was ugly?"

He answered without thinking. "No! Never."

Blair cupped his cheek with her hand. "Then why can't you believe I feel the same way about you?"

Garrett stared at her for long seconds as understanding finally dawned. She meant it. And God help him, he believed her. She'd seen his body in the light, all the scars, the imperfections, the missing pieces, and she hadn't turned away in revulsion. Two years of pain and heartache and self-doubt melted away as she smiled at him. For the first time in two years, he was whole.

A slow smile curved Blair's lips. "Like I said, you're beautiful, Garrett."

She reached out her hand and he grasped it, pressing a kiss into her palm. The words *I love you* tumbled through his head, demanding to be spoken. He held them back, afraid. It was too soon to talk about love. After all, they really hadn't known each other as adults for very long. They needed time, he told himself.

But deep down Garrett understood he was lying. He was afraid if he said the words, Blair wouldn't be able to say them back. That she'd never be able to say them back. Sometimes he sensed in her a barrier he couldn't cross, a wall she'd erected around her heart designed to keep everyone out, save a select few, like her grandfather. He hoped someday she'd trust him enough to talk about the reasons she'd built that wall.

For now, he'd take whatever she had to give.

After affixing another condom, Garrett covered her naked body with his, raising her hands over her head and holding them tightly with his own. He slid into her body with ease as if he belonged there. He hoped to hell he belonged there.

Garrett never took his eyes off hers. He needed to see her face, see the emotions that flashed through her eyes as he made slow, careful love to her. She moved in perfect time with him until she tensed, her body bowing. Her release came then, her body trembling for long minutes. Only then did he join her, shouting her name and silently chanting, *I love you. I love you. I love you.*

****

Blair woke to the sound of distant thunder and rain gently pelting the windows of the shed. The storm had passed, leaving the earth washed clean and fresh.

She relaxed against Garrett's side and breathed in his spicy, masculine scent. It was heaven to be with him like this, to touch him, to hold him.

If only...

She cut off that line of thinking immediately. Instead, she snuggled closer and rested her hand against Garrett's heart, reassured by its strong, steady beat.

Garrett stirred and linked his fingers with hers. "Sounds like the storm is mostly over."

"Yeah."

Stretching over her, he reached for his cell phone from the crate that served as a bedside table.

"Almost two a.m." He kissed her temple and sighed. "I should go."

He sat up and switched on the lantern. Blair sat as well, pulling the blankets over her breasts. Panic roiled in her gut as Garrett reached for his jeans. He was leaving her. It wasn't like that, not really. She'd been the one who'd insisted he leave before morning. It was her idea to hide the fact they were sleeping together, though her grandfather had had little trouble figuring it out. She'd wanted to be cautious, she believed.

But now, watching Garrett getting ready to leave, she wanted to throw caution to the wind. She wanted to wake beside him in the morning, wanted to see the morning light slant across his face, feel the stubble of his unshaven face. The only thing that mattered any more was being with Garrett. She was complete only with him. Happy with him.

But there was something more than that, a longing on the edge of her consciousness that called to her. The longing frightened her because she was very much afraid it was a lot like love. She pushed it into the shadows where it couldn't hurt her.

"Wait." Blair swallowed nervously and lifted her gaze to his. It was possible Garrett didn't want to stay with her the rest of the night. Maybe he'd rather leave right now. "Stay."

Garrett's arms froze in the act of pulling his T-shirt over his head. His face gave no clue to his thoughts. Only his eyes showed any hint of emotion. They burned with intensity as he stared at her.

Slowly, he lowered his arms. "You want me to stay until morning?"

"Yes," she whispered.

"What about your grandfather? My parents? I thought you were concerned about them knowing we're together."

"My granddad already knows, and I'm guessing your parents have figured it out, too."

Blair held her breath while he stared at her, his expression giving nothing away. Finally, he spoke.

"Why do you want me to stay, Blair?"

"Because it seems ridiculous to disrupt your sleep this way."

His gaze didn't leave hers. "Is that the only reason?"

She looked away. He was going to make her say it. She settled for a half-truth. "I like being with you."

"I like being with you, too."

She slowly brought her gaze back to his. "I think I'd very much like to wake up with you in the morning."

"Yeah." He tossed his T-shirt to the floor and unzipped his jeans. "I'd like that, too."

Blair smiled and reached out her hand to him, tugging him back down to the mattress.

****

Morning light streamed through the windows of the shed. Garrett lay motionless, trying not to disturb Blair's sleep. She was snuggled against his side, warm and sweet smelling, one hand on his chest. He resisted the urge to wake her with a kiss. A shiver trembled through him as he remembered sinking into her welcoming body.

God, he loved her. He prayed she could someday feel the same.

With a sigh, Garrett listened to the sounds of the morning. Birds sang in nearby trees, happy the rainstorm of last night had moved on. From the barn he heard the soft whinnies of the horses. They were probably anxious for their breakfast and to get outside into the sunshine. The smell of freshly cut grass and wet earth combined to give Garrett a sense of well-being. A sense of home.

Strange that he should feel that way about Blair's

farm. He'd never wanted a life in the country. At eighteen, he couldn't wait to leave to experience the wider world. He'd been too restless to be tied to one place the way a farmer or rancher inevitably was tied to the land.

Now, he couldn't imagine leaving this place.

Or this woman.

Beside him, Blair began to stir. As she stretched her arm over her head, her gaze collided with his, and she smiled.

"Good morning."

"Good morning."

Garrett leaned over to kiss her. She evaded him, covering her mouth with her hand.

"I haven't brushed my teeth."

Grinning, he gently removed her hand. "I'll risk it."

"Don't say I didn't warn you."

He claimed her mouth, his tonguing stroking hers. Her moan made him instantly hard and ready. He rolled her on top of him, settling her softness over his solid length. Blair's laugh was full of amusement, but her eyes were heavy lidded with desire.

"Are you sure you won't let me brush my teeth first?"

"Nope."

She grinned. "Okay, but be warned. Next time I won't shave my legs either."

"Living dangerously. I like it."

Garrett swallowed her chuckle with another kiss before she lifted her head.

"Condom."

She reached for the box of condoms on the crate, picked up her cell phone instead, and gasped. "Oh, my

God! It's seven-thirty! I have to be at work at eight."

Garrett tightened his hold around her waist. "Couldn't you be a little late?"

"No, of course not."

He loosened his hold, knowing he wouldn't win this argument. Blair's work ethic was too well developed to skip work, even for a few minutes. She immediately jumped to her feet and began gathering her clothes.

"I need to get dressed for work and make breakfast for Granddad." She stepped into her panties and pulled them up her legs. "Can you feed the horses and let them out of the barn?"

"Sure." Seeing her beautiful, partially naked body in the full light of the morning sun made him harden painfully. Garrett stifled a groan of frustration.

She pulled her T-shirt over her head. "You okay?"

"I will be. But I'd better stay out here till things…settle down."

Blair glanced at the tent over his crotch. "Sorry. I'll make it up to you. I promise."

"I'm gonna hold you to that promise."

She leaned over to kiss him. "I look forward to it."

She backed away when he tried to deepen the kiss. Picking her jeans off the floor she slipped them on. "The horses each get a bowl full of pellets. The feed's in the lean-to attached to the barn."

"I'll take care of it." He watched her slide one foot into a flip-flop and turn in a circle as she searched for its partner. "Are you going to tell Everett I spent the night?"

She hesitated before answering, using the time to retrieve the second flip-flop from under his discarded shirt.

"Yes, I'll tell him. He'd figure it out anyway, so what's the point in lying? I've got to run."

She hurried to the door, giving him an apologetic smile before she left. Garrett groaned and sat up. He hoped the cool morning air would put a damper on his raging hard-on.

After fastening his prosthetic, he dressed in last night's discarded clothes and made his way to the lean-to where Blair kept feed for the horses in covered bins. Before he could unlatch the door, he heard a scream.

"No!"

Blair. His stomach flipped over at the horror he heard in her voice. Garrett ran out of the barn as fast as his prosthetic could carry him, afraid of what he'd find.

"Garrett! Granddad's not moving. Dear God, he's not moving!" She ran toward him as he did his hop-skip run toward the house.

"Where is he?"

"In his bed." She started to weep. "I heard Jake whimpering. I found them both in his bedroom."

Was he dead? Garrett's heart missed a beat at the thought.

Blair tugged on his arm, urging him to hurry. She was a coiled spring stretched to its limit and on the verge of breaking. If Everett was dead, she'd be devastated.

Once in the house, Blair ran ahead of him to the bedroom. Garrett followed as quickly as he could. He found Everett face down on the bed and Blair crouched beside him, rubbing his back.

"Please, Granddad, wake up. Please wake up."

Beside Everett on the bed, Jake whimpered, head

on his front paws. Everett wasn't moving. Garrett had seen that stillness before. He knew even before feeling for a pulse on the cold skin at his neck that the old man was dead.

"I'm sorry, Blair. He's gone."

"No!" Her eyes blazed with anger. "No, he isn't. I've called nine-one-one. They'll be here in a minute and everything will be all right."

Garrett reached for her. "Blair, sweetheart—"

She recoiled from him. "Don't touch me! I should have been here. If I'd been in the house instead of out in the shed with you, this wouldn't have happened."

Her words hit him like a hammer. "You don't know that. Everett had a weak heart. He probably had a heart attack in his sleep and there was nothing you could have done to help him."

"No, I should have been here." Blair wrapped her arms around her up-drawn knees. She began to rock, her gaze vacant. "I should have kept him safe. I never kept him safe. I'm to blame. I'm always to blame."

"Blair, there was nothing you could have done differently. Everett was ill."

She shook her head. "No, it's my fault. I put my pleasure before his safety. And now he's gone. It's my fault."

She was scaring him. Garrett touched her shoulder. "Blair, sweetheart—"

She slid away, her eyes full of recrimination. And distaste. "Don't touch me. Don't ever touch me again."

Her words were cold, flat, and final. Garrett rose slowly to his feet. Sirens sounded outside signaling the arrival of the paramedics. "I'll let them in."

Blair didn't acknowledge him. He made his way

back through the kitchen with slow deliberation, carefully putting one foot in front of the other. This was a nightmare, and he was sleepwalking his way through it. Except it was all too real.

Everett was dead, and Blair blamed herself.

Blamed him.

By the time he got to the front door, the paramedics were already climbing the porch stairs with their equipment. Garrett opened the door and pointed them to the bedroom. A short time later, they carried Everett's body out of the house on a stretcher, a sheet pulled over his face. Blair followed behind the stretcher, her face stony and expressionless.

He had to try one more time. "Blair, this wasn't your fault."

"I think you should go." The dead look in her eyes frightened him.

"I could help you. I haven't finished feeding the horses—"

"I'll do it. Go. Please."

Her last word was said on a choked whisper. Blair was hanging on to her composure by a thin thread, and if his presence upset her this much, he had to leave.

"All right, I'll go. But I'll finish feeding the horses first."

She nodded and followed the attendants to the ambulance. She watched as they loaded Everett's body into the back, her arms wrapped around herself as if trying to ward off a winter chill. She looked lost and alone and unbearably sad.

Garrett needed every ounce of self-discipline he possessed not to go to her. But she didn't want him, and his presence would only upset her more. He made himself walk away.

After he'd fed the horses and let them out into the paddock, he climbed into his truck and backed it out of its hiding place beside the barn. As he drove through the yard, he saw that Blair's truck was gone. She'd probably followed the ambulance to the hospital in Bismarck. Or the funeral home. He didn't know which.

He couldn't believe Everett was dead. Despite his advanced years and sketchy health, he'd always seemed the kind of person who would live forever.

Garrett blew out a breath. That was only a fantasy, but for Blair's sake, he wished it were true.

She'd said she was to blame because she hadn't kept Everett safe. That she was always to blame. What had she meant?

She was in shock right now. As soon as she had a chance to think things through rationally, she'd realize she couldn't have saved Everett, even if she'd been in the house the entire night. He'd been old and sick.

Images of making love to Blair last night swam in front of his eyes, overwhelming him with guilt. Even if she couldn't have saved Everett, she believed she could have. And that meant she blamed him.

Perhaps she was right.

Chapter Nineteen

Blair busied herself mixing pancake batter and frying bacon. Her brothers were asleep upstairs, having arrived late the previous evening. She was grateful they'd been able to drop everything to hurry home.

Funny she should think of Masonville and the farm as home, since the three of them had only visited during summer vacations. Their parents had been only too happy to be shed of them for a couple of months. Every summer, from the time she was six until she was sixteen, she'd spent with her grandparents. They'd been the happiest times of her life.

For the thousandth time she wondered how two down-to-earth people like her grandparents had produced a daughter so utterly different. Victoria Greyson cared about power and money and social status above family and home. Or at least it had always seemed that way to Blair.

She'd moved through the last two days in a haze. She did and said the things she was supposed to, but inside she was numb. She accepted condolences and casseroles from well-meaning neighbors and old friends of her grandfather's. The obligatory phone call to her parents to inform them of Granddad's passing had sucked her dry. Her mother expressed little emotion and hadn't offered to help with funeral arrangements, asking only to be informed of the time and place.

So the arrangements had fallen to her. Blair had dreaded meeting the funeral director. She had no idea what her grandfather would have wanted; they'd never talked about a funeral, mostly because she couldn't bring herself to think about it. And she worried about how she'd pay for it. Even if her mother had offered to help, which she hadn't, she wanted to do this one last thing for Granddad. Fortunately, Blair discovered that Everett had already planned his funeral, right down to the flowers in the church and the music to be played. He'd prepaid for everything as well. Her granddad continued to look out for her, even in death. Even so, the tasks had taken all her reserves of strength, leaving her barely breathing.

The worst was yet to come. Her parents would arrive later today. The only saving grace was that they'd insisted on staying at a hotel in Bismarck rather than at the farm. And, of course, there was the funeral itself tomorrow. Blair had no idea how she was going to make it through the day alone without breaking down.

Alone? She whisked her eggs a little harder. She wouldn't be alone. Her brothers were with her, as well as long-time neighbors of her grandparents, and her co-workers, whom she'd come to think of as friends. Her parents would be at the funeral, God help her. She wasn't alone.

But Garrett wasn't with her. She'd sent him away. It was for the best, really. She couldn't be what he needed. He deserved better.

The thought made her eyes sting, but she pushed the tears back. She hadn't allowed herself to cry since Granddad's death. She was afraid if she started, she wouldn't be able to stop.

The sound of a vehicle driving into the yard provided a welcome diversion. Inhaling deeply, she blew out her breath, wiped her hands on her apron as she untied it, and went to the door. Despite the early hour, it was likely one of the neighbors come to pass along their condolences. Blair steeled herself for their remembrances of her grandfather as she opened the door.

She froze as she stepped onto the front porch. Garrett got out of his truck and came toward her. He stopped at the bottom of the stairs.

"Good morning." The dark circles under his eyes told her he hadn't been sleeping any better than she had. He hadn't shaved for a couple of days, and his thick hair was mussed as if he'd just rolled out of bed. An image burst into her head. Garrett looming over her in their makeshift bed in the potting shed, his body inside hers. She ruthlessly pushed it away.

"Why are you here, Garrett?"

He lifted his chin a notch, his mouth unsmiling. "I've got a job to finish. I said I'd fix the fence, and I don't intend to go back on my word."

Blair nodded. For one moment, she'd hoped he was going to say he'd come for her, to see if she was all right. But that was stupid. Whatever they'd had was over.

She'd made sure of that.

"Would you like some coffee before you go?" she asked.

"No, I'm fine. Thanks." Instead of heading to his truck, he remained standing at the bottom of the stairs. "Blair, I'm sorry."

Blair swallowed and nodded again. Was he sorry

for her grandfather's death, or for sleeping with her?

"It wasn't your fault." His voice was so soft she had to strain to hear him. "Please don't blame yourself."

She looked away. Of course it was her fault. She'd only been thinking of herself and what she wanted. The way she had with Eve.

Garrett mounted the first step. "Blair—"

"Garrett? Garrett Saunders? Is that you?" Blair heard her brother Ben behind her. "It's good to see you."

Garrett smiled politely. "It's good to see you, too, Ben. I'm sorry it's under such unhappy circumstances. Everett was a hell of a man."

Ben stepped out onto the porch and put his arm around Blair's shoulders. "Yeah, the best."

She looked up gratefully into Ben's hazel eyes and smiled. Thank God her brothers were here. With their help she could make it through the next few days. She hoped.

"Why don't you come in and have breakfast with us? Looks like Blair's been busy cooking."

"Thanks, but I really should get to work. I've been fixing fence for Everett, and I want to get it done so the horses can be let out into the pasture."

Fixing fence for Everett. Perhaps he didn't want her brother to know how intimately connected they'd been.

"Come on, how 'bout some coffee at least? I'd really like to catch up with you," Ben insisted. Blair knew her brother was sincere. He and Garrett had been friends back in the day and had always liked each other.

She made herself smile at him. "Yes, why don't

you come in for coffee?"

Garrett's gaze met hers, and she held her breath. Despite knowing a relationship with him was impossible, she craved his company.

At last, he nodded. "Okay, thank you. I'd love a cup of coffee."

He ascended the steps, his gait stiff. Had he injured himself? She wanted to ask but didn't want to bring attention to the injury in front of her brother. If Ben noticed, he didn't mention it.

Her brother Damon descended the stairs as they entered the kitchen, his hair still wet from his shower. His face broke into a smile when he saw Garrett.

"Man, you're a sight for sore eyes!" He eyed Garrett's disheveled appearance. "Or maybe just a sight."

Garrett laughed and clapped him on the shoulder. If Ben had liked and respected Garrett, Damon had idolized him. He'd wanted to be like Garrett. Hell, as a teenager, he'd wanted to *be* Garrett. He'd fallen short for a while, but he'd turned his life around, and Blair was proud of him.

Blair bustled around the kitchen, pouring coffee for the men before turning her attention to making pancakes. It helped to keep busy and have a task to accomplish. If she was busy enough, she didn't have time to remember that her grandfather was gone. Or that she'd never wake up in Garrett's arms again.

"Are you home on leave?" Ben asked.

"No, I'm retired from the military," Garrett answered. "I was injured out. I'm trying to find a new career direction, but in the meantime, I've been doing odd jobs around my parents' place, and with my brother-in-law Cole, and I helped Everett here."

"You said you were fixing fence."

"Yeah, and we also fixed the barn floor. Jackhammered out the broken concrete and poured a new floor."

"We? You mean Granddad was doing heavy physical labor?"

"No, not Everett." Blair felt Garrett's gaze land on her. "Your sister got pretty proficient at wielding a jackhammer."

Both of her brothers turned to stare at her. She glared at their surprised expressions. "Why is that so shocking? I got pretty good at pushing a wheelbarrow full of concrete debris, too."

"When you didn't dump it on the ground." Garrett's smile was partially hidden by his coffee cup.

"Once. That happened once." Blair cleared her throat and turned her attention back to her brothers. "I had to fix the floor for my horses. The broken concrete was too dangerous for them."

"How many horses do you have now, Sis?"

"Only the two rescues I brought with me from Minnesota. And we've been boarding Garrett's horse the last couple of months. Harry's his rescue horse."

Damon groaned. "Don't tell me Blair talked you into one of her crazy rescue schemes."

"No, I managed to be crazy all by myself."

While Blair flipped pancakes and scrambled eggs, he told them how Harry had come into his life. He paused and turned to Ben.

"Blair and Everett told me about your wife, Ben. I can't tell you how sorry I am," Garrett said.

Ben nodded. "Thank you. I appreciate that."

"Where are your girls staying while you're here?" Blair asked.

"With friends in Chicago. I didn't think another funeral so soon after Olivia's would be good for them." He stopped and cleared his throat. "I think Granddad would have understood."

Blair stopped stirring. Everyone went silent at the mention of her grandfather. It didn't seem real. He couldn't be gone.

And Olivia. She'd been only thirty-three. Why was life so cruel?

"Blair probably told you I'm in California," Damon said. "I'm a psychologist specializing in helping adults overcome trauma."

"Sounds like a tough job," Garrett said.

"Not as tough as being a soldier who's seen action in the Middle East, but yeah, it can be tough. Totally rewarding, though."

Blair was proud of her brothers. Life had thrown them obstacles they'd had to overcome. That they continued to overcome. From the outside looking in, her family appeared to have every advantage. Her mother had married into a wealthy, prominent Minnesota family, and as children, she and her two older brothers had been given everything money could buy, but nothing they really needed. If it hadn't been for those two months a year spent with their maternal grandparents, they wouldn't have known what it was to be loved.

Garrett finished his coffee and stood. "I'd better get to work. It was good seeing you again."

Her brothers stood and shook his hand and walked him to the door. Garrett nodded at her.

"I'll see you tomorrow."

Blair nodded and swallowed around the lump in her throat. *Tomorrow*. The funeral.

He opened the door to leave. "I almost forgot. Everett gave me an envelope. He asked me to give it to you, Ben."

"To me? Do you know what it is?"

"Copies of his Will. He asked me to be one of the executors. I'll bring it by the day after tomorrow."

"Sounds good. Thanks."

With a nod he left the house. All the warm air seemed to rush out of the house with him. Blair rubbed at the goose flesh on her bare arms.

Damon filled his coffee cup once more. "What do you think's in the Will, Ben?"

"Granddad had other property aside from the farm, and he likely wanted us to know his wishes for it."

"I hope he wrote an iron-tight Will that Victoria and Peter can't manipulate to their advantage. I wouldn't put it past them." Damon's voice was bitter. Blair noted he couldn't bring himself to call their parents Mom and Dad. Of the three of them, perhaps he had the most reason to be bitter.

"One step at a time. After the funeral we'll look at Granddad's Will. I promise you I'll fight tooth and nail to make sure his wishes are kept."

Damon nodded. Blair met Ben's determined gaze and breathed a sigh of relief. If anyone could keep a promise, it was Ben.

****

The morning of her grandfather's funeral dawned bright and hot. Blair and her brothers dressed in black and drove to town for the ten-thirty service at the church her grandparents had attended for over fifty years. She smiled at the thought of Granddad watching from heaven as the service he'd so meticulously planned played out. He'd get a charge out of being the orchestra leader at his own funeral.

The church parking lot was filled with cars and the nearby streets were clogged. Ben maneuvered into a spot reserved for the family.

"Looks like the whole town is here," he said.

"Everyone liked Granddad," Damon murmured. "He volunteered and sat on committees in the community for years. Remember the summer he headed up the committee to build the new swimming pool? He was the kind of guy who got things done, and people respected him."

"They loved him," Blair said. Her heart warmed to see so many people here to pay their last respects. Granddad would have loved it. He would have seen it as a big send-off party.

A send-off. It wasn't like he was going on a trip he'd eventually return from. Granddad wasn't ever coming back. Her throat closed at the thought.

Ben turned off the engine. "Are you ready for this?"

"No," Blair said with a smile as she squeezed his hand. "But it's time to go."

Blair held her brothers' hands as they entered the church vestibule. Victoria and Peter were already there. Her mother reached for her, wrapping her arms around her neck. The familiar scent of her perfume wafted around Blair, bringing back old, painful memories.

"Darling." Her mother kissed her cheek while her father shook hands with her stony-faced brothers. "This must be so difficult for you."

"Yes, it is." Her mother was dry-eyed and composed. She could have been going to the funeral of an acquaintance rather than a beloved father.

The door to the sanctuary was open, and Blair could see it was full. The funeral director greeted them. "The basement is full as well. Your grandfather was well-liked."

Blair nodded. The open casket was sitting at the front of the church. Memories of her grandmother's funeral, less than a year ago, swamped her. She'd been devastated to lose the woman who'd been more of a mother to her than her actual mother had ever been. But at least she'd still had her grandfather. He'd held her hand through the whole service, giving her comfort, though his own heart must have been shattered.

Olivia's funeral six months ago had been overwhelming. The funeral of a woman so young, with so much to live for, had been emotionally draining and had left her angry. Why had this happened to Olivia? Why had this happened to Ben and the girls? The unfairness of it all had made her want to scream.

God, she hated funerals.

"Would you like to pay your last respects to Everett?" the funeral director asked.

They looked at each other and nodded. Her parents went into the church first. They stood in front of the casket for a moment, and her mother dabbed her eyes with a tissue while her father put an arm around her shoulders. How long had it been since they'd visited Granddad? The last time her parents had been in Masonville had been for her grandmother's funeral, and to her knowledge, Victoria hadn't telephoned Everett in the last year. Once their show of grief was done, they sat at one end of the front pew. Ben nodded at her and Damon. *Time to go.* Hand in hand they walked together to the front of the church and stood in front of the casket. It comforted Blair to see that Everett looked peaceful. But seeing him in the casket put emphasis on the fact that he was really gone.

He was never coming back.

Damon put his arm around her waist, his fingers clutching her side, and she was reminded that she wasn't the only who was grieving. She rubbed his back, hoping to give him a bit of comfort.

After a few moments, they turned to take their places in the front pew. As she turned, Blair's gaze collided with Garrett's. He sat three rows from the front with his parents and sisters. He'd shaved and neatly brushed his hair, perhaps even had it cut. His broad shoulders filled out his elegant charcoal gray suit. She'd never seen him dressed up before, never seen him more handsome. A painful pang of longing made her chest hurt.

Garrett gave her an imperceptible nod, his way, she supposed, of lending his support. Blair quickly turned to sit on the front pew between her brothers. But the painful longing, along with bone-deep grief, made it hard to breathe.

The service was mercifully short, likely at Granddad's request. He was a simple man who liked simple things. She could almost hear his voice: "Nobody wants to sit around a hot church for hours listening to a preacher go on and on about an old fart like me. Get in, get out, and everything's right as rain." The thought made her smile.

The family, including her parents, piled into the funeral car and followed the hearse to the Masonville Cemetery. The silence was deafening inside the car, the tension palpable. The cemetery was only a short distance from town, but the journey was made a little longer by a short detour to Grandad's farm. The funeral director told them Everett had requested the cortege drive past his beloved farm one last time before he was laid to rest.

Finally, they arrived at the cemetery. Blair was relieved to get out of the car and into the sunshine. The interment ceremony was also short. After a brief but heartfelt prayer from the minister, the casket was lowered into the ground.

Granddad's life had officially concluded. Blair closed her eyes. *Goodbye, Granddad. I love you.*

After shaking hands and accepting condolences, they made their way back to the funeral car for the ride back to the church. As was tradition in Masonville, a luncheon was to be served in the church basement, with the women's auxiliary in charge. Blair dreaded this event as much as the funeral itself. All she wanted was to go home and crawl into her bed. But she was expected to show up and make small talk with her grandfather's friends and neighbors. For his sake, she'd do it.

The ride back into town was quiet until Victoria removed her delicate black lace gloves and asked the driver to raise the privacy glass.

"Blair, I want to prepare you. Your father and I plan to sell the farm as soon as possible."

Blair went cold inside. She'd been afraid of this. What would she do with the horses, with Jake? The thought of having to leave the farm was wrenching.

"The farm doesn't belong to you yet. Nothing will be done until we read Granddad's Will and find out what *he* wanted. We will adhere strictly to the terms of his Will." Ben's tone brooked no arguments. But Victoria had never been one to take no for an answer.

"Surely the needs of the living are more important than the wishes of the dead."

Ben opened his mouth to speak, but before he could, Damon leaned toward their mother, his eyes blazing with fury. "I don't give a damn about your needs. You've never cared about anyone but yourself."

Victoria leaned back, her eyes wide with shock. Peter finally spoke, his voice hard.

"Have some respect for your mother."

Damon laughed, but the sound was bitter. "Respect? I lost respect for the two of you a long time ago."

Blair reached over and put her hand over one of his clenched fists. Gradually Damon's fist unclenched and he interlaced his fingers with hers.

The wounds of the past still festered.

The car stopped, and Blair saw they'd arrived back at the church. Victoria pulled on her gloves once more, her face hard and unsmiling.

"I expect you to produce the Will tomorrow morning. I want to get out of this town as quickly as possible."

"Of course, Mother," Ben said.

Victoria and Peter scrambled out of the car and slammed the door. Ben turned to Damon.

"We don't have to do this. We can get in my rental car and go back to the farm. Right after we stop at the ice cream shop for a chocolate-covered double scoop."

One side of Damon's mouth curled in a grin. "As tempting as that sounds, we owe it to Granddad to go to the church basement and eat tuna on white bread and drink tepid coffee."

Blair made herself smile, though her stomach was churning with nerves. "You make it sound so appetizing."

He squeezed her fingers. "For Granddad?"

She looked at Ben, and he nodded his assent. She turned back to Damon with a smile, a genuine one this time. "Yeah. For Granddad."

The basement was full by the time they arrived. A table for the family had been reserved near the front. Victoria and Peter were already seated, their faces stony. For Damon's sake, Blair wished they could sit anywhere but at the same table, but all the other tables were full, and it would surely be noticed if the family didn't sit together. Ben put himself between their parents and Damon. As the oldest, he'd always tried to protect them and had always blamed himself if he couldn't.

As soon as they sat down, a couple of church ladies set down plates of sandwiches and dainties and offered coffee and tea. Blair accepted a cup of tea, and though she put a sandwich on her plate to make the ladies happy, she wasn't able to eat it.

After people ate and visited with each other, they rose to leave. A line formed in front of their table as people paid their respects and said goodbye. Many left sympathy cards, and some said they'd given donations in Everett's name to the local old folks' home foundation, which her grandfather had spearheaded.

Their heartfelt condolences helped ease some of her grief.

Garrett stepped up to their table with a somber-faced Morley Walker. They shook hands with her brothers and offered condolences. Garrett turned his back toward her parents and lowered his voice.

"Morley has something he wants to tell you."

Morley glanced toward her parents. They were occupied with accepting condolences from Garrett's parents and sisters. Blair wondered if Garrett had asked his family to run interference while he and Morley spoke to them.

"There could be fireworks. Be prepared."

Blair blinked up at Garrett. What did Morley mean? Garrett merely shrugged. Morley wouldn't have talked about the contents of the Will before he told the family, and Garrett was too honorable to open the envelope and read the contents.

"We'll be ready," Ben said. "Can you both be at the farm at ten tomorrow morning?"

Garrett nodded. Morley glanced at Victoria and Peter once more, his distaste obvious in the curl of his lip.

"Can't wait."

Morley clapped Garrett on the shoulder as if ready to move on, but Garrett stood in front of her, not budging. He extended his hand to her in a shake, and she accepted it. His hands were big and warm and calloused, and her memory immediately flew back to him caressing her body with those hands. Though large, they'd touched her with infinite gentleness.

"I'm sorry for your loss, Blair."

"Thank you." Her tight throat barely allowed her to

get the words out.

She wasn't sure how long they stood staring at each other, her hand in his. The spell was only broken by Morley as he cleared his throat.

"We should move on, son. We're holding up traffic."

There was indeed a line of people waiting to extend their condolences. With a last nod, Garrett released her hand and walked away.

Finally, most of the guests left, aside from the church ladies who were cleaning up in the kitchen. Blair could hear them chatting, dishes clinking as they were washed. Victoria pulled on her black lace gloves once more.

"I'm glad that's finally over. Come along, Peter. Perhaps we can find an adequate lounge in Bismarck to have a few drinks."

Blair and her brothers watched their parents walk toward the stairs. At the last moment, Victoria turned toward them. "Remember, tomorrow morning at ten sharp. We have a plane to catch at two, so don't waste our time."

"We'll be ready," Ben said.

They walked up the stairs and disappeared. Blair closed her eyes in relief. For today, at least, they were gone.

"We should leave, too," Ben said.

Blair rose and slung her purse over her shoulder. "I want to thank the ladies in the kitchen before we go."

At Ben's nod she walked to the kitchen and knocked against the frame of the open door.

"Excuse me, ladies. I want to thank you for all your work in putting on the luncheon today. It was wonderful."

A plump woman with short, curly hair smiled at her. Blair couldn't remember her name, but she'd worked at the library when she was a kid and always helped her find the right book.

"We were happy to do it, dear. Your grandfather was a wonderful man. He did so much for this town. Making a few sandwiches was the least we could do."

"He would have been very pleased."

"Yes, there was a lovely turnout, wasn't there?"

"Yes, there was."

Her throat closed, making it impossible to say anything more for a moment. She swallowed, willing herself to stay strong. She couldn't break down. Not here, not now.

Not ever.

Finally, she made herself smile for the ladies. "Well, I wanted to let you know how much my brothers and I appreciated everything you did for us."

"You're most welcome, dear."

With a final smile, Blair turned and rejoined her brothers near the staircase. She looped her arm through Damon's.

"Let's go home. Right after we stop for ice cream, Ben."

He chuckled. "No problem."

Chapter Twenty

Garrett arrived at the Branson farm at twenty minutes to ten and saw that Morley Walker's Cadillac was already there. Apparently, Morley was getting an early start. He'd said he expected fireworks today, and it looked like he was getting ready for battle.

He picked up the large brown sealed envelope on the seat beside him. What had Everett put into his Will to make his lawyer believe it would be so controversial? He got out of the truck cab and headed to the house. Whatever it was, he hoped it didn't cause Blair any more distress. She'd been through enough already.

Ben answered his knock. "Come on in. We're setting things up in the living room."

Garrett handed Ben the envelope and followed him to the living room. Damon was helping Morley attach a DVD player to the television.

"If you'd told me we were watching a movie, I would have brought popcorn."

Morley gave a cackling laugh. "Not a movie, Garrett, but damn fine entertainment, I can tell you that."

"What do you mean?"

"Apparently Granddad videotaped his Will," Damon replied.

Morley nodded. "He wanted to leave no doubt that

238

he was in sound mind, and he wanted his last wishes to be crystal clear. To everyone."

By "everyone," Garrett assumed he meant Everett's daughter and her husband. Yesterday at the funeral had been the first time he'd seen Victoria since he was a little kid. It was hard to believe Everett and Anna could have born a child so different from themselves. Though he'd only spoken briefly to her at the funeral, Victoria Greyson struck him as superior and disdainful, everything her parents were not. The salt-of-the-earth gene had skipped a generation and landed on Blair and her brothers.

"Where's Blair?" he asked.

"Upstairs, getting ready," Ben said. "We let her sleep late this morning. She hasn't been getting much rest the last few days."

Garrett nodded. She'd looked exhausted yesterday. He wished he could see her, make sure she was all right, but he should leave before Victoria and her husband showed up. This was a private family meeting, and he didn't want to intrude.

"I should go. Good luck with everything."

"Hang on there, Garrett." Morley walked toward him, leaning heavily on his cane. Anyone who assumed the old lawyer was feeble-minded as well as feeble of body had a rethink coming. Morley might be over seventy, but his brain and wits were as razor sharp as ever.

"Everett wanted you at the reading of the Will. It was important to him that you be here. Besides, you're one of the executors. You need to know the contents of the Will."

Garrett still didn't understand why Everett had

named him as one of the executors. Morley read his mind.

"He trusted you. He gave you those papers, didn't he?"

"Well, yeah, but—"

Morley held up a restraining hand. "No buts. You want to honor Everett's last wishes, don't you?"

"Of course."

"Good. Get yourself a cup of coffee and pull up a seat."

Garrett glanced at Ben, who simply shrugged and shook his head. He'd have to trust Morley on this one.

Ben clapped him on the shoulder. "Come on, there's fresh coffee in the kitchen. And Blair made cookies."

He followed Ben into the kitchen and helped himself to a mug from the cupboard. "Are you expecting your parents to contest the Will?"

"If they don't like what's in it, yeah, it's possible. My mother doesn't like not getting her way."

There was bitterness in his voice. Even as a kid he'd known there was something not quite right about the Greyson family. He was beginning to get a clearer picture now, but he was sure there was much he didn't understand. Did Blair's past have anything to do with why she'd told him she didn't want to be with him anymore? Did it have anything to do with her suicide attempt?

"How's Blair? I mean, really. How's she doing?" he asked.

"She's grieving, of course, but she's hanging on." Ben sipped his coffee. "Of the three of us, Blair was always closest to Granddad. His loss has really hit her hard."

He got that, and he certainly understood. But Blair's reaction to Everett's death had an element of magical thinking in it, as if she believed she'd had the power to keep him alive but had failed to use it.

"Why would Blair believe she didn't keep Everett safe, that it was her fault he died? Why would she say it's always her fault?" Those words had haunted him. What was it he didn't understand?

Ben's eyes widened in surprise, then shuttered. "You'll have to ask Blair those questions."

"She won't answer them, so I'm asking you. I want to help her."

"What exactly is your relationship with my sister?" Ben folded his arms across his broad chest, a big brother intent on protecting his little sister. As a big brother himself, he could respect that, so he told the truth.

"I love her. I want her to be happy, and I want to be with her."

"I see." Ben cleared his throat. "Have you told her this?"

"No," Garrett confessed. "I was afraid I'd scare her off. But she scared off anyway when Everett died. She blamed herself, and me, because she wasn't in the house at the time of his death. She was with me."

"I see," Ben said again. His expression didn't give away his thoughts, a good trait for a lawyer, Garrett supposed. "Like I said, talk to Blair."

"Talk to me about what?"

He and Ben both turned toward the bottom of the stairs where Blair stood watching them, a mutinous look in her eyes. Ben looked from him to Blair and back again.

"I'll leave you to it." He clapped Garrett on the shoulder and walked out of the kitchen, leaving them alone.

She lifted her chin slightly. A gesture of defiance? Of fear? He didn't want her to be afraid, especially not of him. "What did you want to talk to me about?"

"Why would you take the blame for Everett's death? There was clearly nothing you could have done to prevent it. What did you mean that it's always your fault?"

He saw her swallow, her gaze somewhere over his left shoulder.

"It has nothing to do with you."

That stung. But he wouldn't let her avoid him. "It has everything to do with me. What hurts you hurts me. I love you, Blair."

Her gaze shot to his, and he read the panic in her eyes. It hurt to see her in such distress at his declaration.

"I don't expect anything from you, sweetheart. I only wanted you to know how I feel, to know you're not alone. You've got your brothers, and for what it's worth, you've got me."

She stared at him silently, eyes wide with anxiety. He rubbed her shoulder, needing to touch her. Finally, she averted her eyes and began to speak.

"Garrett, there are things you don't know about me. I've made mistakes, done things I'm not proud of."

He grasped both of her shoulders. "There's nothing you could have done to make me love you any less. I *know* you, Blair. You're a good person, a compassionate person."

"Please Garrett." She pushed against his chest, and he recognized she was hanging on to her composure by a thin thread. "You don't know."

"Then tell me!"

She stepped back, blinking and holding one arm out as if to ward him off. He swore softly. He hadn't meant to yell, and he certainly hadn't wanted to scare her. He made himself calm down and lower his voice.

"I'm sorry." He shook his head. "Whatever's wrong, we can fix it. I promise you."

Her chin trembled, but her eyes remained dry. The hopelessness and disbelief he saw in them terrified him.

"No one can fix this."

A knock sounded at the door. Blair's parents had arrived for the reading of the Will. Garrett suppressed a howl of frustration at the interruption.

"I won't give up on you," he whispered. "Not ever."

She closed her eyes briefly. After taking a deep breath, she opened her eyes and went to the door to admit her parents. Wordlessly, she ushered them inside and closed the door.

"I hope this doesn't take long. We have a plane to catch." Victoria glanced around the kitchen. "Same old place. Some things never change."

Garrett knew the remark wasn't meant as a compliment. Morley appeared in the kitchen and nodded politely at them.

"If you'll follow me into the living room, we can start."

Once they were all seated, Morley cleared his throat and began. "The details of the Will are set down in writing. However, Everett recorded the highlights of his Will in a video the two of us made earlier this summer. He wanted to speak directly to all of you to make his last wishes perfectly clear." He made a move toward the DVR.

"Wait." Victoria pointed to Garrett, suspicion in her expression. "What is he doing here? This is for family only."

Morley straightened to his full height. "As Garrett is one of the executors, Everett specifically asked for him to attend this event, and I intend to carry out his wishes to the letter."

Victoria glared at Morley, her displeasure obvious. "Fine. Get on with it."

"Thank you."

He pressed the play button, and Everett's face filled the screen. The old man cleared his throat.

"Are we ready?" he asked. Jake lifted his head from the carpet and barked at the sound of his master's voice.

In the background, Garrett heard Morley reply. "We're ready. Go ahead, Everett."

"All right." Everett cleared his throat once more. "If you're watching this, it means I've finally kicked the bucket. I can't regret it because I believe I'll be reunited with my Anna once more, and that will be reward enough for me.

"But I regret any pain my passing causes any of you. Especially you, Blair. You've always been a sensitive girl, blaming yourself for things that were beyond your ability to control. Know that Anna and I always loved you, no matter what."

Garrett glanced over at her. She stared straight ahead at the screen, transfixed by Everett's image.

From across the room he couldn't be sure, but he thought her eyes were dry.

"I have one favor to ask, Blair," Everett continued. "If I should predecease my old dog Jake, I ask you to please care for him when I'm gone. Make his last days comfortable and happy. I know I can count on you, Blair girl."

"I'll look after him, Granddad," she whispered.

"Several years ago, I began speculating on the stock market. It was a hobby at first. I enjoyed researching different companies and trying to figure out which ones would blossom and which would die on the vine. Turns out, I'm pretty good at it. I've put together a nice little portfolio, which will be dispersed among my heirs in the fashion I lay out in my Will. So let's get on with it, shall we?"

Everett began with a list of charities and community projects that he wished to contribute to before he got to the main event.

"To my young neighbor and friend, Garrett Saunders, I leave the gold pocket watch I inherited from my father, and his father before him. I leave the watch to you as something to remember me by, and as a reminder of strong men who came before you. My father lost his arm in the Second World War, but he never let the loss of it stop him, and I don't want anything to stop you either. You're a warrior, Garrett. Fight for what you want."

Garrett swallowed, touched beyond words. The watch was incredibly meaningful to Everett, and so it meant a lot to him, too. Garrett would treasure it always.

He glanced at Blair, wondering if Everett was

talking about his granddaughter when he urged him to fight for what he wanted.

"To my grandson Damon I leave a property I bought a few years ago in downtown Masonville. Most of the building is rented out, especially at street level, but there are offices on the second floor that would be suitable as consulting rooms for a psychology practice, if you want to go in that direction. The third floor contains apartments and one could easily be fixed up to suit you. The building is yours to do with as you wish. I also leave you a sum of three hundred thousand dollars in cash."

"To my older grandson, Ben, I leave the possibility of a career in Masonville. My old friend Morley here is getting on in years, and he's ready to hand over the reins of his practice to a younger lawyer. I want that lawyer to be you, but it has to be your decision. Masonville would be a fine place to raise those little girls of yours. They could be safe and happy here. To each of them I bequeath one hundred thousand dollars to be held in trust for their education. I also leave you three hundred thousand dollars and a nice, solid little house on Prairie View Road, close to the elementary school. I think you and the girls would like it, but if it's not what you want, you're free to sell it."

Ben shook his head in wonder. "Thanks, Granddad. The girls thank you, too."

"To my beautiful, sweet granddaughter Blair, I leave you the farm and the house and everything in it. You always had a feel for the farm and especially for the animals. I want you to fill up that barn with as many rescued horses, dogs, cats, and whatever else as you can fit in there. Love your animals, Blair girl, but don't forget you need one special person to love as well. Anna and I had that, and I want it for you, too." Everett's voice broke, and he had to stop a moment. He cleared his throat and continued. "I'm leaving you three hundred thousand dollars cash like I did with your brothers, and you'll also have the money from the rent of the land to support what you want to do with the farm."

Garrett glanced at Blair. Her chin quivered, but she kept her back straight and her hands clasped tightly in her lap.

Everett straightened his shoulders, his demeanor changing. "To my daughter Victoria, I leave the sum of three hundred thousand dollars. And I also leave this." He produced a ring box from his pocket and opened the hinged lid to reveal a sapphire circled by diamonds. "This is the ring I gave your mother fifty years ago. I saved up for months for this ring. I wanted to give Anna the best. Sapphire was her birthstone, and she loved it." He sighed, set the ring box on the table in front of him, and stared into the camera once more. "I know that by your standards it's not much, but it meant the world to Anna and me. It was a symbol of our commitment to each other and our love. I want you to have this ring to remind you of that love."

He paused and drank water from a glass on the table before picking up the ring box once more. "I'm grateful to you for blessing us with three wonderful grandchildren. They have been the lights of our lives. But the way you and your husband have treated them is abysmal. You bullied them, blamed them, and failed to keep them safe. I give you this ring to remind you of love because you don't know the meaning of the word.

It pains me to acknowledge what a self-centered person you've become. I expect some, if not all of that, is my fault. I spoiled you horribly as a child, gave you everything you wanted, gave in to all your demands. Anna warned me, but I didn't listen."

Everett paused again, looking exhausted. "So I give you this ring. And hope you learn something from it." He nodded to Morley behind the video camera. "That's all I have to say."

The screen went dark. No one spoke until Victoria rose to her feet, stunned disbelief twisting her mouth.

"I'm his only child. *I* should have inherited everything. Why would he treat me like this?"

No one answered. Garrett thought Everett had spoken his reasons quite clearly, but Victoria was unwilling to listen.

She turned to Morley. "I want to see a copy of the Will."

"Of course." Morley calmly pulled a sheaf of papers from his briefcase and handed them to her. Next, he pulled a ring box, the same one as in the video, from his pocket and held it out to her. "And here is your inheritance."

She accepted it reluctantly. Garrett noted the trembling of her hands as she opened the box and looked at the ring.

"This ring always meant more to my parents than I ever did. They were so consumed by each other they never had time for me." She snapped the lid shut. "It's a decent sapphire. I should be able to get a few bucks for it."

Blair put her hand over her mouth, her eyes wide with shock. But she didn't utter a sound.

Dear God. What kind of person sells her mother's wedding ring? He hated that Victoria's callousness was so upsetting to Blair.

Morley leaned heavily on his cane. "This concludes the reading of the Will of Everett Branson. If you wish to contest the Will, Victoria, that's your prerogative, of course, but I wouldn't recommend it. I consulted with some of the top estate lawyers in the country to ensure the terms Everett set out would be upheld in any court. His wishes were very clear."

Victoria lifted her chin. "We'll see about that."

She walked out of the house with Peter trailing behind her. Garrett heard their rental car roar to life and squeal out of the yard.

No one spoke for several minutes. Beside him, Blair was pale, lines of stress marring the perfect skin around her mouth and wrinkling her forehead.

"Can she contest the Will? Can she take the farm away from me?"

Morley shook his head. "I'm quite confident she has no grounds to do so. Everett was of sound mind when he made his Will, and we made sure all the legalities were in place. Victoria can't contest the Will simply because she doesn't like the terms."

Blair nodded. Garrett's heart broke at the sorrow on her face, but he didn't know how to help her. Some kind of trauma had colored her childhood; that was now clear to him. Unless she opened up at some point, there was little he could do aside from simply being there for her.

If she'd allow it.

Anger spread through him until he wanted to punch a wall. What the hell had her parents done to her?

Finally, Blair looked up with a smile. "I could use a cup of tea. Would anyone else like one?"

"Love one," Morley said. "And if you've got some more of those homemade cookies of yours, even better."

Blair reached for Morley's hand. "You can have as many as you'd like, Morley."

They walked hand in hand to the kitchen. Garrett got to his feet. He didn't really want tea, but he wasn't ready to leave Blair yet.

"Do you think Victoria is going to make trouble?" Damon asked quietly. Anxiety showed on his face.

"I think she'll try." Ben wearily closed his eyes. As he reopened them, fresh determination sparked in them. "We'll be ready for her."

For the first time, Garrett realized Blair wasn't the only one who'd somehow been traumatized in childhood. Even if she asked for his help, he was ill prepared to offer any. What did he know about childhood trauma? His childhood had been idyllic in comparison.

But he understood pain. If nothing else, he could listen and hold her hand when she was ready to talk. If she was ever ready to talk.

****

The next morning Blair rose early. After feeding Jake and giving him fresh water, she went out to the barn to look after the horses. The way they ran to her as she climbed through the fence rails made her smile.

She stroked their soft noses and murmured sweet words to them, taking comfort in their presence. They seemed to sense her pain. They stood close to her, as if trying to tell her she wasn't alone. At least, that was how she wanted to interpret their actions.

"Thanks, guys. I love you, too."

I want you to fill up that barn with as many rescued horses, dogs, cats, and whatever else as you can fit in there.

Her grandfather's words from the video came back to her, and she was filled with gratitude. As she fed the horses and made sure they had water, the rest of her grandfather's words played in her head.

Love your animals, Blair girl, but don't forget you need one special person to love as well.

Garrett immediately came to mind. He was never far from her thoughts. And he was never out of her heart.

She swallowed hard and leaned her forehead against Harry's side.

"He deserves so much better than me."

Blair stood leaning against Harry until he started to move away, clearly tired of her feeling sorry for herself. With one last pat to each of them, she made her way to the potting shed. Everything was exactly the way they'd left it that last morning. The electric lantern. The carelessly tossed blankets. The mattress where they'd made love and woke in each other's arms. She could almost feel the strength and tenderness in Garrett's arms as he held her, could almost smell his clean, masculine scent.

God, she missed him.

She sat on a wooden crate. Even though she'd seen Garrett every day since her grandfather died, it hadn't been the same. They'd never been alone or had the opportunity to talk, except for those few brief moments yesterday morning before her parents arrived. But even if they'd had the chance to talk, what could she say? For years now, whenever she'd tried to talk about Eve and what had happened, the words stuck in her throat, refusing to be spoken. Even in the safe confines of her therapist's office, she'd had trouble talking about her.

Garrett had said he loved her. She had no idea what to do with that.

Blair got to her feet. There was no point hanging around here torturing herself. She carefully closed the door to the potting shed and walked back to the house.

Her brothers were busy preparing breakfast in the kitchen. Ben made coffee while Damon cracked eggs into a bowl and scrambled them.

Blair washed her hands at the kitchen sink. "I'm sorry, guys. I should have at least put coffee on. I wanted to feed the animals first."

Ben slipped a couple of pieces of bread into the toaster. "I've become an almost passable cook these last few months. At least the girls haven't complained about my cooking. Much."

"How are they doing, really?" she asked.

"Okay, I think. They're sad sometimes, and confused, but mostly they've accepted that their mother is gone and isn't coming back." He turned back to his task and Blair saw his throat work. "I wish I could."

Her heart broke for her brother. "A change would be good for all three of you. Would you consider accepting Granddad's inheritance and moving here to Masonville?" Blair asked.

Ben plucked the bread from the toaster and buttered it. "I'm not sure how I feel about moving. I finally have work I love and can be proud of. I'd hate to give that up. And I don't want to uproot the girls."

Blair nibbled on her breakfast. "What about you, Damon? How do you feel about your inheritance?"

"It's definitely intriguing," Damon said around a mouthful of bacon. "But I've got a life in California, a job. I'm not sure either of those two things can transfer easily here."

Blair pushed scrambled eggs around her plate. "I plan to stay. I love my job here, and I love the farm. I love the opportunity I have to rescue more horses. The only thing missing is family. It would be amazing if you guys moved here, too."

"What about Garrett? You didn't include him on your list."

Blair lifted her gaze to look into Ben's eyes, then focused her attention on her plate once more. "I...I don't think we have a future together."

"Why not? I know for a fact he's crazy about you. And he'd be damn lucky to have you."

"He needs someone...stable. We all know that's not me."

"Because of your suicide attempt?" Damon asked softly.

"Of course because of my suicide attempt! I come with a lot of baggage." Mostly guilt, her constant companion. "Not to mention I'd never want to inflict our parents on him. He doesn't need that kind of crazy."

Damon wasn't about to give up. "Have you told him about your pregnancy?"

"No."

"Why not?"

"Don't play psychologist with me." Blair pushed away her plate, her appetite gone. "Go shrink someone else's head."

He only grinned at her, the bastard. "But shrinking your head is so much fun."

Ben pointed his fork at her. "Garrett told me you blamed yourself for Granddad's death. He said you told him you didn't keep him safe, that you were at fault. That it was always your fault."

Blair looked from Ben to Damon, her heart pumping with panic. "I don't need the two of you ganging up on me."

Damon's demeanor sobered. "Have you ever talked to a counselor about the baby?"

She nodded. "After my suicide attempt. And again at college. I saw someone at student services for a while." It had helped to talk to someone who didn't judge her. Her counselor had helped her cope with a lot of negative feelings, at least enough to be able to finish school. But they'd only scratched the surface. Once she graduated, her counselor had suggested Blair find another therapist, but she never did. Perhaps she was afraid to dig deeper.

"Have you ever considered that blaming yourself is an excuse for not moving forward?"

"That's ridiculous. I've got a new job, new friends, and a new passion rescuing horses. I'm moving forward all the time. I'm a freaking train."

"Okay," Damon agreed. "But I'm willing to bet that, emotionally, you're stuck at age seventeen. You're still that scared girl, afraid to let anyone get too close because the people who were supposed to love and protect you—your boyfriend and your parents—turned their backs on you. They blamed you for the pregnancy and were ashamed of you. And they blamed you for the aftermath. You accepted that blame and never moved past it."

Blair pushed her chair away from the table. "You don't know what you're talking about."

Damon grasped her hand. "We can talk, Blair. You and me and Ben. We can help you. Or if you don't want to talk to us, we can find a psychologist who can help you."

She pulled her hand from his and backed away. "Don't. Don't try to fix me. I'm perfectly fine the way I am."

"Are you?"

A little voice in her head screamed that she was a mess, that she should grab onto the lifeline her brother was offering her and hang on tight. But pride and fear won out.

"Yes! Don't try to analyze me, Damon. I'm not one of your patients."

A knock sounded, and Blair jumped, startled. Ben rose to open the door, and Garrett stepped inside. His gaze met hers, and his dark eyes filled with concern.

"What's wrong?"

The desire to step into his arms and press her face against his broad chest nearly brought her to her knees. She needed all her strength to lift her chin and offer him a smile, however wobbly.

"Aside from my brothers acting like know-it-all assholes, nothing. What are you doing here?"

"Just checking in before I go back out to the pasture and work on the fencing."

"How would you like some help? These two strapping young men happen to be free today."

"Hey!" Ben said.

Garrett's lip quirked. "They pissed you off that

much, did they?"

Her conscience kicked in and she had to tell the truth. "I'm a little touchy today. I think it's a good idea if we don't see each other for a couple of hours."

He stepped next to her and tucked a strand of hair behind her ear. "Okay. We'll give you some space."

Her eyes filled, and she had to turn away and make a joke to cover her distress. "Good, because if I have to spend all day with them, I can't be held responsible for my actions."

To her surprise, Garrett pulled her into a hug and kissed the top of her head. "It's okay, baby."

Blair allowed herself to cling to him for a moment and breathe in his scent before putting her hands on his chest and gently pushing. Garrett smiled into her eyes before turning to her brothers.

"You heard the lady. Let's get to work."

"I'm not dressed for fixing fence," Ben grumbled.

"I'll find a couple of pairs of Granddad's overalls."

Blair left the kitchen in search of the work clothes, grateful to have a moment to compose herself. Was Damon right? Did she have the emotional capacity of a scared seventeen-year-old? Why was Garrett being so kind to her? He deserved someone whole.

She was so messed up no amount of counseling was going to help her.

She found the overalls and returned to the kitchen. Her brothers grudgingly accepted the overalls and put them on over their street clothes. Her Granddad's old work clothes were long sleeved and zipped up the front, covering her brothers from ankles to wrists to throats. Damon wriggled in discomfort.

"We're going to sweat like pigs in these outfits,"

he said.

"Lucky for you, it's much cooler today." Garrett clapped Ben on the shoulder. "I've got a couple of extra pairs of work gloves in my truck."

Ben blew out a breath. "Fine. Let's go."

He followed Garrett outside to his truck. Damon hung back and closed the door.

"I meant what I said, Blair. You can talk to me, or we can find another counselor, but until you move past the hurt and guilt, nothing will change. And that would be a damn shame. For both you and Garrett."

With that he quietly opened the door and left. Blair watched the three men pile into Garrett's truck and drive out of the yard.

For the next couple of hours, Blair washed floors and scrubbed toilets. She dusted and polished every inch of the old house. But no matter how hard she worked, she couldn't outrun her brother's words.

He thought she needed help. Maybe he was right, but shame swamped her at the thought of confessing her sins. She was afraid no one could help her.

Jana Richards

Chapter Twenty-One

After breakfast the next morning, Blair's brothers brought their luggage down the stairs and prepared to leave. Despite what happened yesterday, she hated to see them go. The thought of rattling around this big, old house alone depressed her.

She made herself smile for them. "Looks like you're ready."

Ben set the strap of his bag on his shoulder. "Yeah. By the time we take back the rental car, Damon's plane will be ready to board. Mine leaves about an hour after his."

"I'm so glad you were both able to stay a couple of extra days. I know it wasn't easy with your jobs, and your kids."

Ben pulled her into a hug. "It was great seeing you, sweetheart."

Blair kissed his cheek. "Give Bella and Sophie a hug for me. And think about Granddad's offer. Masonville's a great place to raise kids. I think it would be good for you as well." She honestly believed it, though she might have had slightly selfish motives.

Damon wrapped her in a hug. "And think about what I said, too, okay?"

"Okay." She hadn't thought about much else.

He kissed her forehead. "Take care of yourself."

She walked them out to their car. Ben put their

bags in the trunk and opened the driver's side door. Blair set her hand on his arm, needing one last moment of contact.

"I want you both to call me as soon as you get home so I know you're safe."

"We will. Look after yourself, Blair. And give Garrett a chance. He cares for you," Damon said.

She nodded, unable to speak for a moment. How she wished she could simply accept whatever Garrett was willing to give.

They got in the car and, with a wave, they were gone. Blair watched until the dust from their rental car settled. How she wished she could tell her brothers how much she loved them. How she wished she could hear them say it to her. But they hadn't been raised with words of love, so saying it didn't come easily.

Loneliness pressed on her heart. She swallowed, climbed up the front porch steps, and went back into the house.

Damned if she was going to cry. If she started, she might never stop.

She scrambled up the stairs to the second floor and stripped the beds her brothers had slept in. After throwing the sheets in the washing machine and putting fresh towels in the bathrooms, she checked the time. Only ten a.m. She groaned.

Keep busy. Keep working, Blair. Aside from the laundry and a few dishes, there was nothing to do since she'd scrubbed down the house yesterday. She'd fed Jake and the horses before breakfast, leaving her little to do outside. She couldn't wait to go back to work. Lauren had told her to take the rest of the week off, but she'd go crazy here alone. She'd go back tomorrow morning.

After washing the breakfast dishes, she found some carrots in the fridge and chopped them into pieces. Outside on the porch, Jake gave a desultory thump to the floor with his tail, his head resting on his front paws. Blair crouched beside him and stroked his soft fur.

"I know you miss Granddad as much as I do, but he'd want us to carry on, wouldn't he? He wouldn't want us to be sad forever." She stood and snapped her fingers. "Come on, Jake. Let's go visit the horses."

At first Jake didn't move, but after some coaxing, he pushed himself to his feet and followed her down the steps.

As soon as they reached the paddock behind the barn, the horses trotted to the fence to greet her, and her heart lifted, even though she knew they were simply looking for food. She climbed between the wooden rails, and they followed her as she put pieces of raw carrot in their flat-bottomed bowls.

She heard a vehicle pull into the yard. Blair crawled back through the wooden rails to see who had arrived. Excited butterflies danced in her stomach as Garrett emerged from his truck.

Don't do that. If she reacted this way every time she saw him, she'd go crazy. Straightening her spine, she walked toward him, with Jake close beside her.

"Hi."

He flashed her a smile and bent to pat Jake's head. "Hi. Sorry I'm late. I had to pick up some fencing supplies in town." He gestured at the rolls of barbed wire in the back of his truck.

"Make sure you give me the receipts and I'll

reimburse you."

"It's not necessary."

"Oh, I think it is. Besides, I'm a woman of means now, remember?"

She'd happily give back the money and the land if it meant having her Granddad with her again, even for a day. She looked away.

"When did your brothers leave?"

"Right after breakfast, a couple of hours ago." At the reminder, she saw her day stretching out in front of her with infinite loneliness. "Would you like some help? I'm off the rest of the day."

He didn't answer right away. She looked away once more, embarrassed that he didn't want to spend time with her. She couldn't blame him. She'd been blowing hot and cold, sending crazy mixed messages ever since they met.

"It's okay—"

"I'd appreciate an extra pair of hands."

She lifted her chin to look at him, and he cupped her cheek. "It gets easier after a while. You never get over losing someone you care about, but in time the pain becomes more bearable."

"You're talking about your friend Tommy." The words were out before she could stop them. She didn't want to share his pain. She already cared too much.

His smile was fleeting. "Yeah."

"And you feel guilty because you survived, and he didn't." Being the honorable man she knew him to be, he'd hold on to that guilt.

"In my head, I know Tommy's death wasn't my fault and surviving was simply the luck of the draw. But in my heart..."

He swallowed and looked away. Blair laid her hand on his cheek. "It's not your fault, Garrett."

His gaze found hers once more. "I could say the same to you."

She withdrew her hand. He was talking about her grandfather, and maybe he was right. But he didn't know about Eve.

They stared at each other until Garrett finally broke the silence. "So. You want to do some fencing today, do you?"

"Yeah. If you give me a couple of minutes, I can put together a lunch for us."

"I'll give you a hand."

Blair nodded and started toward the house with Jake close on her heels. "Can we bring Jake?" The old dog didn't want to be alone any more than she did.

Garrett gave Jake another pat. "Sure."

They assembled a lunch and, after loading Jake into Garrett's truck, drove out into the pasture. The fence in this part of the pasture was in bad shape. Large sections of it were broken, the fence posts lying rotten on the ground and surrounded by spirals of rusting barbed wire.

Garrett stopped the truck and turned off the ignition. "There's no fixing the fence here. We'll have to totally rebuild it."

It was worse than Blair had thought. She blew out a breath. "I guess we'd better get at it."

They worked together easily, only speaking about the job at hand. With each holding one side of the two-man gas-powered auger, they dug several new holes for the new posts. Managing her end of the heavy machine required every ounce of Blair's strength. But if she didn't do her part, Garrett would have to dig the holes manually, a difficult, backbreaking job. So she gritted her teeth and hung on.

After a few hours they broke for lunch. Blair spread an old blanket on the ground and opened the cooler. She tossed a dog treat to Jake, and he caught it neatly in the air, then stretched out on the ground next to the blanket to eat it. Garrett eased himself to the blanket and reached for the thermos of water she'd packed.

"I'm starved," he said after taking a drink.

Blair handed him a couple of sandwiches. "Nothing like good honest labor to work up an appetite."

They ate in silence, but it was a comfortable silence that soothed Blair. Bird songs and insect sounds surrounded them. A light breeze rustled the tall grasses that, with autumn approaching, were brown and dry. The smell of rich earth wafted on the breeze. Blair breathed it in, more at peace than she'd been in days.

After they finished eating the cookies she'd packed, Garrett pushed himself to one knee.

"I guess it's time to get back at it."

"Yeah, I suppose so."

Blair scrambled to her feet and resisted the urge to offer him her hand to help him stand. She wanted so much to make things easier for him, but she understood how important it was to him to stand on his own two feet. Literally and figuratively.

Once Garrett got to his feet, she packed the remains of their lunch into the cooler, then folded the blanket and stowed both in the back seat of the truck. Returning to the fence line, she grabbed one end of the auger while Garrett lifted the other. As he was about to start the machine, his phone rang. He gave her an apologetic look.

"I should probably check this."

"Go ahead."

They set down the machine and Garrett pulled the phone from his pocket. He frowned at the screen.

"Chris's wife is calling." He clicked the speaker phone. "Hi, Alison. What's going on? How's Chris?"

"Chris is…he's having a hard time adjusting to life at home, harder than we'd hoped." Alison's voice broke. "I'm afraid he's going to end up in the hospital again."

Garrett pinched the bridge of his nose. "Tell me what's happening."

"He's alone too much." Blair could hear the anguish in her voice. "I'm at work all day, and the girls are at daycare and school. He goes to his sessions at the VA hospital once a week, but he has too much time on his hands, too much time to think. I know he's trying, but…he gets quiet and won't talk, and next thing I know, he'll explode over some small thing, like the girls making too much noise. Just like…just like before."

She didn't have to add, "When he threatened to kill himself."

Garrett drew in a sharp breath, and without thinking, Blair grasped his hand. He squeezed it hard, as if needing something, or someone, to hang on to.

"What can I do?" he asked.

"I don't know exactly. Chris needs time, and some peace and quiet, so he can slowly make his way back to us. Do you think…do you think he could stay with you for a while?"

Garrett closed his eyes. "I'm sorry, Alison. I'm living with my parents. I'm burden enough to them. I couldn't ask them to take in Chris as well."

"Yes, of course," Alison said. "I'm sorry. I shouldn't have asked."

"I'll ask around, check VA sites on the Internet," Garrett said. He stared out over the prairie, though Blair doubted he saw the gently waving grasses or the gophers scurrying between burrows. He maintained his grip on her hand. "We'll figure something out."

"Thanks, Garrett." Alison sounded as if she was holding tight to her emotions. "I should go—"

"Wait!" Blair squeezed Garrett's hand, and his gaze flew to hers, surprise in his eyes. "Chris could stay with me."

"I'm…I'm sorry," Alison stuttered. "Who is this?"

"I'm sorry, Alison. My name is Blair Greyson. I'm a neighbor of Garrett's and his parents. He's been helping me fix things around the farm. We're fixing fence right now. I'm sorry to eavesdrop on your conversation, but Garrett's told me about Chris, and I know how much he wants to help him."

"You want Chris to stay at your farm," Alison said cautiously. "How would your…your husband feel about having a stranger in the house?"

"I'm not married." She could imagine how it sounded to Alison. A single woman alone with her husband on an isolated farm. "Perhaps while Chris stays here, Garrett can move in as well. I've got lots of room."

Garrett's eyes lit with relief. "Yes, I could do that."

"I don't understand," Alison said. "Why would you

do this? You don't even know Chris."

"No, I don't, but I know Garrett, and Chris is important to him." She cleared her throat. "I've got my own selfish reasons. If Chris is here, perhaps he wouldn't mind helping Garrett finish fixing fence. I've got horses I can't let out of their small paddock until the fence is back in place. And I work full time. I don't always have enough time to look after my horses the way I'd like to. Chris can help me with that, too."

"I don't think Chris knows anything about horses," Alison said.

"That's okay. I can teach him everything I know." Garrett winked at her, and she grinned back at the shared joke. "There's no shortage of work around here. I could really use Chris's help. I really think spending time outside, working with the horses and having a purpose, will be good for him. I know it's been good for me."

"It sounds exactly like what Chris needs. If you're certain…"

"I am." He tugged Blair closer. "As long as Blair is sure she's okay with the two of us underfoot."

"I'm sure." She stared into Garrett's eyes. She was terrified. Was inviting Garrett into her home the smart thing to do? How could she live with him and not want him in her bed once more? She had no idea, but she did know she'd go crazy if she had to spend her evenings and weekends alone.

"I'd like to talk to Chris first," Garrett said. "Make sure he's okay with the idea of staying here on the farm for a while."

"You and your kids could visit any time, Alison. Like I said, I've got lots of room."

"Blair, thank you. Thank you so much. You don't know what this means to me." Blair heard the tears in Alison's voice. They caused her own eyes to well up in response.

"It's my pleasure. Truly."

"Is Chris at home right now?" Garrett asked.

"Yes. Can you call him right away?"

"I will. If he agrees, I'll drive to Minneapolis tonight. I'll stay overnight, and he and I can drive back here tomorrow."

Blair could hear the relief in the long breath Alison expelled. "Thanks, Garrett. You're such a good friend."

"Chris deserves any help we can give him."

"Yes, he does." Alison took another shaky breath. "I've got to run. My break's over, and I need to get back to work. Can you let me know what Chris says?"

"I'll text you as soon as I talk to him."

"Thanks. Bye, Garrett. And Blair, thanks again."

"Goodbye, Alison."

As soon as Garrett ended the call, he dragged Blair into his arms and held her tight. She clung to him, allowing herself a few precious moments to touch him before stepping back.

"You don't know what this means to me, Blair." His voice was raw and husky.

"I think I have an idea."

"You don't even know Chris. Why would you invite him to stay in your home?"

For you. She attempted a nonchalant shrug. "I guess I'll do anything for free labor."

One corner of his mouth turned up in amusement. "Tell it to someone who doesn't know you as well as I do."

She knew him, too, she realized. She knew how determined and resourceful he could be, knew the tender heart that beat in his warrior's chest. She understood what made him happy, what frustrated him, what made him crazy. She understood his desire to find his way in the world and make a difference.

Blair swallowed and went with a version of the truth. "It'll be nice to have company."

He nodded. "I know, but I'm afraid this is a case of being careful what you wish for. Whenever you get tired of having us around, you can tell us to leave."

Blair couldn't imagine getting tired of having Garrett in her life. But she wasn't who he needed. With an effort, she made herself smile. "I'll remember you said that if I find dirty dishes and stinky socks lying around the house."

Instead of laughing, he cupped her cheek, smoothing the tender skin beneath her eye with his thumb. "You're a beautiful, generous person. Everett would be so proud of what you're doing for Chris."

Blair couldn't speak. She stared into Garrett's dark eyes, unable to look away. He looked at her as if he believed in her. As if she were something special.

Her granddad had always told her she was special.

Oh, Granddad.

The tears started and she was helpless to stop them. She missed her grandfather so much. He'd been her rock, her anchor all her life. He'd loved her, protected her, cheered for her. How would she go on without him?

Garrett pulled her into his arms and held her as she cried, soothing her with gentle words. She clung to him as grief and pain washed over her.

Eventually, her tears slowed and finally stopped. Blair made herself push away from Garrett. He held tight for a moment, and with a sigh, dropped his hands.

"I'm sorry, Blair. I know how hard it's been for you to lose your grandfather."

She nodded. "Yes."

"I didn't mean to make you cry." He closed his eyes and shook his head. "I only wanted you to know how much I appreciate what you're doing for Chris."

"It helped. To cry, I mean." She swallowed. "I haven't cried since he died. Haven't let myself. But it helped."

"Good. I'm glad." He sighed. "I should phone Chris and make sure he's on board with our plans."

"Yeah."

"You're sure you're okay?" The look he gave her was tender, but worried.

"Yes, of course." She made herself smile for him. "I'm fine, Garrett. Really. Go phone Chris."

He blew out a breath and pulled his phone from his pocket. "Okay."

Blair went back to work, setting posts in the holes they'd already dug, backfilling the holes with earth and tamping it down. A few moments later Garrett joined her. "It's all set. I'll drive to Minneapolis later today and stay overnight with Chris and Alison. Tomorrow Chris and I will leave first thing in the morning. We should be home in the early afternoon."

Blair wondered if he realized he'd called her farm home. "So Chris is okay about staying here, and about being away from his family?"

"He's not happy about being away from them, but he knows he's not coping. He's willing to do whatever it takes to get back to them. We're going to contact the VA center in Bismarck to see if he can continue his counseling sessions there." He sighed, a worried look on his face. "I hope this works."

"It will. I have faith in you."

He grinned in that slow, easy way she loved so much. "From your lips to God's ears. Come on, time to get back to work."

"We should wrap up so you can be on your way."

"I've got plenty of time. Unless you're ready to call it a day?" She heard the teasing note in his voice.

"Not at all. It's my fence, remember?"

"I have a stake in it as well. I'm sure my boy Harry will enjoy roaming around out here."

Blair looked around the pasture, to the gently rolling hills and the vast blue of the sky. There wasn't anywhere else she'd rather be.

"Yeah, Harry will enjoy this place. We'd better get it ready for him."

They worked together for another couple of hours. Once they'd finished a section of fencing, they packed up and headed to the farmyard. Garrett dropped her and Jake at the house, and she showed him where she kept an extra key to the house, in case they arrived while she was at work. With a wave and a promise to call her when he got back to Masonville with Chris, he was off. Blair waved as he drove out of her yard.

She missed him already.

****

The following day Garrett pulled his truck to a stop in front of Blair's house in the late afternoon. He'd expected to be at the farm earlier, but the long drive and the close confines of the truck cab had made Chris anxious. They'd stopped frequently to stretch their legs, sometimes talking, but more often walking together in companionable silence.

"Here we are."

Chris nodded. "It's nice."

"Yeah."

Garrett took in the neat, well-tended farmyard with its trimmed shrubs and weed-free flower beds. Keeping the farm in shape was a full-time occupation. Blair worked hard to look after what was hers.

She worked too hard. Garrett hoped he and Chris could ease some of her burden.

After sending Blair a quick text to tell her they'd arrived, they stepped out of the truck and headed to the house. Jake thumped his tail on the porch floor a couple of times and made his way down the steps. He briefly greeted Garrett with a lick to his hand before going straight to Chris and looking up into his face as if he recognized another soul in pain.

"Jake was devoted to Everett. He's been pretty sad since he died."

Chris stroked Jake's head. "Poor old boy. It's tough to lose a good friend, isn't it?"

Garrett's thoughts immediately flew to Tommy, and for the thousandth time he wondered why his friend died and he'd survived.

You survived to make a difference.

Garrett blinked, stunned by the out-of-the-blue thought. To make a difference in what? To whom?

Chris lifted his head and gave a brief smile. "It's nice here. Quiet."

"It is," he agreed. "Come on. I'll introduce you to the horses."

Chris grimaced. "You know I'm a city boy, right? I've never been up close and personal with a horse before."

"Don't worry. We'll get you countrified before you know it."

They headed to the paddock behind the barn. Harry and the other horses ambled to the fence to greet them. Garrett climbed between the rails and stroked Harry's nose and scratched him behind the ears the way he liked. Blair's horses nuzzled his hair, looking for their share of attention. Chris stayed several feet back on the other side of the fence, apprehension on his face.

"Blair hopes to rescue more horses. Too many are abandoned when they get old or their owners can't afford them anymore."

"She sounds like a very compassionate person," Chris said. "She must be, to offer to take me in."

"Blair is amazing." The most amazing woman he'd ever known.

Chris gave him a knowing grin. "Sounds like you've got it bad."

He had it real bad for Blair, but that wasn't the issue right now. "Shut up and meet the horses."

Chris slowly walked up to the fence. "Now what?"

"Stick your hand through the rails and let them smell you."

"Do they bite?"

"Only city boys."

"Very funny."

Chris slowly stretched his arm between the wooden rails, his hands fisted as if getting ready to defend himself. Harry sniffed all the way up his arm.

"Harry, meet my friend Chris. Chris, meet Harry."

"Geez, he's big."

"Trust me, he's a pussycat. Scratch behind his ears. He likes that."

Chris slowly lifted his arm and scratched behind one ear. Harry snorted and shook his head, making Chris pull back in alarm.

"It's okay," Garrett said quietly. "You tickled him, that's all. Try again."

Chris blew out a breath and reached out once more. This time Harry stood unmoving as he scratched and petted. Chris visibly relaxed.

"You're doing great, buddy."

"So what made you buy Harry?" Chris asked. "Did you have horses as a kid?"

"No, we never had horses." Garrett stroked Harry's side. "I can't really explain it, but when I looked into Harry's eyes, I knew I couldn't let him be sold for meat. I didn't know the first thing about horses. If it weren't for Blair, I couldn't have kept Harry. Anything I've learned, she taught me."

Chris grinned. "Like I said, you've got it bad."

This time Garrett didn't push aside the remark. He wanted to be honest with Chris. Perhaps honesty would help them both. "She makes me want to be a better man."

Chris nodded in understanding. "That's why I'm here. I want to be a better man for Alison. She deserves that from me."

"Yeah." He only wished Blair would trust him with her secrets.

A vehicle drove into the yard. Jake, who'd been sleeping nearby on the grass, barked and ambled around the side of the barn to see who'd arrived. Garrett climbed through the wooden rail, and he and Chris followed. Garrett was surprised to see Blair emerge from her truck. He lifted a hand in a wave, and she waved back.

"Hey." Though he'd only been away overnight, he'd missed her. He longed to pull her into his arms. "I didn't expect you home this early."

"I went in to work a little earlier this morning." She turned to Chris with a smile. "I'm happy to meet you, Chris. I'm Blair Greyson."

"It's nice to meet you, too, Blair. I want to thank you for inviting me to stay on your farm. You're very generous."

"Not so generous. Like I told Alison, I plan to put you to work. You'll be earning your keep."

"I'm looking forward to it. I've been sitting around too long. It'll be a relief to work up a good, honest sweat."

"I'm pretty sure we can help you with that." Blair grabbed a bag of groceries from the back seat of her truck. "Come on inside the house. Are you hungry? I've got chili in the slow cooker that should be ready. I picked up fresh bread and pie for dessert at the bakery on the way home."

Garrett laid his hand on her shoulder, needing to touch her. "We don't want you going to a lot of trouble while we're here. We can help with the meals and the cleanup. Chris here is a pretty passable cook."

"Is that right? What do you like to cook, Chris?"

Chris's smile was shy. "I love to bake. Bread mostly. There's something very satisfying about kneading and working with the dough."

"Feel free to bake anything you like while you're

here. Just tell me what ingredients you need."

"Chris and I will pay our fair share for groceries." Garrett wanted both of them to know she wouldn't be taken advantage of. "We don't expect you to cook for us or pay for our food."

"But—"

"Garrett's right. I don't want to take advantage of your hospitality. You're doing me an enormous favor."

"You're doing me a favor, too. And I'm not talking about working around the farm, though I appreciate that immensely." She glanced at Garrett, and he saw vulnerability and pain flash in her eyes before she turned back to Chris. "Garrett probably told you my grandfather died recently. It's been very quiet without him. I'm glad for the company."

"I'm sorry for your loss, Blair."

"Thank you."

He understood Blair was having a hard time with Everett's death. But this was the first time she'd come close to admitting how lonely she was, at least in his hearing. Garrett wanted to drag her into his arms and keep her safe. He wanted nothing more than for her to be happy.

Once they mounted the front steps, Garrett grabbed the grocery bag from her as she fished out the key from her purse and unlocked the door. They were greeted by the delicious smell of Blair's chili.

"Smells great," Chris said.

"If you're hungry, we can eat right now." For the first time, Blair turned to him, her expression unreadable, her gaze not quite meeting his. "Do you remember where the dishes and utensils are? If you don't mind setting the table, I'd like to change out of my scrubs."

He touched her arm, and she didn't shy away. It gave him hope.

"Of course. Chris and I can take care of it."

"Thank you." She finally met his gaze. "I'm glad you're back."

He squeezed her arm, wishing it could be a more intimate caress. "So am I."

Garrett watched her leave the kitchen and head for the stairs. How was he going to sleep tonight knowing Blair was only a few steps down the hall?

Chapter Twenty-Two

Blair sat bolt upright in her bed, heart pounding in fear but too disoriented to know what had awakened her so abruptly. Then she heard it again, a keening cry followed by a scream of sheer terror.

Dear God, was that Garrett?

She pulled back the blankets and fumbled out of bed, searching in the dark for her robe and slippers before rushing to the door of her bedroom. In the dim light of the hallway she saw Garrett leading Chris down the stairs, speaking quietly and calmly to him. Her first reaction was relief that it wasn't Garrett. The cries she'd heard spoke of deep pain, and she couldn't bear to think of him suffering that way.

Chris mumbled incoherently as they descended the stairs, and Blair made out a few words. He was sorry, he shouldn't have come here. Blair's heart broke for him. Tightening the belt of her robe, she followed them.

In the kitchen, Chris paced back and forth in agitation. Garrett stood at the sink, filling the kettle with water. Blair's eyes met Garrett's, his tired and full of resignation. And acceptance. Whatever happened, he'd stand beside his friend.

A bark sounded, accompanied by scratching at the kitchen door. As soon as Blair opened it, Jake brushed past her and headed straight for Chris. Surprised, Chris stopped pacing. Jake sat on his haunches, staring up at him and making a whimpering sound in his throat.

Chris reached out and stroked the top of his head. "It's okay, boy. Don't worry about me."

Blair cautiously approached them. "Are you okay?"

Chris blinked, as if noticing her for the first time. "I'm fine. I'm sorry, Blair. The nightmares get me sometimes. I didn't mean to wake you."

"I know. It's all right. What can I do to help?"

He shook his head in misery. "There's nothing you can do. There's nothing anyone can do. I shouldn't have come here."

He tried to move away, but she stopped him with a hand to his arm. "You absolutely should have come here. This is only a small setback. You were probably disoriented because this place is new to you. You're going to get stronger every day."

She hoped she was speaking the truth.

Chris lifted his gaze to hers, his eyes bleak. "I hope you're right."

Garrett set a pot of tea on the table. "I've made chamomile. Would you like some, Blair?"

She gave Chris's arm one last pat. "Sure. Thank you."

She brought the sugar bowl and a carton of milk to the table while Garrett found cups and spoons. Taking the seat next to Chris, she put a spoonful of sugar into the cup Garrett passed her. The adrenalin that had shot through her veins at the sound of Chris's screams had worn off and weariness took its place. Glancing at the clock on the wall, she saw it was four a.m. Blair stifled a yawn. In a couple of hours she'd have to feed the horses before preparing for work. Maybe she should simply stay up. The sun would rise soon, and she likely wouldn't be able to sleep anyway.

Jake settled himself beside Chris, sitting close to his chair with his head on his lap. Blair had never seen him react this way to anyone aside from her grandfather. Chris laid one hand on the dog's head as he quietly drank his tea. He appeared calmer now, as if he'd derived comfort from contact with the dog.

"It looks like you made a friend," she said.

Chris smiled at Jake. "He's a good boy."

"Jake went straight for Chris as soon we got out of the truck." Garrett lowered himself into the chair across from Blair. "Must be your animal magnetism, buddy."

"Jake's always been a one-man kind of dog. He tolerated me because I fed him, but he was Granddad's dog. They were devoted to each other."

Chris held out his hand for Jake to sniff, and the dog licked him. "He's probably missing your grandfather."

Blair's heart gave a painful kick. *He's not the only one.* "Yeah."

They quietly drank their tea, the only sound in the kitchen the ticking of the clock. Finally, Chris rose.

"I'm going back to my room. Thanks for the tea, Garrett. And Blair, again, I'm sorry to wake you."

As he turned to leave, Jake began to whimper. Chris stopped, a look of distress on his face.

"It's okay, boy. I'll see you in the morning."

Jake apparently didn't like that answer. His whimpering turned to loud, anguished crying that tore at Blair's heart.

"Chris, would you mind taking Jake to your room?" she said. "I think that would settle him down."

Chris nodded and from the look of relief on his face, Blair knew it was what he wanted, too. "Yeah, sure. Come on, boy."

Jake immediately stopped crying and followed Chris up the stairs. A moment later she heard the door to his room close, and all was quiet.

Blair was suddenly aware she and Garrett were alone. The night cocooned around them, reminding her of the nights they'd spent together in the potting shed. Precious nights when they were the only two people in the world. Garrett's bare chest reminded her, too. Each taut muscle, each scar called to her, begging for her touch. Making her long for what she couldn't have.

She closed her eyes and looked away.

"Chris and Jake will be good for each other."

Blair made herself turn to Garrett with a smile. "I hope so."

"I'm sorry," Garrett said. "I wouldn't blame you if you changed your mind about Chris staying here."

"I won't change my mind." *Because Chris is your friend and he's important to you.* "I can't say being woken by screaming at four a.m. is something I bargained for, but it's the first night. Once Chris is used to the place, I'm sure he'll settle in." Or at least she hoped so.

"I appreciate that, Blair. More than I can tell you."

His soulful brown eyes held hers, and she found it impossible to look away. He was making this difficult, and so tempting. A part of her wanted to give in, to allow her body and her heart free rein. She'd take Garrett to her bed right now and spend what was left of the night making love to him.

But once the morning came, her old fears would

rise, and shame would consume her once more because she didn't deserve Garrett.

What right did she have to be happy?

Blair rose quickly, almost tipping her chair.

"I have to go. I have to…" She had no idea what she had to do.

Garrett rose as well. "Blair, please. Talk to me. Tell me what's wrong. Is it something I did? Have I upset you?"

"No, of course not."

He moved quickly, suddenly in front of her and grasping her shoulders. "Then what is it? I love you, Blair. I want us to be together. Whatever is wrong, we can work it out. We're stronger together."

She wanted to believe him. But she found herself shaking her head, overtaken by the guilt that had been a constant part of her life these last ten years.

"I can't do that to you, Garrett. You deserve so much better."

He stared at her, his mouth opening but no words coming out. Blair turned and ran up the stairs. Once inside her room, the tears came. She curled into the fetal position on her bed and cried, holding her hand over her mouth to stifle the noise. She cried until she was exhausted. Until she had nothing left.

****

For the next few days, Garrett was scrupulously polite to her, but didn't try to touch her or talk privately with her. Blair missed him, though he was right in front of her. She told herself she had no right to be upset with him. He was only doing what she asked.

But that didn't stop her heart from aching.

The first morning after Chris's arrival had been the

worst. Blair could barely look at Garrett without tears threatening. He made small talk and smiled as he ate breakfast, but that was likely for Chris's benefit. Neither of them wanted any awkwardness between them to affect Chris's recovery. Blair was relieved to escape to work that morning and the rest of the mornings that week. She volunteered to stay late some days and worked an extra shift on Saturday, her day off. If Garrett recognized she was avoiding him, he didn't say anything.

On Sunday the clinic was closed, so she had no excuse to leave the farm. She kept herself busy by cleaning house and baking cookies. Garrett seemed to be doing the same. He and Chris spent most of the day working on the new stalls in the barn. The only time they spent together was during meals.

God, she missed him.

Shortly after dinner, Charlotte drove into the yard, and Blair was relieved by the distraction. She liked Charlotte a lot but hadn't talked to her in a while. They both had busy work schedules and the upheaval of her grandfather's funeral meant they'd only exchanged a few words in the last couple of weeks.

Blair headed toward Charlotte's car and was surprised to discover she wasn't alone. Charlotte opened the back door of her car and a dog of indeterminate breed jumped out. The dog was of medium size, with short, mostly brown fur that gave him the appearance of a small chocolate lab, until you noticed his long, pointed nose, patches of black fur, and pointy ears that suggested a German Shepherd or perhaps Doberman heritage somewhere in his gene pool. Somehow the disparate parts came together to produce a remarkably ugly dog. Then Blair realized with a start that his left eye was missing, and she felt a rush of sympathy for the mutt.

"Who do you have here?" she asked.

Charlotte clipped a leash to the dog's collar. "This is Frisco. He's been a resident of the shelter for over two years." She gave Blair an apologetic smile. "I have an ulterior motive for bringing him here today."

Warning bells went off in Blair's head. "What do you mean?"

"Frisco's not the prettiest dog in the world, and aside from that, no one wants a dog with one eye. Now he's been in the shelter so long he's developed some bad habits, like barking and whining for no reason. He's become terribly anxious. I'm afraid Frisco's been deemed unadoptable."

"And you brought him here because…?" She was afraid she already knew the answer.

Charlotte's face twisted, and for a moment Blair thought she was going to cry. Instead she drew herself up and looked her in the eye. "They were about to put him down. I couldn't let that happen. I fibbed and said I'd found a home for him. With you."

"Charlotte! Why would you do such a thing without asking me? I've already got a dog to look after. I don't want another one!"

"I'm sorry, Blair, but it was a matter of life and death. Besides, you like dogs, right? You talked about rescuing a dog from the shelter."

She watched Frisco as he sat obediently beside Charlotte, looking like the best-behaved dog in the world. As if he knew his life depended on it.

"This isn't a good time. I don't have the energy for

a new animal right now."

"There's no one else, Blair." Charlotte sounded desperate. "I tried keeping him, but with my crazy schedule I'm not around enough, and Frisco got anxious and started chewing the furniture. Besides, I've adopted River, the pup I was fostering, so I've already got two dogs."

"I'm away at work, too, Charlotte. What if he doesn't get along with Jake? I won't subject Jake to any kind of trauma. He's getting up in age."

"Garrett told me he's staying here while his friend recovers, and I thought with them here on the farm all day, Frisco would be okay. He only needs some love and attention." She stroked Frisco's head, her voice breaking. "Please, Blair. I'm begging you."

Blair stared at the dog. He stared back with his one eye, somehow aware that he needed to impress her. He stepped carefully toward her and licked her hand before sitting on his haunches in front of her and staring up at her with a hopeful expression.

Blair frowned at Charlotte, but even as she did, she felt herself weakening. "Did you teach him that trick?"

"No, I swear I didn't. That's all Frisco. He's a good dog, really, but he's had a tough life. He needs someone to give him a chance."

"Someone like me, I suppose."

"I was hoping so."

Blair huffed out a breath. She had imagined herself adopting another dog, and perhaps more horses. But since Granddad's death she couldn't imagine lavishing affection on another creature.

Garrett and Chris joined them, and Garrett introduced Charlotte to his friend. He nodded at the dog.

"Who do you have here, Char?"

"This is Frisco, from the shelter in Bismarck."

He shook his head. "That has got to be the ugliest dog I've ever seen."

"She's trying to guilt me into adopting him. He's on death row."

Even as Blair said the words, she realized she couldn't allow the dog to leave her farm and face certain death. She only wished she really wanted him.

Garrett frowned at his sister. "That's dirty pool, Char. Isn't there another alternative?"

"Believe me, I've exhausted them all. Blair's my last hope." Charlotte raised hopeful eyes to her. "Please?"

"I'll help look after him as long as I'm here," Chris offered. "Maybe that will ease his transition to living here on the farm."

Blair glanced at Garrett, and he shrugged. "It's up to you. If you decide to keep him, I'll help any way I can, but don't let Charlotte guilt you into it."

Blair turned her attention back to the dog who stared pleadingly up at her. With a sigh she turned to Charlotte.

"Okay, he can stay, but only if he and Jake get along."

Charlotte pulled her into a hug. "Oh, thank you, Blair. You won't regret this, I promise you."

She already regretted it. *It looks like I've adopted an ugly, one-eyed, anxiety-ridden dog*, she thought with chagrin. Exactly what she needed.

Charlotte handed her the leash, and Blair spoke to the dog. "Okay, Frisco. I'll introduce you to Jake. But

I'm warning you. One wrong move and you're out."

Frisco cocked his head at an angle in order to look at her with his one good eye. Despite herself, her heart turned over at the comical, and hopeful, expression on his face.

She led Frisco up the front porch stairs to where Jake was lying on his favorite blanket in the sunshine. At their approach, he lifted his head and barked twice. To Blair's ears, there was a warning in the sound.

"Jake, this is Frisco. He's going to be staying with us." She held tight to Frisco's leash. "Pending your approval, of course."

With a growl deep in his throat, Jake got to his feet and sniffed Frisco from nose to tail. Frisco stood perfectly still and allowed himself to be given the once-over. Suddenly he dropped to the floor and rolled over, exposing his belly to Jake in a gesture of submission. After a thorough sniff, Jake sauntered back to his blanket. In minutes he was asleep again.

Behind her Garrett chuckled. "Looks like Frisco made a conquest."

"Or Jake established who's the alpha dog around here."

Charlotte beamed. "He's going to fit right in here, Blair. I can feel it."

For Frisco's sake, Blair hoped she was right.

****

Garrett straightened his back and stretched, trying to work out the kinks from long hours spent hauling around heavy fence posts and wrangling barbed wire into submission. In the two and a half weeks since he and Chris had been working together on Blair's fence, they'd put in countless hours. They'd accomplished much more together than he could have managed on his own. Blair might have been doing Chris a favor, but his friend was definitely paying her back.

He was proud of Chris. He worked hard and never complained, even if the work was unfamiliar and uncomfortable for him, like grooming the horses. Though he was obviously intimidated by their size, he made himself get close enough to brush them with the curry comb. By the end of the first week, he seemed to enjoy working with the horses enough to derive comfort from being with them.

The first few days, they'd barely spoken while they worked. Chris seemed to prefer silence, and Garrett followed his lead. Slowly, conversation started, and they began talking about their time in Afghanistan as they worked. Garrett wasn't sure he was any more eager than Chris to cover that ground. But neither of them could fully heal until they faced that part of their lives. So they talked, mostly about the fun times they'd had, and their friends. Except they never talked about Tommy Carmichael. Garrett tried to bring him up a couple of times, but Chris immediately shut down that line of conversation.

At least Chris was sleeping better. Since that first night when his nightmares had woken them all, things had been quiet. He sometimes heard Chris walking the halls in the middle of the night, Jake's nails tapping on the wooden floors as he followed him. But at least the night terrors and the screaming had stopped. Jake was spending nights in Chris's room, and the dog's presence seemed to have a calming effect on him. He went everywhere with Chris. While they worked on the fence, Jake slept on the grass in the shade of the truck, with Frisco stretched out next to him.

Maybe, this time, Chris really had turned a corner in his recovery.

Chris's progress had made Garrett wonder if there was a need for a place where other veterans could heal and recover. Someplace quiet where they could work out their problems, perhaps with the help of trained therapists. If he could buy some land in the area, it might be possible to get something going. With a little help from Harry.

"Is there any water left?" Garrett asked.

"Some." Chris handed him the thermos. "Do you think we could take a short break? There's something I'd like to talk to you about."

Garrett poured water from the thermos into a cup. "Sure. What is it?"

Chris's gaze didn't quite meet his. "Alison and the girls are supposed to come here this weekend."

"Yeah, I know. It's all you've talked about for days."

"I don't think I can do it."

"What do you mean?"

Chris turned to stare at the straight row of new fence posts they'd fitted in the last few days. "The more I think about it, the more I realize it's better if I stay away from the girls for a while. I need more time."

"Yeah, but you've made a lot of progress since you got here. You're much calmer."

"That's because I'm not around the kids. As soon as I'm with them again…" His voice trailed off, a world of hurt behind his words.

"They'll be disappointed." So was Garrett. He'd been so sure Chris was getting to the point where he could better handle the pressures of everyday life.

Chris blinked as if holding back tears. "I know. So am I. I don't know if I'll ever be ready to go back home to them."

What could he say to that? They'd all had such high hopes for Chris's recovery. But now...

They resumed their work and spoke only a few words to each other for the rest of the afternoon. Shortly before six, they packed up their tools and headed back to the farm. Blair's truck was already in the yard. Garrett's heart fell at the prospect of telling her Chris's decision, knowing how gutted she'd be.

Blair was at the stove, stirring a pot of pasta sauce on the back burner, as they entered the kitchen. As always, Frisco went directly to her, looking up at her in adoration. She turned to smile at them, and Garrett couldn't help but smile back, despite his somber mood.

"You're right on time. By the time you wash up, I'll have the food on the table."

"There's something I have to do first." Chris cleared his throat and lifted his gaze to hers. "I have to call Alison and tell her not to come here tomorrow."

"Tell her not to come? You've been looking forward to seeing your family for days."

"I know, but the closer the time for them to come gets, the more I realize I'm not ready. I can't see my children, Blair. I'm no good for them."

Blair turned off both burners on the stove, then fisted her hands on the counter, her head bent.

"What are you saying? That you don't ever want to see your children again?"

"It's not that I don't want to see them." There was a plea in Chris's voice. "I *can't* see them. There were things that happened in Afghanistan…I'm no good for them."

She twisted around to face him, and Garrett was shocked by the anger on her face. No, there was more than anger. There was disbelief and disappointment. But mostly he saw rage, along with deep pain and unbearable sadness.

"That's a damn cop-out, and you know it." Blair's voice shook. "I've seen the pictures. You've got two beautiful, healthy daughters. They need you to be their dad."

"Don't you know I want to be their dad?" Chris raised his voice to match hers. "I can't be what they need. I can never be what they need. I'm broken, Blair."

"So you won't even try to put yourself back together? I thought that was the whole reason for coming here." She tore off the apron tied at her waist and threw it on the counter. "Do you have any idea what some people would do to see their children again? Do you have any idea what I'd do?"

Garrett's heart stopped at her words. "Blair—"

She ignored him, focusing all her attention, and her anger, on Chris. "I never had a chance to be a mother to my child. I never even got the chance to hold her, not once."

Garrett closed the distance between them, but she shook him off when he tried to touch her.

"You've got two little girls who need you, but you're willing to throw them away because…why? You're not willing to do the work to be part of their lives? Do you know what I would give to have my daughter with me for one day? You have no right to be so selfish. No right at all."

For a few moments, none of them spoke. Blair began to shake, her hands trembling so hard she had to clutch them together. She looked at Garrett in shock as if she just realized what she'd said.

"Blair, I'm sorry. I didn't know." Chris's voice shook. "I wouldn't upset you for the world."

Blair's eyes were full of panic. "I'm sorry…I shouldn't have…I have to go."

She ran out of the kitchen, not bothering to shut the door. Frisco barked once and tore after her. Garrett stared at the open door and then at Chris, uncertain who needed him more.

His friend read his mind. "Go. I need to talk to Alison. And to think."

Garrett nodded once and left the kitchen. He headed for the barn but changed course at the sounds of distress coming from the paddock. He found Blair leaning against Harry's neck, her sobs echoing in the silence of the farmyard. Harry stood still, while the other horses made agitated movements nearby, and Frisco whimpered at her feet. Blair cried as if her world had fallen apart. As if she was broken.

Garrett eased himself between the wooden rails of the paddock and stepped inside. He approached her slowly, not wanting to spook her or the horses, and unsure of his welcome. All he knew was that he needed to be there for her.

He touched her shoulder. "Blair, sweetheart."

She slowly turned to him and lifted her gaze. Tears had created little rivulets down her cheeks and her curly, unbound hair blew wildly in the breeze. She swallowed hard as if to quell the tears.

"The things I said to Chris—I had no right."

"He'll be all right. He understands."

"It wasn't my place to judge him. I know what that feels like."

She'd lost a child. Garrett ached for her. What could he possibly say to her? What could he do to ease her pain?

"I'm sorry." The words were inadequate.

She nodded. "It was a long time ago."

The bleakness in her eyes told him it could have been yesterday. "Even if it was, I'm still sorry. The pain of losing someone you love doesn't go away easily."

She blinked, and her mouth twisted as fresh tears rolled down her face. "No. Time doesn't make it hurt any less."

Garrett gathered her in his arms and held her as she cried. He'd give anything to absorb her pain, to take it on himself so she wouldn't have to.

But that was impossible, so he simply held her closer.

****

Blair wasn't sure how long they stood in the paddock, their arms locked around each other. But it was long enough that the sun had begun to lower in the western sky. She sniffed back the last of her tears and stepped away from Garrett. At first he resisted her departure, but eventually he sighed and dropped his arms. He wiped the tears from her face with gentle fingers.

"Feel any better?"

Not really. "A little."

"Do you think you can talk about her, about your daughter?"

Blair shrank from him. She'd wanted to avoid this

292

conversation, but now that he'd heard part of the story he might as well hear the rest, even if it changed the way he saw her. She gulped in a shaky breath and nodded.

"Would you like to go back to the house?"

"No." After the things she'd said, she couldn't face Chris right now. "We can talk in the potting shed."

She led the way, Frisco at her heels. Memories assaulted her the moment she stepped inside. Garrett had made love to her here. She could almost feel him looming over her, his body inside hers. She could feel his hands on her, bringing her pleasure, bringing her to release.

She could have wept for the loss.

Garrett switched on the lantern in the corner. The lantern gave the room a soft, intimate glow that unnerved her. She hit the switch for the overhead light, and stark, bright light lit the room. What she had to say needed to be said in the light. Despite the reaction she was sure her story would receive from Garrett, she was tired of holding it inside.

"Would you like to sit?" Garrett asked.

"No, you go ahead," Blair said, gesturing to the mattress. She was far too keyed up to sit.

Garrett lowered himself onto the mattress and leaned his back against the wall so he could sit comfortably. He said nothing, letting her tell the story in her own time.

She gathered her thoughts and began to pace the small shed. Frisco paced with her, looking anxiously up at her. "I was seventeen when I found out I was pregnant. I stole a home pregnancy kit from a pharmacy and locked myself in the bathroom one morning to take the test. It was positive. I was terrified of what my parents would say and do, but a part of me was glad. I was going to have a child who would need me. Someone of my very own who would love me. Right from the beginning I loved my baby more than anything in the world.

"I told my boyfriend I was pregnant, and he promptly dumped me. It hurt, but I wasn't surprised. He was a kid, even less mature than I was. The only thing I asked was that he didn't say anything about my pregnancy to anyone, and he was only too happy to comply.

"I hid my pregnancy as long as I could, but eventually I started to show, and my mother figured it out. She took me to a doctor, hoping to secure a quick abortion. A pregnant teenage daughter and an illegitimate grandchild were not on my mother's agenda. Dad was in the state legislature in St. Paul, but she had plans for him to go to Washington. There could be no skeletons in our family's closet."

But what had hurt the most were the names her mother called her, the way Victoria treated her like dirt under her feet. She made no secret of her contempt for Blair.

"Unfortunately for my mother, I was too far along in my pregnancy to have an abortion. So she found me a place in Rochester at a home for unwed teenage mothers and left me there. It was a relief to be away from her and her constant scrutiny. All I had to do at the home was keep up with my studies and look after myself and the baby.

"When I was nearly at term, my mother showed up and said she'd found a nice couple who wanted to adopt my baby. I fought with her, raged at her. I told her there was no way I was giving up my child. She said I would have to give her up because I'd receive no support from her or my dad, either financial or emotional, and there was no way I could raise her on my own.

"She was right. I had no money, no job, no prospects. But I had my grandparents. If I could get to Masonville, they'd help me, no questions asked. So while my mother was making arrangements with the home's director for the birth of my baby and the hand-off to the nice, childless couple, I grabbed my mother's car keys from her purse, snuck out of the home, and stole her car.

"I had my learner's permit but little experience driving. I was upset and frightened. I wasn't even sure how to get to Masonville. I hadn't gone more than a few miles before going through a red light. The car was T-boned on the driver's side by an oncoming car. They told me later they needed the Jaws of Life to get me out. I don't remember anything. I woke up a day after the accident and was told my baby was dead.

"I didn't believe them. I couldn't. I screamed and cried and demanded to see her. Finally, they brought her to me, swathed in a blanket. They wouldn't let me hold her, but I could see her face. Her eyes were closed, and she looked as if she was asleep, but I knew she was gone. She was so beautiful. I'll remember her beautiful little face till the day I die."

She squeezed her eyes shut. The memory of Eve's sweet face rushed over her, the pain sharp even after all these years. "I called my grandparents. As soon as I was able to leave the hospital, they took me home with them, and we buried Eve in the Masonville cemetery. It gives me comfort now to know she's only a short distance away from them. I know they're looking out for her."

She closed her eyes, and the little white casket her baby had been buried in flashed into her memory. She pushed the image away. "I spent what was left of the summer here in Masonville with Granddad and Grandma. I would have stayed with them forever, but my parents insisted I move back to St. Paul. My mother enrolled me in a fancy private school where nobody knew me. I was so angry they forced me to leave Masonville. So I lashed out."

"What do you mean?" Garrett asked when she stopped talking.

"I wanted to make my parents angry, to embarrass them. I wanted them to hurt as much as I was hurting."

"How did you do that, sweetheart?"

Blair opened her eyes and looked directly at Garrett. He had to understand exactly who she was. "I slept with any boy who would have me. My parents treated me like a slut, so I played the part."

She hated even thinking about that time. Her actions had only succeeded in hurting herself. All her anger and grief turned inward as self-loathing, building up to a crescendo that culminated in her suicide attempt. It was only after she received help in the hospital that she was able to piece her life back together. The pieces were ragged-edged, but her work with animals and her experience rescuing horses gave her life a meaning and purpose that had sustained her.

Blair felt a cold nose against her hand and opened her eyes to see Frisco at her feet. Garrett stood in front of her as well. She'd been so caught up in old memories she hadn't noticed him leave the bed. He reached out to wipe her tears with the pad of his thumb.

"I'm so sorry for what you went through, sweetheart."

More than anything, Blair wanted to step into his arms and accept the solace and forgiveness he offered. But she didn't deserve it. She stepped away from his touch.

"Don't you see? If I hadn't been so selfish, Eve would be alive today. My mother was right. I couldn't look after a baby. I was a kid myself. A stupid, selfish, mixed-up kid. If I hadn't tried to run, she could have had a life. At least I'd know my baby was alive somewhere in the world. It's my fault she's dead."

Garrett grabbed her by the upper arms. "It's not your fault. It was an accident. You loved your child and you were trying to protect her. You are in no way responsible for her death."

"No. You're wrong," she whispered.

With a frustrated growl, he pulled her into his arms and held her tightly. "Don't do this, Blair. Don't do this to yourself and don't this to us. I love you, and I think you love me, too, but you're so caught up in guilt and blame that you won't allow yourself to acknowledge it."

He tipped up her chin so she was forced to look up into face. "I know I'm not much, but everything I've got, everything I am is yours. I love you, Blair."

His mouth descended on hers in a fierce, tender kiss. She kissed him back, letting her feelings flow through. She'd tried so hard not to love him, but it was a losing battle. Garrett was the bravest, the strongest, the most loving man she'd ever known. And she loved

him down to the marrow of her bones.

But there was no future for them.

Reluctantly, Blair ended the kiss. Shame washed over her at the thought of the way she'd yelled at Chris and chastised him for neglecting his children. She had no right to lecture him after what she'd done.

"I have to go back to the house and apologize to Chris," she said. "The things I said…"

"Chris understands. Give him some time. He said he needed to think about things and to talk to his wife."

Blair nodded. If Chris cancelled his family's trip to see him, he would regret it for the rest of his life. His children wouldn't understand his reasons. All they would know was that their father didn't want them.

She should know. Her parents had never wanted her.

Overwhelmed by fatigue, Blair lowered herself to the mattress. "I think I'll stay out here for a while. You should check on Chris."

"No. I'm with you."

He kneeled on his good leg to untie her shoes and slip them from her feet. Blair could have wept at the tenderness in the gesture. He pushed her back onto the mattress, placing a pillow under her head as she curled onto her side. Warmth enveloped her as he threw a blanket over her. Frisco jumped onto the mattress and settled himself next to her, tucking up against her stomach. Garrett snuggled close, his chest touching her back, one arm wrapped protectively around her waist. He kissed her hair and whispered in her ear.

"Rest now, sweetheart."

Blair tensed, torn between the urge to run and the need to accept the comfort he offered.

To accept the love he offered.

She closed her eyes and allowed the oblivion of sleep to overtake her.

****

Garrett held Blair while she slept, his mind racing. She'd lived with the guilt of her child's death for over ten years. It had colored her every decision and especially the way she saw herself. So many things made sense now.

She didn't deserve this hell she'd made for herself, but he had no idea how to help her. If he knew anything about guilt, it was that she had to move past it on her own. He could support her, but he couldn't make the guilt go away. He held her closer.

After a couple of hours, she began to stir. Reluctantly, he loosened his hold, and she moved to sit on the edge of the mattress. Frisco sat at her feet, looking at her with love in his one good eye. Blair patted the dog's head, her tension showing in the rigid set of her jaw.

Finally, she spoke. "I need to apologize to Chris."

"There's no need. He understands."

"There's every need." She got to her feet and turned, looking at him from under her lashes. "I appreciate what you said earlier. I really do. But I'm not who you need, Garrett."

He pushed himself off the mattress to stand in front of her. "Maybe you should let me decide who I need."

She squeezed her eyes closed, and her mouth twisted as if she was fighting to hold back tears once again. But when she reopened her eyes and looked at him again, they were dry and the look of determination in them scared him. "I don't want to hurt you."

Jana Richards

"You won't."

Blair only sighed and opened the door. "We need to go."

They walked back into the house together. Chris and Jake were sitting on the living room couch watching TV. As soon as he saw them, Chris turned off the TV with the remote and got to his feet.

"I'm sorry, Blair."

She made an attempt at a smile. "That's supposed to be my line. I'm the one who yelled at you. I shouldn't have—"

"No. You were right. I was being a coward. While you were out, I called my counselor in Minneapolis and then Alison. I finally told them why I was having so much trouble being with my kids. I need to tell you, too." He nodded at Garrett. "Both of you."

He motioned for them to sit on the couch. Frisco jumped up to sit between them while Jake paced with Chris. He blew out a breath before starting to speak.

"The day of the explosion, I was riding shotgun and Tommy was driving. You were in the back. I'd made a deal with Tommy, and so he was driving instead of me. I'll regret that decision until the day I die, but I know now I had no control over who lived and who died."

Garrett sat up straighter. Perhaps he needed to take a page from his friend's book and come to the same realization. But in any case, this was real progress.

"Do you remember anything about that day, Garrett? About our trip to the forward operating base?"

Garrett shook his head. "Some, but it's all muddled up. I had a pretty bad concussion."

"You don't remember the children?"

300

Garrett wracked his brain but couldn't come up with anything. "The children?"

"Yeah. Two little Afghan kids, couldn't have been more than six years old. Around the same age as my girls."

Chris stopped pacing to stare at the ceiling as he relived the moment. Jake sat at his feet, looking up at him.

"They popped out of the ditch and stood on the side of the road. We were in the middle of nowhere, so Tommy and I wondered how they got there. We were concerned about their welfare, but kids were sometimes used as decoys. These ones were so young. Little girls dressed in loose fitting clothes."

"Tommy slowed down, leaving a gap between us and the rest of the convoy ahead. The kids stepped toward the Humvee—and all hell broke loose. The explosion was strong enough to blow us off the road."

"I don't understand." Garrett couldn't get his mind around Chris's words. "I was told, *you* told me, suicide bombers approached the convoy. You never said anything about children."

"At first, I suppressed the memory. I didn't want to think about it. But the faces of those little girls haunted my dreams, and eventually my waking hours. Soon I started seeing my children's faces instead of the little Afghan girls."

Blair gasped and covered her mouth with her hand.

Chris sighed. "I didn't want you to know. The army called them suicide bombers, and that's what they were. Only they didn't know they were committing suicide. At least I hope not."

Garrett leaned back against the cushions of the

couch, barely able to process this news. What kind of sick bastard could do such a thing to a child? There had to be a special place in hell for someone who would strap a bomb to a little girl and detonate it from a safe distance.

"I've been afraid to be with my children, to have that ugliness brush off on them. I was afraid to talk about what happened. But after what you said tonight, Blair, I realized I owed it to them, and to myself, to somehow find a way past it. It starts by telling the truth, by exposing all the ugliness to the light."

Blair jumped to her feet and flung her arms around Chris. "I'm so sorry. So sorry."

They held each other until Chris said, "Alison will be arriving with the kids shortly after lunch tomorrow. My oldest says she wants chicken fingers for dinner."

Blair made a sound somewhere between laughter and tears. "We can make that happen."

"Yeah." Chris grasped her hands. "I'm going to work really hard to forgive myself...for surviving unhurt when Tommy died and Garrett was injured, for not being the father my children need. I want you to forgive yourself, too. Whatever happened, Blair, it wasn't your fault. I know that because I know you. It wasn't your fault."

At first she simply stared at Chris. Her chin began to quiver, and Garrett saw a tremor race through her body.

"I want to believe you." Her voice was a husky whisper.

"Believe it," he said fiercely. "It's the truth."

"Thank you. I appreciate you saying that." Blair offered a wobbly smile. "I'm so proud of you. I can hardly wait to meet Alison and the kids."

"They're going to love you." Chris sobered, his smile disappearing. "I know I've got a lot of work to do. I'm probably going to stumble and fall a few times. But if you guys are in my corner, I think I can get there."

Garrett got to his feet and clapped his friend's shoulder. "We're in your corner, buddy. Always."

Chapter Twenty-Three

Blair cut a chicken breast into strips. She smiled to herself as she worked. Chris's girls had loved her chicken fingers so much at their first dinner at the farm on Saturday that they'd insisted on having them again for Sunday dinner, their last meal before they headed back to Minneapolis tomorrow morning. She was pleased she could make them something they enjoyed so much.

Would Eve have liked chicken fingers, too?

She pushed aside the guilt and sadness that usually accompanied thoughts of her baby and allowed herself to remember and imagine. If Eve had lived, she'd be ten years old by now, a little older than Chris's daughters. She would have had many firsts by now; first steps, first day at school, first time riding a bicycle without training wheels. Blair was acutely aware she'd missed all those firsts.

But she was also acutely aware that her guilt had not allowed her to remember Eve with anything other than shame and sadness and guilt. Blair had carried her for nearly nine months, and she had loved her fiercely. She wasn't honoring Eve's memory by associating that time only with misery.

And she wasn't honoring Eve's memory by refusing to accept love into her life.

Her hand shook as she sliced into the meat, the

chicken finger taking on an uneven shape. Blair pushed away the thought. One thing at a time.

Alison tied an apron around her waist and washed vegetables at the sink. "Thank you for being so accommodating to the girls. I know it's extra work for you to cook a separate dish for them."

"I'm flattered they like my cooking so much." Through the kitchen window she saw the girls playing catch with Chris and Garrett, Frisco leaping for the ball while Jake watched the proceedings from his blanket on the porch. "They're wonderful girls. You must be very proud of them."

"I am," Alison said with a smile. "Hannah and Chloe are my life. Chris's too. For the first time in a long time, I have hope that he can make his way back to them. To us."

"I know he's going to try really hard. They mean everything to him."

"Yeah." Alison put down the knife she had used to slice carrots into sticks. "It's done him so much good to be here, to get away from the city, and spend time with Garrett. And with you."

"I've enjoyed having him and Garrett here." She didn't know Alison well, but she felt she was someone who understood pain. "After my grandfather died, I was afraid to be alone."

"Afraid?"

"Not in the physical sense. Afraid to come home to an empty house, to have no one to cook for and look after. Afraid to be alone. Especially to be alone with my thoughts."

Alison nodded sympathetically. "Even if I'm not alone, my thoughts can take me places I don't want to be."

Blair smiled at her, glad she understood. "Yeah."

"Chris and I have had time to really talk this weekend. Thank you for keeping the girls occupied so we were able to spend time together."

"It was my pleasure."

She and Garrett had put the girls on Harry's back and led them slowly around the paddock and the yard. All three horses had been patient with the girls' efforts at brushing them, and when they'd offered them bits of carrot in their flat-bottomed bowls, the horses had devoured them, much to the girls' delight. The horses seemed happy with the attention, not to mention the carrots.

The four of them had played with the dogs, and Chloe proclaimed she wanted a dog like Frisco with one eye because they were the smartest. Blair thought Frisco's intelligence was questionable, but she agreed that Frisco was a fine dog. The mutt was beginning to grow on her.

What she noticed most of all was Garrett's patience with the children, his obvious enjoyment in being with them. He'd be a wonderful father.

Could she be his children's mother? The thought caused a pang of anxiety in her chest.

Alison continued. "We threw around the idea of the girls and me moving here."

Blair turned to her, surprised. "Here to Masonville? Do you mean permanently?"

"Possibly. We talked about how happy Chris has been here. Perhaps it's the slower pace of life. Now that his military career is over, we can live anywhere. I have a sister in Minneapolis, but aside from her, we don't have any ties there."

"Chris said you're a nurse. Have you thought about looking for a job here? The nearest hospital is in Bismarck."

"As soon as I get home, I'll check their website and see if there are any job prospects."

"Garrett's sister Charlotte works there. I'll ask if they have any openings."

"Thanks." Alison picked up her knife and sliced carrots into sticks. "Don't say anything to the girls. Moving to Masonville is only an idea at this point. I don't want them to get excited, or worried, about something that may never come to be."

"Of course. But I hope it does happen. I think it would make Chris very happy. And I'd like it, too. It would be nice to have friends close by."

Alison smiled. "Yes, it would."

They worked silently for a few moments until Alison asked, "So, you and Garrett seem close. Are you a couple?"

Blair blinked at the direct question. And then she laughed. "So is this what being your friend is going to be like?"

"I'm sorry," Alison said with a blush. "I'm being nosy."

"It's okay. I'm not sure I know what Garrett and I are to each other." She decided to trust Alison. Charlotte and Lauren were good friends and she loved them, but they were Garrett's sisters, and she didn't feel comfortable talking with them about their brother. "He says he loves me."

"And how do you feel about him?"

Blair stared out the window and watched as Garrett

chased a shrieking Hannah around the yard, Frisco following and barking madly. "I love him, too."

It was the first time she'd said the words out loud. She waited for panic to strike, or for the world to fold in on itself because of her admission, but nothing happened.

"Garrett's a wonderful man. He deserves someone like you who's equally as wonderful. But I get the feeling it's not that simple."

"No." Blair swallowed and closed her eyes. "I'm not who Garrett needs."

She told Alison an abbreviated story about getting pregnant at seventeen and the accident that ended Eve's very short life. Alison listened without interruption, and Blair found that telling her story was easier this time around.

"I'm really sorry." Alison set down her paring knife. "Losing your child must have been awful for you. I can't imagine how I'd feel if I lost one of my girls."

"The thing about losing a child is that it's never over. I relive it again and again. What I did, what I should have done. But in the end, it's all the same. My baby died because of my actions, and I have to live with that."

Alison blinked at her. "Wait a minute. You blame yourself for your baby's death?"

"I was the one who stole the car. I was the one behind the wheel even though I had no business driving. I was the one who went through that red light."

"You were a scared kid. You weren't more than a baby yourself. All you wanted was to keep your child."

Blair shook her head. "I was selfish."

"Oh, Blair." Alison's face was full of compassion. "I've only known you this short time, but I know for sure that you're the least selfish person on the planet. If you were running away it was because you believed staying would be far worse for your child. You wanted to save her. It would have been the easiest thing in the world to simply stay, deliver your baby, and have your mother adopt her out to some anonymous couple. You could have gone back to your life without a backward glance. *That* would have been the selfish thing to do."

Blair stared at Alison, shocked at her words. She'd never considered her actions this way. It was true she believed she was keeping her baby safe. But in the aftermath of the accident, her mother had told her she had no one to blame but herself for Eve's death. In her grief she'd accepted the blame as her due.

"Not many people would welcome Chris into their home knowing his problems. But you did it without hesitation. When I made that phone call to Garrett, I was at the end of my rope. I had nowhere to turn. You were my lifeline, Blair. You're compassionate, kind, and brave. If she were here, I know your daughter would be proud of you."

If Alison's previous words shocked her, these words shook the foundations of her world.

Your daughter would be proud of you.

She stared at her, unable to speak. Her mind whirled, her thoughts a jumbled mess. A part of her wanted to hang on to her guilt with both hands. In a weird way she'd become comfortable with guilt in the last ten years. Hanging on to it meant she never had to put herself out there, to give or receive love.

She never had to take the chance of losing someone

else she loved.

But the world didn't work that way. She'd loved her grandparents and she'd lost them. Ben had loved Olivia and now she was gone. There were no guarantees.

Hannah and Chloe ran into the kitchen, their excited laughter filling the room. Jake and Frisco followed close behind, Frisco with a ball in his mouth. Chris entered next, looking more relaxed than Blair had ever seen him. Garrett followed him into the house and closed the door behind them. His brows knit together in concern as his gaze met hers. She clearly read the question in his eyes. *You okay?*

She nodded and made herself smile at him. *I'm fine.*

How was it they could communicate without words?

With help from Chris and Garrett, she and Alison finished dinner preparations. There was much laughter around the table, and much love. Blair sensed it each time Alison and Chris looked at each other.

Though she talked and smiled through dinner, Blair's thoughts were far away. Alison's words played over and over in her head, challenging what she'd believed to be the truth for so long.

Garrett watched her through the meal, and later as they cleaned up and washed dishes. When Chris and Alison excused themselves to take the girls upstairs for their baths, he reached for her hand.

"Do you want to talk about it?"

There was no point denying something was on her mind. "No. At least, not yet."

He tugged on her hand, bringing her closer. "You

know you can tell me anything, right? Anytime you need to talk, I'm here."

She laid her palm against his cheek, loving the slightly rough texture of his three-day growth of beard. "I know."

He rested his forehead against hers. "I love you, Blair."

Her heart expanded so quickly she was afraid it would burst from her chest. She wrapped her arms around his neck and burrowed her fingers into his thick, silky hair.

This man...Oh, God, this man.

"I wish…" He stopped and shook his head.

Blair pulled away far enough to look into his eyes. "Tell me. What do you wish?"

With a sigh he closed his eyes and inclined his head. His shoulders slumped. "I wish you could say the words back to me."

Oh, Garrett.

She wished she could say the words aloud, too. They stuck in her throat, fear keeping them locked inside. But she felt them in her heart. She loved him. She loved him so much.

Blair wrapped her arms around him and held him tightly, hoping he could feel her love.

****

After breakfast the next morning Alison and the girls prepared for the long drive to Minneapolis. Chris had decided to stay on the farm. He'd found a counselor in Bismarck he thought he could work with, and he was eager to begin the healing process. The separation from his family, especially from Alison, was difficult for him, but Blair was glad for his sake that he was staying and working on his recovery. But she was also glad because if Chris stayed on her farm, so would Garrett.

Alison gave Blair a hug and whispered in her ear, "Remember what I said."

Blair nodded. She'd thought of little else since their conversation yesterday.

"Like I said, I'm going to be looking at nursing opportunities around Masonville."

"I'll get Charlotte to email you."

"Thank you. I appreciate you putting me in touch with her."

"It's my pleasure."

"Thank you for all you've done for my family. Without you…" She stopped and shook her head.

"It's going to be okay, Alison. Everything's going to work out."

Alison held her tightly for a few more seconds. There was a smile on her face as she stepped away.

"If it does, I have you to thank. Take care of yourself, Blair."

With that she ushered her children into the car and buckled them into their car seats. She and Chris embraced and kissed one last time before she got behind the wheel and drove off. Chris sighed, looking like he missed them already. Blair gave him a smile.

"They'll be back in a couple of weeks. Maybe by then Alison will have found a job close to Masonville."

"Yeah, maybe." He turned to her. "It was a wonderful weekend. Thank you for not letting me call it off."

"You're the one who made that decision. I just yelled at you a lot."

He grinned. "I needed someone to kick my ass."

"Any time." Blair checked her watch. "I've got to get to work. I'll see you tonight, Chris."

"I'm making pasta. You'll love it." He exchanged a look with Garrett before turning back to her. "I'll go wash up the breakfast dishes. Have a good day, Blair."

"Thanks. You, too."

With Jake at his heels, he walked back to the house, leaving Blair alone with Garrett. "Will you walk me to my truck?"

"Sure."

They said nothing as they walked the short distance, though Blair's mind whirled with unspoken thoughts. But mostly she wanted to hear him say he loved her one more time.

"What are you doing today?" she asked as they reached her truck. She was stalling. She should get to work, but she couldn't make herself leave.

"We'll be out in the pasture, fencing. I figure there's three to four more days of work out there."

"You've worked so hard. If I haven't said it lately, thank you."

A smile whispered across his face. "It's been my pleasure, Blair. I'd do anything for you, you know."

Sudden tears burned behind her eyes. "The feeling is mutual."

They stared at each other, neither of them speaking. Blair wished she could pour out all the things in her heart, tell him she loved him.

Her cell phone rang, breaking the tension. She saw her brother Damon was on the line, and her stomach clenched, knowing he only called when he had serious news.

"Damon, hi. Isn't it kind of early in California?"

Damon chuckled. "Ridiculously early, but I wanted to talk to you before you left for work."

"Is everything okay?"

"Everything's fine. I've been thinking a lot about the place Granddad left me in Masonville, and I think I want to move there."

Blair covered her gasp with her hand. Garrett stepped closer, concern in his expression. "Are you serious?"

"I am, but my decision depends on you."

"Damon, Garrett is here with me. I'm going to put you on speaker phone." She clicked the button and caught Garrett up on the conversation. "He says his decision whether to move here depends on me. What do you mean, Damon?"

If Damon wondered what Garrett was doing at her place at seven-thirty in the morning, he kept his questions to himself. "The legacies we received from Granddad give us the rare opportunity to pursue our dreams. You can rescue horses on the farm and I can set up a private counseling practice. But if we pool our resources, we can accomplish so much more. We can rescue animals while giving veterans a place to heal."

Garrett's eyes lit with excitement. "How do you suggest we do that?"

Blair wondered if he realized he'd said "we."

"Working with horses is a recognized form of therapy for people with PTSD. As part of their therapy, vets would care for the horses and bond with them. You'd be able to rescue many more horses than you could if we worked separately."

It was an exciting possibility. "Where would these vets stay while they're in Masonville?"

"At the building Granddad left me in his will. I'd have to convert some of the space into dormitories. I'd probably have to buy a van to transport people back and forth."

"How would you finance this endeavor?" Garrett asked. "The money you got from your grandfather would probably be eaten up pretty quickly, and most vets I know couldn't afford the kind of treatment you're talking about."

"I've already approached the Veterans Administration to see if a project like this would be something they're interested in. We'd be private contractors, providing a service to them. There's no deal yet, mainly because I have nothing to show them, but they're definitely interested."

"You've gone to the VA already? What if I say no?" Blair asked.

"Then I'll buy another farm and hire someone who knows how to look after animals. But I'd rather work with you."

The idea was intriguing, especially the prospect of being able to rescue several more horses, and perhaps dogs as well. But did she really want strangers in her home?

Damon sensed her reticence. "You don't have to give your answer this minute. I want you to think about it for a while. Call me with any questions you have."

"All right, I will. I've got to get to work." Her gaze met Garrett's. She sensed this was something that interested him. "Garrett can tell you about a friend of his who's been staying here on the farm, and the progress he's made." She gave a brief rundown of Chris's history. "I'll text you Garrett's number and the two of you can talk."

"Sounds good."

She smiled. "We'll talk soon, okay?"

"Okay. Bye for now."

"Bye."

She sent him a quick text message with Garrett's cell phone number before opening the door to her truck. "So what do you think?"

"I think it's an intriguing possibility."

Blair nodded. "Yeah. Is working with fellow vets something you could see yourself doing?"

"I have to admit I've thought about setting up a sort of retreat in the country for veterans. But I'm not a trained psychologist. I'm not sure there'd be a place for me in the project Damon is proposing."

If there wasn't, there should be. Garrett was instrumental in Chris's recovery. His empathy, his compassion, and his own experience made him the perfect person to work with other veterans. She'd have a word with Damon.

"I've got to run. See you after work."

"Have a good day, Blair."

"You too."

She hesitated, one hand on the open truck door. "Garrett, what you said last night about wishing I could say those words back to you…"

"That you love me?"

"Yeah." She stared at her shoes, then squared her shoulders and lifted her gaze. "Aside from my grandparents, no one's ever said they loved me. I don't know what to do with those words."

He lifted his hand to gently rake his fingers across her cheek. "It's okay, Blair."

"No, it's not okay! Garrett—"

"Shhh." He brushed a kiss across her lips. "When—if—you're ready, you'll say the words. And if you can't feel the way I do, I understand."

She looked into his eyes and nodded, her emotions plummeting. He deserved so much better.

Blair longed to be the woman who deserved a man like Garrett.

Chapter Twenty-Four

Blair opened the windows of her truck so the wind could blow across her face. It was unseasonably hot for mid-September in North Dakota. The air conditioner had stopped working at the clinic today, and she was sweaty and probably stinky. All she wanted was to go home and jump into a cool shower.

So why had she turned into the parking lot of the Masonville Cemetery?

For the past week, Blair had thought about what Alison said. After accepting the weight of responsibility for Eve's death for so long, she was having trouble accepting Alison's contention that she wasn't to blame, that her selfishness hadn't caused her baby's death, and in fact the selfish path would have been to give her child away and move on.

She'd gone over and over that time in her mind, trying to come to grips with her decision to steal her mother's car to make an escape. She remembered her panic after her mother told her she'd found a couple willing to take the baby off their hands.

Willing to take the baby off their hands.

Those were her exact words, Blair remembered, and they chilled her now almost as much as they had back then.

If she'd had the chance to meet the couple who'd wanted to adopt Eve and had been able to assure herself that they would love and care for and cherish her baby, she might have been able to make the decision to give her up. But those words from her mother had frightened her. Victoria didn't care what kind of people these prospective parents were. She was only interested in protecting the family name from the scandal of having a daughter who was an unwed teenage mother. Blair didn't even know if Victoria had gone through an adoption agency or through the black market. It probably wouldn't have made any difference to her as long as the problem went away.

She'd run because she was afraid for her child. Because she didn't, couldn't, trust her mother.

Blair gripped the steering wheel. Though her actions had ended in disaster, her motives had been unselfish. It was a startling, and freeing, realization.

She opened the truck door and got out, walking past the trees circling the cemetery and through the main entrance. This was the first time she'd been at the cemetery since her grandfather's funeral, and she wasn't exactly sure why she was here now.

But something about the peacefulness of this place—the sounds of birds and insects, the endless blue of the sky—compelled her to walk between the rows of headstones.

She soon found the spot where her grandparents had been laid to rest. The dirt over her grandfather's side of the grave was still fresh; it had only been five weeks since his death. Eventually the ground would settle and the caretakers would seed grass.

She wished she'd brought flowers. Her grandmother had so loved flowers. Another time she would.

Blair got to her knees and touched the smooth granite of the headstone, tracing the carved rendering of her grandmother's name with her finger.

"I want to thank you for everything you did for me, Grandma and Granddad. You were my rocks in a very scary world. I could always count on you. But mostly I want to thank you for loving me unconditionally, no matter what I'd done. If I have children someday, I'll know how to love them because you showed me the way. Thank you for loving me."

The sun was warm on her back as she listened to the birds flit from tree to tree. Peace flowed over her.

After a while she pushed herself to her feet and stood looking over the grave. "I have to go now and do something I should have done a long time ago. But I'll be back soon. I love you both."

Blair kissed her fingers and pressed them to the sun-warmed granite before moving on.

She wasn't exactly sure where she was going. She wandered up and down the rows, reading the inscriptions on the stones, until she found the one she wanted. Blair knelt in front of the grave and read aloud.

"Eve Greyson, beloved great-granddaughter of Anna and Everett Branson. Always loved."

The day of her birth, and death, one and the same, was included. It was a pretty headstone, if there was such a thing, carved with cherubs and teddy bears. Her grandparents must have picked it out. The only time she'd been here was on the day they'd buried Eve. There was only her and her grandparents, the minister from their church, and the people from the funeral home. There'd been no formal funeral in the church, only a short graveside service. The minister had said a few words of which Blair could remember nothing, and they'd lowered the tiny white casket into the ground.

She'd wanted to die that day. She'd wished with all her heart that she'd died in the accident along with Eve. Later, back with her parents in St. Paul, she'd almost succeeded in ending her life.

But eventually she came back to life. Her grandparents' love had helped. She survived her final year of high school and living with her parents by focusing on her goal of working with animals, and in particular, rescuing horses. She studied hard and worked a part-time job at a grocery store to save money to go away to school. The day after her last day of high school, she loaded up her car and moved to Rochester, Minnesota, where she'd been accepted into a veterinary technology program. To their credit, her parents had bought her a used Honda and paid her college tuition, even though her mother had made it abundantly clear she thought such a career was too lowbrow for their family. Perhaps it was their way for making up for past mistakes. More likely, they were ready to wash their hands of her.

It didn't matter anymore. She'd never have a close relationship with her parents. All she could do now was move forward, and she couldn't do that if she continued to cling to the pain of the past.

She traced her finger through Eve's name. "I loved you so much, from the moment I knew you existed. I'll always love you. You'll never be forgotten, my sweet baby girl."

With a sigh, Blair sat back on her heels. A dandelion, now gone to seed, had grown against the side of the headstone. She plucked it, and as she blew on it, the breeze picked up the seeds and lifted them high into the air. Blair smiled as she watched them scatter across the cemetery. Along with the seeds, she released the pain and the guilt that had weighed so heavily on her for so long. She could almost feel the dark emotions leaving her body.

Blair got to her feet, and as she'd done with her grandparents' grave, she kissed her fingers and pressed them to Eve's name carved in the granite.

"Goodbye, my darling. I'll be back soon."

She walked back to the truck and sat behind the wheel. Now that the weight of guilt had lifted, everything was clearer. Guilt had blocked her from seeing everything that was possible, and everything she wanted her to life to be. She wanted to *live,* not merely exist. She knew what she needed to do, but first she had to talk to her brother. She fished her phone out of her purse and called Damon.

"Hey. How are things going?"

Blair looked toward the cemetery and smiled. "Surprisingly well. That's why I'm calling. I'm in. I want to be part of your veterans program."

"That's great news!"

"Don't get too excited yet. I've got some conditions."

"Okay. What are they?"

"You have to commit to staying in Masonville for a reasonable period of time. At least a couple of years. If we do this, you've got to be there."

"Agreed. What else have you got?"

Blair was surprised he'd agreed to her first demand so easily. "I want Garrett to be part of this program. He's not a trained psychologist like you, but he's a veteran who's gone through his own struggles, and I know other vets would relate to him. He'd be an amazing addition to the program."

"You don't have to sell me on Garrett, Blair. I've been talking to him, and I think he'd be perfect as a peer counselor. All I needed was the go-ahead from you."

"You've got it." She was thrilled Garrett had earned the position on his own. "We'll talk later and work out all the details of this venture."

"All right. I'll send you some information. I'll be in Masonville permanently soon, and we can get started." Damon laughed. "I can't wait."

"Neither can I. Talk to you soon."

Blair ended the call with a smile and started the engine. It was time to go home to Garrett.

****

Garrett checked the clock on the stove once again. It was long past the time Blair usually got home from work. He'd tried her phone, but each time it had gone straight to voice mail.

His gut churned with apprehension. All day long he'd had the unsettling feeling that something had happened.

Damn it, if she didn't get home within the next fifteen minutes, he was going to look for her.

Chris clapped a hand to his shoulder. "I'm guessing she stopped to pick up a few groceries after work, probably in Bismarck."

"Yeah." But she usually called if she was going to be late, and it didn't explain why her phone was turned off. Garrett fought the rising panic in his chest.

Where was she? Was she all right?

The sound of gravel crunching under tires alerted them that a vehicle had pulled into the yard. Garrett hurried to the window over the sink, his heart in his throat. Chris stepped next to him and pushed aside the curtains. "Here she is. I told you not to worry."

The overwhelming relief made him lightheaded. Garrett rushed out of the house and into the yard. As soon as her truck came to a stop, he wrenched open the driver's side door.

"Where the hell were you?"

Blair smiled and hopped out of the cab. "And hello to you, too."

"I'm sorry." He blew out a breath and pulled her into his arms. "You were so late, and I couldn't reach you by phone…"

He was embarrassed now by how panicked he'd been. But something was off with Blair. She'd been quiet the last few days, and distracted, as if she'd been trying to work something out.

He squeezed his eyes shut and held her tighter. He only hoped she wasn't trying to work out how to tell him goodbye.

"I'm sorry." She looped her arms around his waist, her head against his shoulder. "I didn't mean to worry you. There was something I needed to do."

"What?"

Instead of answering she linked his fingers with hers. "Will you walk with me?"

He nodded and she led him toward the barn. Chris walked out onto the porch, and Blair waved at him. "Keep dinner warm for us, will you? We'll be back soon."

She led Garrett past the paddocks and into the

pasture. The horses saw them and ran toward them. Blair laughed.

"They probably think we have treats."

She seemed happy, at peace. Not like a woman ready to say goodbye. At least he hoped not.

"I didn't realize how late it was getting. I went to the cemetery and visited my grandparents' grave." Rainbow reached her first and nudged her with her nose. "I haven't been there since the funeral."

"I would have gone with you." The visit must have been difficult for her. He wished he'd been there to support her.

She smiled at him. "I know. We'll go together another time. This time I had to go on my own. I visited my daughter's grave, too. For the first time."

Garrett's breath hitched. What did this mean? He squeezed her fingers. "Are you okay?"

"Yes, I'm fine. I finally realized something. Eve will always be with me in my heart. What happened was awful and tragic, but it was an accident. I'll probably always assume much of the blame, but I can't allow it to stop me from living. Or stop me from loving you."

His heart expanded, soared. He held his breath.

"I want a life with you, Garrett. I want us to work together to rescue horses and veterans and anything else that needs rescuing." She lifted her eyes to his, and he saw love and hope in them. "I want children with you. Not to replace Eve, because no one could replace her. But because we love each other, and children are a natural extension of that love. Do you want that, too?"

"Yeah." He could barely get the word out. Blair constantly threw him off balance, constantly amazed him. "I want that, too."

She smiled and lifted her hand to his face. Garrett grasped it and pressed a kiss into her palm.

"I love you, Blair."

"I love you, too. Very much."

For now, that was all he needed to know.

****

Three months later

Katie, the new rescue horse, made an anxious circle of the paddock, shaking her head in distress. Fog-like plumes rose above her as her warm breath met the cold December air. She was afraid, poor thing, but with love and kindness and patience she'd soon learn she was safe here.

Just as she had.

Blair smiled at the thought. She did feel safe here on the farm. And loved. All because of one amazing, incredibly sexy man.

The man in question stepped into the paddock and walked toward her. Garrett had become very proficient with the horses in the last few months. He'd been studying up on horse behavior and physiology with online classes and by following Cole on some of his equine veterinary cases. He was currently enrolled in a farrier program at a local college. His aim was to look after the horses' physical needs as well as their emotional needs. Blair would assist him as often as she could, but for now she continued to work full time at the veterinary clinic. Garrett would spend time with veterans in his capacity as farm manager. Though his focus was on the animals and the farm, he'd be a shoulder for veterans to lean on and a sympathetic ear any time they wanted to talk.

She was so proud of him. Blair nearly burst with love and pride.

Garrett climbed between the wooden rails and kissed her, holding her close.

"Hey, baby. How was your day?"

"It was good and busy. Just the way I like it." Blair snuggled closer to him and wrapped her arms around his waist. "But this is the best part of my day."

"Best part of my day, too." His chuckle rumbled through her. "I take that back. Later, in our bedroom, is the best part."

Anticipation made her shiver. "Good point."

Their lovemaking had been wonderful before, but since Blair had admitted her feelings for Garrett, sex had taken on a whole new meaning. It meant commitment and love and acceptance. And passionate, wild lovemaking.

Garrett brushed a warm kiss across her lips. "Chris is in the house making dinner, and Damon should be home shortly. He said he had to meet with his contractor in town. There were some details on the renovations to the building they needed to work out."

"What about Alison? Will she be home for dinner?"

"No, she's working till midnight tonight. It's the four of us adults and the kids."

It was a full house, and Blair loved it. Alison had started working at the same hospital as Charlotte about a month ago. Chris would continue to work at the farm, helping with the cooking and other chores while working on his recovery. They were looking for a house, but until they found the right one for their family, they were staying on the farm. Blair was in no hurry to see them leave.

Damon, too, was a guest until his apartment was ready. The building he'd inherited from Granddad was going through extensive renovations to turn it into a multi-unit dwelling with space for common rooms for recreation and for group counseling sessions. It would likely be a few months before he could move in.

In late October, Ben and his stepdaughters had surprised her by moving to Masonville, into the house Granddad had left them. They were frequent visitors to the farm, and Isabella and Sophie had already made friends with Alison and Chris's girls. Blair was thrilled to have them close by, but she couldn't help worrying about the reason for the sudden move, especially since Ben had seemed uninterested in leaving Chicago back in August. She'd asked what had prompted the move, but he'd only said that small town life would be good for his kids. She sensed there was much more he wasn't telling her.

Blair reluctantly left Garrett's arms. "I should change and have a shower. I had a run-in with a goat today, and I probably smell."

"Wait." Garrett stopped her retreat. "Before you go, there's something I need to tell you. I love you, Blair."

Hearing him say the words never got old. "I love you, too."

He got down on his good knee and looked up at her, not releasing her hand. "I want to be with you for the rest of my life, Blair. I want us to have children together. I want us to fill our house with dogs and cats, and friends and family. But mostly with love. Will you marry me?"

She couldn't speak, could barely breathe. Marriage hadn't crossed her mind. She was happy simply being with Garrett.

She hadn't allowed herself to believe in forever. Not really. Though she'd been working with a therapist the last three months, it was still difficult to accept that she deserved happiness.

Her therapist kept telling her that until she loved herself, she couldn't fully love anyone else. Garrett deserved all the love she could give him. He deserved all of her, a whole, healthy partner. So did their future children.

In that instant, she made up her mind to throw off the last traces of guilt over Eve's death. She would hold on with both hands to the precious love Garrett offered and never relinquish it.

"Yes. Yes, of course I'll marry you."

Smiling, Garrett produced a ring from his pocket, pulled off her warm mitten, and slipped the circle of diamonds and gold on her finger, where it glistened in the light from over the barn door.

"It's beautiful." Tears clogged her throat. "It's the most beautiful thing I've ever seen."

Garrett pushed himself back to a standing position. "It's freezing out here. Let's put Katie in the barn and tell everyone the good news."

Blair wanted to tell the whole world how much she loved this man. "Let's go."

A word about the author...

Jana Richards has been making up stories since childhood, but she was in her thirties before she began to put pen to paper. While romantic suspense is one of her favorites, romantic comedy holds a special place in her heart. She loves writing romance fiction because of its message of hopefulness and its steadfast belief that love makes people better human beings.

When not writing or working at her day job as an office administrator, Jana can be found reading, gardening, spending time with her family or tearing up her favorite golf course. Jana lives in Manitoba, Canada with her husband and daughters.

Visit Jana at http://www.janarichards.net

or at http://www.myspace.com/jana_richards